# Rock 'n' Roll Suicide

P-P HARTNETT

# Rock 'n' Roll Suicide

SCEPTRE

First published in Great Britain in 2002 by Hodder and Stoughton
A division of Hodder Headline

The right of P-P Hartnett to be identified as the Author
of the Work has been asserted by him in accordance
with the Copyright, Designs and Patents Act 1988.

A Sceptre Book

2 4 6 8 10 9 7 5 3 1

A CIP catalogue record for this title
is available from the British Library

ISBN 0340 73342 X

Typeset in Sabon by Hewer Text Ltd, Edinburgh
Printed and bound in Great Britain by
Mackays of Chatham plc, Chatham, Kent

Hodder and Stoughton
A division of Hodder Headline
338 Euston Road
London NW1 3BH

For Lisa and Claire, the girls in my life

'Ever tried? Ever failed? No matter. Try again, fail again. Fail better.'

Samuel Beckett (A quotation which appears on the internal CD sleeve of *Ocean Spray* by Manic Street Preachers

'Everyone needs a psychic shield, otherwise too much of the world gets in and you've had it.'

Thom Yorke of Radiohead, *NME*, 2001

*Q:* What did Kurt Cobain's suicide mean to you?

Morrissey: I felt sad and I felt envious. He had the courage to do it. I admire people who self-destruct and that's not a new comment for me. They are taking control. They're refusing to continue with unhappiness, which shows tremendous self-will. It must be very frightening to sit down and look at your watch and think, in thirty minutes I will not be here. Thinking, I'm going to go on that strange journey. Modern life is very pressurising. We're all on the verge of hysteria. There are people around who'll shoot your head off because you forgot to indicate.

*Q* Magazine, 1997

Part One

# Part One

# 1

Sitting by the window, from where she spent hours just gazing out at the big wide world down below, the cat was dreaming of meeting a tom. On those rare occasions when she managed to escape between the legs of her mistress to the corridors, elevator and staircase of the building, there was always the chance of a quickie.

She *knew* there were others like her in the building. She had heard them, scented them. Insemination, even at her age, was still a possibility. She longed for the neighbouring toms to be neatly lined up by the door, allowed in one by one for a series of five-second fucks. Her body craved to be pregnant, then the joy of pretty little kittens to lick clean, nurse and play with. A vain dream, alas, for all the male cats in the building had been doctored.

The cat, named Minty, was an affectionate and devoted animal, whose sweet, wide-eyed, innocent expression and soft coat had long made it captivating and as lovable as a teddy bear. It was a cat that was an individual, with its own distinct personality, unique in the way that it viewed the world and responded. Never completely tamed or understood, that imprisoned animal was so often aloof, enigmatic. Loving one moment, indifferent the next. Coquettish, then fiery.

For the last seven years the cat had inhabited a sturdy body, with a compact bone structure. Short in length, broad in the beam and low on the legs. Until recently, the overall impression had been one of roundedness. Round body, round head, round cheeks.

Signs of age showed in the way the cat now carried herself, the look in her eyes, the condition of her coat. Her metabolism was beginning to slow. There was a general loss of sparkle and tone to her. Noticeably thinner of late, her chic lines and gently sloping shoulders were, like the spine and hips, beginning to protrude. Normally weighing somewhere between eight and ten pounds, the cat had slipped to six. Hair growth had recently started to be sparse, and her owner had noticed a mild scaliness to the skin, calluses on the hocks. Her pads were thickening, her muzzle on the verge of whitening.

Minty, a good creature, never made a mess – always using her little tray when the demands of nature called.

The cat was well looked after. Whatever state the owner was in, she was always alert for any signs of a dry nose or watery stool. The reflection of that cat's face in the cold glass right that second, late on a Wednesday afternoon, was anything but happy. While the face was small, possessing the weird stillness of early films, it was capable of an unfriendly glance if things were not to her liking.

That big wide world out there, seven floors down, with its mesmerising pedestrians and cyclists, was a no-go area. Her owner believed that looking out of the window was probably just like watching TV.

There was no cat flap, no little balcony to sun on, no fire escape on which to perform all manner of acrobatics. The world of her mistress was a shared world, and she was stuck there with that woman.

The woman believed that the inside world was the best place for her cat. The outside world was too risky. Minty, her owner felt, could fall victim to not only contagious diseases but also harmful accidents, poisons, parasites and the vicious deeds of inhumane people. Not once had the cat experienced the joy of mousing, or unfeathering a bird. All she had for a harmful bit of fun were her toys.

4

The cat looked over to a small pot of grass, there by the corner of the window. She had not eaten from the pot in weeks, so she had been missing out on a natural emetic and good source of folic acid.

There was something of a Havana Brown or Korat to Minty, and perhaps a strain of typical black tabby. Despite what the cat breeder had boasted as part of an elaborate sales talk, somewhere along the line a rare variety from Thailand had become genetically involved with a moggy. The superior trait dominated in the slender, short-haired nature of the cat. Having lost so much weight in recent weeks, this slight oriental conformation had come to the fore.

Her owner had spent much time hunting through many an encyclopedia of cats in search of the one that flicked some kind of magical internal switch. The woman had liked the look of a Turkish Angora, a shaggy Maine Coon, a sealpoint Siamese. As with the Munchkin variety and Russian Blue, the breeds were expensive. Very.

Minty had been bought from a cattery many miles away. The breeder had told the woman who had needed something to cuddle so badly that the little fluffball was a Manx of 'pet' quality, not 'show' quality. The cat had always carried the term as if in some way sub-standard or defective. Although the variety is best known for its lack of a tail, Minty came from a litter in which there was a rumpy, a rumpy riser, a stumpy and a longy. Minty was the one with the longy, a tail which she swished when annoyed, or lowered fully and tucked in between her legs when in a dignified sulk.

The cat stood, then walked over towards her free-standing scratch post, made of carpet, sisal and wood. As Minty walked, the hind legs were markedly longer than the front legs, making her rump higher than her shoulders. She took a little sniff of the expensive item, which still retained a whiff of the catnip that had been sprinkled upon it just a few days back.

This ignited a whirring, two-way rhythm of inhalation, ex-halation: a purring which grew in volume, then stopped as suddenly as it had started.

Minty stretched, briefly posturing as if to accept a male cat, then shimmied towards the sofa, sniffed, then ducked her head down, gently entering the tight confinement of the dark space in which she felt most comfortable. This is where she did much of her sleeping, around sixteen hours' worth each day.

The highlight of her waking hours had been at around noon. A short, bristly bluebottle had got itself caught in a cobweb at the corner of the window. All that buzzing and bouncing as it had tried to escape the finely spun trap had been quite a show – and it had been no solo performance. The slow advances of a spider every now and then to see whether lunch was ready, just a paw away, had been a real treat. As the fly had expended one last burst of energy in an attempt to be free, the cat's paw had made for it, freaking the spider, which hopped from its web back into a deep crack under the frame. The cat had only managed to scoop up its home into a sticky(ish) rope, freeing the fly. Disappointing, but they were still there, in that apartment. The spider would spin another web, it always did. That fly would make the same mistake as it attempted to reach the blue sky, only succeeding in bashing its head time and time again against the glass.

Dusk was slatting the sky with all the colours of bruises: golden greens, plums, sulphur yellows, grainy blues. The sun was to the extreme far right of the window, which meant her mistress would soon be home. There would be the sound of the elevator shuddering to a halt, those shuffling footsteps, the rattle of keys at the door. This was the time for Minty to crank up something from her vocal repertoire to initiate the greeting ritual. While performing a stiff-legged hop in which the front feet were lifted off the ground together in an attempt at head-to-head contact, the cat would verbalise periodically. This would activate the way to a sing-songy 'Hello, how's my darling?' kiss 'n' cuddle response from her owner. It was a routine that invariably climaxed with a double shake of the dry-food container.

Minty would be the focus of attention for perhaps as long as three full minutes. She would perform the adoring head-to-ankle purring trick, wrapping her tail around the woman's leg, the vertical slits of her big shiny eyes expanded to dark pools of feline expectation and delight. She would watch the round-edged metal bowls being filled attentively: food, water. For the sake of a little exercise she would raise herself up on to her back legs every once in a while to let on that she wanted a better view of the crunchy concoction of some lamb's-heart-and-tuna formula, mushy tinned chicken-and-rabbit mix or, best of all, a bowl of full-fat evaporated milk being prepared.

Minty would alternately beg and try to sing the three syllables of the woman's name: An-gel-a. Using her paw to reinforce her demand, she would put on a good show, really sing for her supper. After just a few mouthfuls she would turn her head to watch, observe the woman. With nostrils quivering, the animal would attempt to sniff out her mood, and where that mood might lead.

The temperature of the little apartment was cooling, more comfortable after the hot afternoon. Soon the sky would be as grey and dirty as the streets she monitored each and every day, each and every night.

An evening of total cloud cover, the cat predicted. A high chance of rain.

The cat let out a little sound. Not a *miaow*, more an *oww*. It had a tearful quality to it.

As expected, there was the sound of the elevator shuddering to a halt, those shuffling footsteps, the rattle of keys at the door.

She was back. Angela was home.

He'd been feeling bad for ages; that day he was feeling worse.

Standing by the window of the backstage dressing room, Max buttoned the flies of his black leather trousers. Based upon the classic design of Levi's 501s, this item of clothing had become a vital component of the rock star's trademark. That, the white satin shirt he would soon don, plus the purple suede boots which were scuffed to fuck, ready to fall apart.

The heavy, black cascade of hair that framed his face like open curtains was a striking contrast to the spooky pale of his translucent skin. That skin, another one of the rock star's trademarks.

He dressed slowly. He had always put on his clothes at a sedate pace, almost tenderly, because he was putting them upon himself. He liked everybody, even his own body, to be gentle with him. That had always been an important part of the preparation, the ritual. That calm, steady pace. That step-by-step timing was not as important, however, as when his body had had some sort of future. Even so, time was time, even with little time.

Tonight would be the last time he'd wear those black leather jeans on stage. In a couple of hours he would throw them from that window to the fans below. There would probably be a fight over them. Those jeans would get torn to pieces, ripped to shreds.

He had worn those leathers so long that they had gained his shape, his smell. There, at the knees: worn thin. There, mid-thigh and at the seat: so soft. Those buttons had become smooth after two years of daily buttoning and unbuttoning. Those same black leather trousers, since day one of international fame. Those pants, a vital part of the Max look, the Max legend.

On the advice of a fashion stylist, no underwear had ever been worn under those pants; outline of cock was a plus. Neat definition of rear, double-plus good. When those black leathers had been new the waistband had scoured the hipbone each time they had been pulled on, skin-tight as they had been. Now they were baggy, almost pitiably so. More than just a fuse wire of hair showed from the navel down; the highest point of his pubic cloud had become exposed, emaciated as he was.

The baggy white satin shirt went on, got repositioned just so. Right there, at the usual spot, resting on the collar bone. Then a decision. No shirt tonight, he decided. No more covering up. No boots either. Barefoot.

The skin was stretching taut across his chest, clingfilm on bone. Diet was not a big enough word for what he had been subjecting himself to over the last two years. Since the moment he had seen himself in all the clarity of his first DVD, he had wanted to be so skinny that he rotted from view. So light that he could walk in the snow and not leave a footprint behind him.

Sitting in front of a long mirror, flicking the theatrical lights surrounding it on and off, Max was enjoying doing nothing. He was not feeling nervous, he was feeling nothing.

On, off. The dressing room was empty, but for a row of stools, and a rack that was not needed. It was cleaner than most, but the floor had been wiped with a sour rag. There was a mighty stench of vomit every once in a while.

The backing band were scattered elsewhere, quite a distance away.

On, off. The crowd were out there getting noisy now that the support act had done their thing.

The door to the en suite bathroom was ajar and a tap could be heard dripping lots of very annoying, very fast little drips. It was to this rhythm that Max started nodding his head, keeping time.

He picked up his guitar, which lay beside him, laid out on that dressing-room table as if it were a meal to get through.

9

For a moment he felt the smoothness of each of the tuning pegs at the machine head, then his fingers moved down for a feel of the waist of the guitar, then the inner curve of the cutaway at the neck. It felt good, all that mahogany. So smooth. The coolness of the metal tailpiece also felt good. Cool, no sharp edges.

Max picked out a plectrum which had been jammed into a gap at the bridge. He inhaled, held that breath, then exhaled slowly. Lowering his head sideways towards the machine head, he began playing a C major triad, using open strings. From the C he went to a G major, no open strings, then back to the C. The four fingers of his left hand curled across the strings, deadening the sound. He enjoyed the feeling of those vibrations buzzing to a halt.

It was a classic jazz guitar he held close to himself, a much-sought-after Gibson ES175, a Charlie Christian pick-up variety, lovingly put together back in 1949.

Again he downstroked the C major triad, slowly. This time the C was followed by a G major triad, then a G7, including the additional F. It felt better than before. Right.

'Don't listen to a word I say,' he monotoned once he had got the sequence near perfect. 'Don't listen to what I can't keep silent.'

He was strangely calm, just a body. The frets of nickel-silver and the position markers of abalone had long been his constant companions. This old Gibson was another vital part of the Max legend, as constant as his long hair and black leather trousers.

Composing a song to the rhythm of a dripping tap just fifteen minutes before he was due to go on stage in front of a capacity crowd of ten thousand might have seemed an odd thing to be doing to anyone there with him – but he was quite alone. One of his rules. Soon, he knew, that rule would be broken. His pig management had insisted a pig journalist from one of the pig broadsheets pop by to 'observe' him ten minutes or so before he went on. Max had been reluctant to agree, but the promised coverage was to be extensive. A rare in-depth interview was due to take place the following day. There was no wriggling out of it, and that pig journalist was the best. One he had never met, one he was a little fearful of. Not the usual kind of pig, not the sex 'n' drugs 'n' kiss 'n' tell variety, not from the plop-plop world of pop. This pig journalist came from a medical background, had her own radio show. She was of the headshrink variety, that kind of pig. Oola Khan.

How far would she venture beyond a skim-read of the clippings and latest press release? Max wondered. How much of the lyric sheet would she give any time to? Which thought-bubble bandwagon would she ride? Would she be just another in a long line of lazy pig journalists, simply requiring the 'radio edit' of Max's life to jiggle about in five hundred words?

Max had never shown any respect for the music industry. To him everybody feeding off the corpse of rock 'n' roll was a pig. The A&R people were pigs; the session musicians and producers were pigs; the photographers, graphic designers, PRs, moronic DJs, accountants and attorneys, tour promoters, management, merchandisers and media: P-I-G-S.

Attention was divided, his thoughts scattered everywhere. Wound up like a clockwork soldier, at the junction of two moods, Max took a cigarette, put it in his mouth, then thought about it. He decided against lighting up. Shouldn't, he thought to himself. Not now. I've only just got started. The cigarette got put behind his ear, as his focus returned to the challenge of his guitar.

Max gently ran the thumbnail of his right hand up and down the wire-wound sixth, enjoying the buzz, the quiet metallic whistle. Then he pushed his index finger against the first, the thinnest of the six strings. It felt cheesewire sharp against his cool fingertip. He gave the string a delicate pluck with his fingernail. The sound made was a shuddering twang.

There was a dull, irregular pulse in Max's left eye. Dull and curt. It hurt. Every fifteen seconds or so he would blink, as if attempting to dislodge dust from his eyes. The song, and the interview, would be his last. That had been decided.

It had been days since he had last pissed. He liked the way he was looking, skin-stretched cheeks, so sunken and despaired. The way he looked, so stripped down to the bone, looked right. *Felt* right. Absolutely.

He could hardly manage to keep up the pretence of what he was supposed to be doing with these last days. Even though he was fulfilling most of what he was contractually obliged to, he was sleepwalking: dazed and vaguely amused that no one could see the sandwich board he had been hulking around with him that said LAST FEW DAYS.

'Tonight, tomorrow night, then goodbye,' Max croaked to the space between his knees. Soon that octave-scaling voice of his would be splintering a single word, a lone syllable, rocking skyward – but not in that dressing room. There, alone, he was the Max no one ever got to see.

He gently rested his guitar against the wall, raised himself, and moved towards the dressing table. Ostentatiously, he began crumbling two bars of light milk chocolate into a small blue-and-white china bowl, watching himself go through this part of the usual routine in the full wall mirror.

'You,' he said, chewing a little mouthful of chocolate, 'are one step away from autopsy.'

He ran a hand over his head, then again, this time allowing his fingers to comb through his shoulder-length hair. The day after he died, would a doctor remove his brain? Cut it out of his head to be measured, weighed and assessed with a few prods? Like a giant cauliflower. Some very big grey vegetable.

There was a double knock at the door. The pig journalist is here, Max thought.

He sniffed, his eyes tightened.

'Come in.'

Walking into the dressing room, the journalist said, 'Hi,' no more. All she got in response was a nod, with eyes directed kind of towards her neck. She was taken aback. In her head the numbers of an electronic clapperboard began to increase at quite a pace. The sudden close proximity to the shirtless star, standing there in front of her, eating chocolate from a little bowl, felt wrong – as if she had invaded a private moment: like wanking or shitting or fixing up. Along with that sudden close proximity came impression number one, that the rock star seemed to have a layer of skin missing: *that* vulnerable, *that* delicate.

Her perfume was distinctive. If Max was reacting to anything, it was that cloud of scent which followed her. Something unusual, expensive. Something with lots of cloves, and something softer. Herself.

Dressed in a little number designed perhaps for leaf-covered shelter from which to shoot a rare species of bird, the journalist took a seat. A blouse the colour of orange squash was teasingly open. She seemed intent on handling herself with TV-script dignity, friendly enough in that formal, shallow, trans-atlantic way that would keep her at a safe enough distance.

Just before she had entered the room, the journalist had pressed the REC and PLAY buttons on a discreet tape recorder that was whirring away within her small, black, silk, hand-beaded evening bag placed on her lap. An extremely compact directional microphone was pointed away from her.

Max gave the journalist the once-over, from UV-tanned legs to a head of hair which had endured much arranging and rearranging. Not for the first time Max had the feeling that he was in the presence of yet another pig journalist who wanted him to exude success like the stale smell of boiled cabbage. Be something five-star.

Surprised to find herself more than a little nervous, the journalist looked anywhere but towards the young man she had been sent to cover for a piece due out the following week, and there he was, now standing by the window of that air-conditioned backstage trap, stacking one chord sequence upon another, preoccupied, almost oblivious of her presence.

His appearance, the journalist acknowledged, has acquired a horrific glamour – broadly built, but frighteningly thin. Straight up/straight down. No ass on him. Simultaneously bloody awful and bloody fantastic. Prod him and he'd snap.

Once described as 'a marvellous boy in black leather, made up by two queers on the phone', Max undoubtedly had an animal beauty that stretched beyond lust. He was nearer seven foot than six, and the temptation to blatantly ogle the gangling, wiry frame of the nineteen-year-old global obsession was a temptation she found hard to resist, but there would be plenty of time to look. Tonight, tomorrow noon, tomorrow night.

While she took in the minimal make-up on the dressing table, the unusual absence of alcohol or upturned mirror in the room, the woman tried to sniff out any outward signs of 'nervous exhaustion' – a standard rock 'n' roll euphemism covering a multitude of sins. That was the angle her editor wanted to chase. The Max backlash was due, and those eyes were short-handing notes very quickly.

The journalist guessed that Max was composing a song, rather than rehearsing. The strumming was jagged, repetitious, building upon fragments. Composing at that moment seemed a weird thing to be doing. Then again, she thought, this is the penultimate gig of a forty-two-date tour which has taken in eleven different countries. Same set for close on eight weeks. Rather as for an actor in a Broadway show, the novelty must have worn off.

Feeling stared-at and alien, Max took the cigarette from behind his ear, put it in his mouth, then lit up.

'You want one?' he asked.

The journalist smiled, gave an economical nod. Game in play, she thought.

A motorcycle accident just one year back had given Max his number-one sexy asset: a bad leg which he dragged a bit. That bad leg gave the impression of a man wanting to avenge, get equal.

As Max moved, he seemed to be approaching the final moments of long-awaited revenge. He extended a pack of cigarettes in the journalist's direction. She took one. Accepted a light. Stuck to the rules, did not say a word. The way she turned her head a little to one side as she exhaled a sharp line of smoke unnerved Max. Her eyes were too hungry, taking in too much information.

Max returned to his seat. He did not like the kind of eye contact this young woman had already locked on him a few times. Eyes that conveyed a certain sorrow and distaste at the same time, even though she was making a passable attempt to crack a minimal smile. Eyes that looked at him as if he were an object of study, a stuffed thing. The woman triggered an anxiety, a discomfort.

Max took a deep suck on his cigarette, inhaling as if in a reversed scream. His head leaned back so far as he did so that to the seated woman only the throat and chin were visible. Although it was a natural, totally undesigned moment, it seemed like a posture made for photographic film to capture. He had a really great jawline, it had an underneath to it. A pointy chin. Then something in him changed. He brushed his hands against the knees of his leathers, as if he had just performed the filthiest of tasks and entered a stare-you-in-the-face-and-psych-you-out moment, which soon melted. From hard to so very vulnerable.

With smoke honking in and out of her little nose, the journalist wondered whether he would talk a little. Break the silence. She was keen to get started. All she wanted was just a little something to take with her from their ten minutes together. Just a little insight into a Max that the public had not seen before. The C90 cassette on her lap was not picking up anything as yet. She hated waste. Wanted something.

Now. Come on. String a few words together. Hit me with something.

Max's ever-chirpy PR had provided the journalist with a stack of clippings. Everything. The entire story of a nineteen-year-old who, bored with his Sega just four years back, had bought a guitar to occupy his hands and to fill/kill the empty hours of a school holiday. His parents had not been happy with the constant strumming so both he and the guitar had been exiled to a nearby subway tunnel to practise in.

Those parents thought it was just a phase he was going through, the music thing all parents dread. What that mom and dad did not know was that their only child was improvising cold-blooded, passionless lyrics on the themes of intensive promiscuity, machine sex, masochism, fetishism, alienation and desperate self-injury just a few blocks away. Day in, day out. First to the attention of commuters, then to the amazement of a record company A&R, a man with a reputation of having ears like satellite dishes.

Max's rise to fame had been sci-fi quick. A crude Hi-8 video led to a day in a dingy sixteen-track studio to a major major record deal. Blending the ancient magical ingredients of rock and making it not only sound like the first time that it had ever been thought of, but also like the most obvious thing in the world, Max's distinctive taut, repetitive, rhythmic, riffing, wistful voice and cocksure, edgy belligerence had everyone at the record company *hooked*. He was anything but the average one-dimensional rocker.

Max had never savoured the bedroom-mirror/tennis-racket stage of many a teenager's fantasy world of fame. He was signed at fifteen, demoing at sixteen, on tour with his first album, *To Be Played at Maximum Volume*, at the age of seventeen. Not bad for a kid who had some kind of severe language-delay condition until the age of eleven, the journalist thought. Not bad for a kid who, according to rumour or a rancid bit of hype, started taking drugs other than dope by twelve. Pretty fucking excellent, actually, for a kid his peers at school avoided like the plague because he was too intense for the casual moment. And so began, wholeheartedly, a career of unhappiness.

Slapping its echoes against bricks in the corridor outside was one very dry cough. Then there was a double knock at the door.

'Five minutes, Max,' the roadie croaked through a two-inch gap.

Max nodded, watched the door close.

'This is when it's so damn easy to cave in,' Max said to the journalist. 'This is when the energy level can either rise dramatically or fall.'

He spoke so slowly, words dragged out on his breath like those advertising banners sometimes seen trailing behind small aircraft. The journalist felt cobwebs could have formed between those words.

That's my boy. Say more. Say anything. Come on, now.

Max cranked open the one small window in the room. Paint splintered. Hinges in need of lubrication whined.

Outside, the air was hung with moth rain: that kind of filmy, suspended moisture which penetrates every stitch. The pig management had already pointed out that the crowd would be arriving damp, so humidity levels in the auditorium would be

17

high. Added to that, the day had been hot. The paramedics would be busy.

'I hate summer,' Max said in a plaintive whisper that seemed to sift through the gap in his teeth. 'I'm sure I get the reverse of Seasonal Affective Disorder. I can't fucking stand it and just wish it was dark at six o'clock. Y'know?'

The journalist was already beginning to draft sentences in her head. This boy is cracking up, this boy is breaking down. Max's appeal, she thought, lies precisely in the fact that he seems so utterly and selfishly doomed – part Narcissus, part Icarus. The fans want him just dysfunctional enough to write all those cool songs with the wistful lilt, the minor key, but not so fucked up that he is not around any more.

Again, a double knock at the door. Max seemed to anticipate what he was about to be told. His posture, the journalist noticed, suddenly shifted, as if half a dozen internal switches had just been flicked. His energy levels had just surged before her very eyes.

Passing over the roadie's ceramic teeth was a tongue that would help the man form a single word.

'Time,' the roadie said.

In gentlemanly fashion, Max allowed the journalist to leave first.

The room was left in silence.

The way Max was humming to himself as he moved along the corridors towards the stage area struck the journalist as dreamy, sad. Kind of lost. The word, she decided, is melancholic.

As the house lights dimmed, Max turned to the woman. Beside her, his body was a long sliver of silver shadow.

'This time tomorrow,' Max half whispered, half croaked into the journalist's ear, 'last gig.' He added, 'And then I'm done.'

A spotlight shone on the crowd. For one full minute the

audience were the live show, and they loved it. A roar went up when certain sections of the arena were projected up on to the massive screens on either side of the stage. Oola Khan thought the first three rows were hideous. To her those faces were huge and crude and hysterical. Faces of fans, awaiting their nineteen-year-old mass hypnotist.

Last gig. Oola was unsure as to what the rock star had meant as he walked on to the stage to the roar of ten thousand cheering people who would soon be thrash-dancing like hooked fish. Last night of the tour, or last gig ever?

# 2

Dawn. Steam rising off the streets.

The air-conditioning system in Room 8063 was totally fucked. It was way too cold in there, like an icebox.

Exactly half asleep, half awake, Max is lying face down on another hotel mattress, the white cotton sheet kicked off. He looks like a Gap advert. He is wearing nothing – that is the way he has slept since the age of sixteen. Since he left home.

Topping myself. Doing myself in. Calling it a day. Hey, three great ideas: something to strive for. My beautiful ambition.

His mind is just about ticking over. His thoughts are fragments that float up together, then crash, forming new ones. The one constant in his line of thought being that ambition, planned so long. He knew its every detail the way a child feels the swerve of a favourite story.

Nights had been bad for a long while, years. He invariably slid out of bed in the mornings as if to get just a little peace before the next bedtime. Lying there, however, Max felt unusually comfortable. Despite the chill of his skin, he felt relaxed. Floaty. Half there, half somewhere else, and that somewhere else was where he was heading.

'This is Thursday, and Thursday means the last gig,' Max croaked to the giant digital alarm clock beside the king-sized bed.

He sniffed in, hard. The day had started. A day like any other recent day. Max felt insignificant. Felt less than modest in his position on earth.

What, he thought, do you do with a light bulb that's a dud?

The bed was warm, so comfortable. Where he wanted to be.

Just five more minutes. Just five more minutes.

Half an hour later he was on auto, practically running on empty as he got himself up, stumbling towards the bathroom. The light had been on all night, or what was left of night after he had been led in, helped into bed, then left like a car in a garage with wires leading to the battery: on recharge. Max felt that he had slept all of five minutes. Felt flat.

He popped his tongue out at the sight of his reflection.

'Last day on earth,' he monotoned. 'Hurrah.'

Once again he popped his tongue out, this time for a squinted self-examination. The sight of his tongue, reflected back at him none too prettily, grossed him out.

He sniffed again, twice.

'Feel *r-r-ough*.'

He ran a little cold water and aimed his penis towards the plug hole in the sink. Nothing.

'Man no drink, man no piss. Man no piss, man die,' he said to his reflection, Rasta style. 'Really feel *shiiit*,' he said in disgust to his screwed-up eyes, screwed-up hairdo. Max thought of all the worst words he could come up with and crammed them into a look grenade.

Although his throat felt sandpapered raw, he craved a cigarette.

His elbow hurt. It had been bandaged. Then it came back to him. The black of another collapse; he had taken another fall. He needed to close his eyes to remember. He could recall being pushed back on stage to do an encore. Could remember hitting the first chord. But that was all.

He was not sure whether he wanted food or to be sick. Both, he decided, but not in that order. Ice cream would be nice, he thought – one big tub of vanilla.

He hawked up phlegm that had a trace of blood in it. This circled lazily towards the plug hole, but did not go down. The glob stuck itself on to the slate-grey porcelain, as if to demand an inspection.

'Oh, fuck it,' Max droned, feeling unable to cope with the demands of the day. He knew what he wanted more than anything in the whole wide world and he was going to have it. Sleep. He knew that someone would wake him soon enough, when it was time to start the schedule of the day. There would be someone to encourage him to swallow orange juice, then coffee. Someone who would pass him a lit cigarette. Someone who would politely avert their eyes as they handed him a bath towel as he stepped from the shower. As far as he was aware, the morning was a blank – all he had to do was get to the office by noon for an interview with . . . Max tried to remember. *Her*. That woman from last night, the pig journalist. That *sexy* pig journalist. Oola.

Max slept for an hour, only to be woken by a couple in the room next door. An argument. Something real.

Standing by the window, Max killed ten minutes just gazing out at the big wide world down below as he listened to the screaming coming from Room 8064. A man, a woman: at war. It was like being a kid again, waiting for the noise to stop, for the coast to be clear.

In the morning sun the buildings were so tall they seemed to be figments. Cartoony. The black silhouettes of cartoons. A bird turned out to be an aeroplane. An airplane turned out to be a kite.

With deliberate precision, a black cloud placed itself in front of the sun. Seemed to drop an anchor in that position. When a few rays managed to break through the cloud it would shift just a little, yet hardly budge – buoyant as a liner.

The ice-blue sky can do nothing about it, Max thought. The ice-blue sky is just background.

Signs of exhaustion showed in the way Max stood there, propping himself up between window and wall. The reflection of his face in the cold glass right that second, early on that Thursday morning, was blank. That big wide world out there, with its mesmerising flows of traffic and on/off lights, was an involvement he felt no part of.

Max stepped over towards a small sofa, settled himself down, lowered his head on to the awaiting flat of his two cool hands.

Max first felt, then heard, the slamming of the door. Whatever had been going on in Room 8064 had come to an end for the moment, punctuated with that angry slam. There was the sound of determined footsteps striding towards the elevator, the rattle of keys. Car keys, Max thought. Someone's going to escape.

Doors opened. Doors closed. Gone. Welcome silence.

There were sparrows on the ledge. Max could see them, but could not hear their chirping, such was the effectiveness of the double glazing. Two of them, side by side. Happy about something.

Before Max closed his eyes, he had watched those sparrows hop from the ledge. Behind those tightly shut eyes were the outstretched wings, frozen in flight. What Max wanted more than anything else for a whole week was to be ignored. Forgotten. Like he did not exist. Just alone alone alone. Absolutely no one.

'It'd be so wonderful,' he whispered to the sky.

Again, Max inspected his face in the bathroom mirror and faded away a faint trace of dry spit around his mouth with a dab of water. He could not be bothered to shave. What the fuck, he thought. I'm not going to turn into a monkey.

He checked his teeth. Decided against flossing.

He brushed away the SR way, then – finished – flashed a TV com smile and whispered, 'Yippee.'

The temperature in Room 8063 stayed constant, too cold. It hurried Max along. Time to get dressed, ride a cab.

The driver nodded, knew where the skinny guy was heading. Max jumped in.

As the door shut, the air-conditioning got busy. Max closed his eyes, feeling the sweat that had accumulated on him in the walk from the swing-doors of the hotel to kerb lift off.

He ran a hand over the freshly laundered white polyester seat covers. They were neatly fitted and sedately frilled, matching the dinky lace curtains over the rear windows. Nodding dog, plastic roses, box of tissues. It was all very home sweet home. Quite a cab.

The driver was old. His ID photo showed a pitted face with bushy moustache – a contrast to the long, clean-shaven neck that Max had a great view of. The driver twiddled his radio until he found a station that he tuned in on just right. A cello played. A lone cello, working a chord sequence which seemed inappropriate for that time of the morning: too sombre. Max responded, involuntarily; he could do nothing about the imminent onslaught of tears. They came, and the driver noticed that they were not wiped away. Poor thing, the driver thought. Another young sufferer in the back seat. Nothing new, nothing so unusual. Just about every human emotion had been expressed on that back seat. Body fluid, too.

Gears shifted within Max. He could feel himself slowing down as the cab began to speed along a vacant stretch of road. And then he was sleeping.

Max could have been taken away anywhere. The driver, checking in his rear-view mirror, knew that. Passengers, so trusting. Cute boy, the cab-driver thought. Not quite my type, though. Too tall.

Just a few blocks away from the record company's main office, Max awoke. The cab had pulled up a little jerkily at lights. The sun seemed twice as bright as usual. Everything turned white, then black. It took a while to readjust.

Like an image developing slowly in a printer's tray, the grainy outline of a cyclist began to form. There, beside the cab. Some guy around the same age as himself, wearing nothing but shiny, black, skin-tight cycle shorts. When the lights turned to green, the play of muscles on the cyclist was visible. Regular, monotonous as in animated photos of the early twentieth century. Shoulders hunched up to ears. Torso, so still, immobile. Feet above the ground, circling. Circling from the calf, knee, long tanned thigh. The hindquarters above the saddle, poised. Almost stripped bare. Cropped, bleached head, shining. With sudden reflections off black glass, the cyclist's body was reduced to a silhouette, lines sharpened as he drew away with speed. Clarified, purified.

Both Max and the cab-driver watched the cyclist flow like water through the net of cars ahead. There was practice in his grace. Daring, too, with all that weaving and dipping while racing forward. It had been a long while since Max had ridden a bike, years.

'Hey, cancel that,' Max said to the driver. 'Take me west at these lights.'

It was an impulse, but part of a thought process that had been woven then unpicked so many times. A decision that had been a dilemma for weeks, the idea of saying goodbye to his parents. Against what he felt was his better judgment, Max had decided to pop by to see those parents of his, just for a few minutes. All he could stand. Just to make the big exit clean, neat. He felt he owed them that.

They were in. First sign of this was the smell of cooking, then the darkening of the spyhole in that front door.

'Max,' his mother said through the door, looking at the gaunt face staring her way, 'is that *you?*'

'As if a burglar would bother,' Max replied huskily.

A moment's hesitation. Then she was there, a sudden full-length vision. Wearing an apron with fading forget-me-nots scattered all over it and a heart-shaped pocket bulging with a cellular phone, as if she were some professional on call.

'Why didn't you use your key?' Max's mother asked.

For a moment Max really was not in the mood to obey the house rules and take his suede boots off. He felt that the impulsive visit was a mistake, that it would be just *too draining*. He did not want to step over that boundary, entering their domain. So he stood there, in the frame of the door, letting a fresh current of air into the place.

Max's mother leaned her right cheek towards him. Max snapped into mode and kissed his mother, then began playing the cheery automaton. What they wanted.

'I'm *ho-ome*,' he sing-songed, and it gave him a scary excellent feeling just for a second, that he could go on like that for ever. Pretending everything was okay – everything jus' fine.

'Look who's come to see us,' Max's mother called out, taking in the sight of her son as if he were some kind of museum exhibit.

Not yet noon and already the lunch was on. A hot meal, Max thought, on a day like this. Only my parents could dream up such torture.

Max's father headed into the hallway, a knife in one hand, half a head of cabbage in the other. By way of greeting, he said, 'Son.'

There was what sounded like an old war movie on the television.

'I, er, I just wanted to say goodbye,' Max began too quietly. Then, too loudly, 'Happy holiday!' It came out all wrong.

'Oh,' Max's mother said, 'that *is* nice of you. We're off at four. Flight's at seven.'

And there were the suitcases by the door. All packed, ready to go.

'Two weeks, right?'

'That's correct,' Max's father said, returning to the kitchen. 'Now that the dog's dead we can come and go as we please.'

Already the familiar edge in the air. Well done, Dad.

'We'll be staying at the usual place,' Max's mother chirped with a little too much glee, attempting to skip over the little hiccup of tension that had already arisen, with her son only just through the door. 'You've got the number.'

'Right,' Max said.

'Cup of tea?' Max's mother asked.

Max nodded.

'Oh,' he said, 'I just need to get something from my old room. Back in a sec.'

It was too much. He had to get away from them, just for a minute. The way they were looking at him was the way they were always looking at him. Max was surprised that his parents did not operate some kind of blood check on entry. They probably had some high-tech gadget hidden away somewhere, to analyse a stray hair.

Nothing had changed in there. They had left it exactly the way it had been when pig management had plucked Max both out of home and school for the intensive coaching he needed before launching him upon the public two full years later. From there, that room, to so many service flats that all felt the same. It had been necessary – pig A&R and pig management had been right. He had needed the singing lessons, the technical advancement with guitar. More than anything else, he had needed to be away from *them*. Those two.

Max had, occasionally in the past, returned to the family home for brief spells. A birthday, not his own. The time his father was sick (the miserable old fuck had recovered – much to everyone's disappointment). Close to the release of the first single, when things had begun to get a bit much, before they got a whole lot worse, Max had come seeking shelter for a month, needing support. He had just been lectured, told that what he was doing was all a big mistake.

He knelt by his old futon. It felt like a stage direction. [Max enters room, kneels.] He had never hidden much. He did not need to. Neither of them had ever enquired about what he had in that old room of his. What all those accumulated possessions meant to him.

Kneeling there, clock ticking down internally, he surveyed the room. Max found the thought of his suicide so comforting at that moment. Less than twenty-four hours to go. Much less.

Lines which Max could not get out of his head were circling his brain. They came to him at the strangest moments. Stepping out of the shower, when having a pee in the middle of the night, on the tour bus. When not thinking about anything in particular. Those lines. *One day after the day of their departure will be the day of mine.* An idea that had consoled the only son for months. *I have passed judgment upon myself. No appeal will be heard.* That is what he thought, over and over. The voice he heard in the silence of his heart.

Those lines, like a couple of chords from a song. Stuck. Repeating. Like a chant. Those lines sometimes surrounded Max with a sustained clarity, a hypnotic buoyancy. A persistence.

I really want to. It's what I need.

All the elements of his boyhood were in that room. Lined up, neatly, in there. All that stuff he had hunted out by himself, too. Books he had somehow managed to hear about and had sought, found, read and kept. While his nose had been in books, his peers at school had been stuck in the mode of chart music and all that went with it, all that shopping they felt compelled to do. Looking over some of the titles, Max was shocked now by what he had worked himself through, things they had no idea of. Them, out there. Those two. Mom 'n' Dad.

And to think that I have put this off so long because I believed that to top myself would hurt them. Ha bloody ha.

No one had ever asked, 'What are you reading?' or 'What's it about?'

They actually believe that the more books you've read, the more intellectual sheen you accrue, the better life'll be some day. Like drips of gasoline, he thought, adding up for some joy-ride into the future. Dark drips, vital sustenance stored in some dirty, greasy tank no one would care to take too close a peek at. Dark, smelly, bitter little drips – producing juicy Class A brains.

It was not as if his room were a shut-off No Entry zone. His mother still cleaned in there, he knew that. Meticulously. And it showed. All those neat lines. But, uncharacteristically, with the unprobing eye of hotel staff, more preoccupied with doing it all in the allotted time than considering what made her son tick. And sick.

Max could not remember why he had gone into that room. He knew he'd said that he had wanted to fetch something. He could not remember what. And now it was raining, and he had to go and stand by the window, look out. It was confident rain, enthusiastic and generous. Flashing, white rain, coming down in show-offy sheets, rain-clouds really strutting their stuff, making sure everyone got some. Splattering down loudly. Rivering down slanted roofs, sneaking in a splash through a slipped tile and a bad bit of pointing in need of repair. Embracing anything dry like a long-lost friend. Saying hi-de-hi to a dry sock, the root of a bulb, the cat's milk saucer.

Seeking out the fax machine by the open window, the hole in an umbrella, the toes of new suede shoes. Rain, going *ha-ha-ha* as it seeped in. Rain, like a nervous, scratching drum pattern. Like rain, a kind of suicidal damp had permeated his life. A mood that had got going in that room, by that window.

It was like being a boy again, standing there. Their boy. Their little machine. Perhaps, stamped somewhere on his butt, there was a discreet MAKE, MODEL and REGISTRATION. Handy. Max wondered whether TYPE OF MALFUNCTION would be neatly annotated close to the beckoning mortuary slab.

'I'm not a slave to a world that doesn't give a shit,' Max muttered under his breath.

What did they think they were doing when they were baby-making, producing me? Max thought, as his mother poured him a cup of tea out there in the kitchen. How do they feel when they look at me? Is it over? Is what they wanted over? Did they get what they wanted, and I'm just the garbage of their dream? Something the therapy queen couldn't fix?

Not for the first time, Max imagined his mother's dilated cervix, and her – obeying the doctor and pushing. Screaming. Panting. And pushing again. He knew it had been a difficult birth. He knew it was a third-time-lucky affair. He knew the birth was a successful event in his parents' marriage. They had got a kid at last. A boy. Smile, please.

His mother had told him, time and time again, that it had been a tough delivery. She had told him often enough. In great detail. And always, often in unison with her husband, his father, that pig of a man, like some comedy sketch on television, so utterly unconvincingly, that same old line – 'But it was worth it.'

'Max,' his mother called out. 'Tea.'

With reluctance, Max left the window. He scanned the shelves. Picked up a MiniDisc that he had put together a while back, something he had entitled 'The Accidental Percussion of Worn-Out Vinyl' at the age of sixteen, a collection of songs that simmered a certain mood. He popped it into the breast pocket of his shirt. Left the room.

'Did you find what you were looking for?' Max's mother asked.

Max patted the pocket over his heart. There. The neat justification.

He lifted the old blue mug that was his mug to his lips. Something he had bought at a foreign fish market many years ago. Aged nine, maybe ten. When the troubles had really begun to accumulate, when life had started to become a very obvious landslide. A mug shaped like an old-fashioned pencil, all geared hexagons. Blue. Decorated with a giant fish.

Max's father took in the sight of his son, leaning against the washing machine. That tatty old grey shirt tucked into old blue jeans – ready to rip at both knees. No socks. You've made a lot of money for yourself, my boy, the man thought, but you look like rent. Cheap.

Max detected the shift of mood within the tiny kitchen as he locked eye contact with his father. That man.

Max put his tea down, then pulled out his shirt. As a gesture it was more shocking to his father than a V-sign. It was *untidy*.

'Hey,' Max said to his mother, 'have this. I never use it.'

He pulled a brand-new digital camera out of his bag. Small, compact.

'Two megabytes internal memory, Web cam function, USB connection, auto white balance, self-timer, the lot,' Max said.

Max's mother shook her head; all that technical information was way too much for her.

'See this?' Max half whispered to his father. 'You just press it, right? Then lay it down on something like . . . er . . . so,' Max said, positioning the camera on the grill section of the cooker, 'and . . .'

31

The camera flashed. Got them. The three of them. Together, one last time.

Max's mother found it such a sweet thought. And odd. Max had never done anything like that before. It made her feel uncomfortable. That, and when he picked up his bag all of a sudden in a rush, only then to turn, looking at his father as if in slo-mo. Up and down, scanning a long, slow, mental picture.

'What's the matter?' Max's father had asked while checking the buttoning of his shirt and the positioning of his tie in the reflection of the small hall mirror.

Max had just said nothing. Just taking in that look of the man. Daddy.

'Time to go,' Max whispered into his mother's ear at the door.

All three had plans to follow.

Max pressed the buzzer. Though his face was turned in the direction of the CCTV camera, his eyes were elsewhere.

*Bzzz.* He was in.

While Max began to climb the stairs, the receptionist continued her telephone conversation.

'Getting hold of coke is as easy as buying candy,' she said. 'It's just like having a beer.' She shrugged, then realised that it was *Max* coming up the stairs. 'Gotta go.' She slammed the phone down, licked her lips, changed her body posture fast as a porn star.

Max never sauntered, he just walked. Plain. As he put it in his song 'Hidden Bruises', 'Never went in for that rock star shit/Just walked straight/Walked tall'.

Max noticed, with horror, that extensive changes had been made to the entrance of the record company since he had been away on tour. The six dwarf magnolias, two olive trees, cypress and four palm trees were all – every one of them – made of plastic. The reception desk was like some kind of high-tech dugout. More flight deck than desk, what with all that fogged glass, underlighting and height.

'Oh, hiya,' the receptionist gushed. New girl. Badge said 'Kayt' something or other difficult to read. Max nodded, but no eye contact. New girl, but part of the organisation, so a pig. In this case, Max thought as he sneaked a sidelong glance, a cute little piglet. Kayt Diekgerdes.

The new girl was all sniffs, Max noticed, as he signed in. It was a very sniffy cold. She would take a sip of that cherry 7-Up fizzing away beside her, then it would be sniff-sniff-sniff. In the amount of time it had taken Max to pick up that Biro and scrawl M-A-X, the new receptionist had made a sweet impression. She was like a seal after swallowing a good-sized fish. With that in his mind he smiled her way and she thought: Ah, bless. He's a dote, so he is.

By the little switchboard that the girl operated there was a big, red, shiny apple. Max leaned over, grabbed it. Took a bite, then returned the apple to where it had been. The girl's jaw dropped an inch, playing mock outrage. She was on the verge of letting out a mini-squeal when Max shook his head fast, like a visual *shhh*.

'Bye,' he said.

She couldn't help but gawp.

'See ya.' Two words that the new girl barely managed to get heard.

Just as the elevator doors were about to bang together, Max glanced her way. Yep, that new girl's focus was upon him, not the flashing lights of the switchboard. And that apple was in her hand. She was having a chew. Max's eyes twinkled for the first time in ages. He gave her a wink.

'Bye,' he said again, alone in the elevator, with only a gold-tinted reflection of himself for company. For the last three months, Max had made it a point not to say 'Hi'. No more hellos. Only 'Bye'. Only goodbyes. He was glad that he had stopped saying 'Hi', only saying 'Bye'. It was tidy and tragically sad.

Max slowly chewed that bite of an apple, savouring the technological and chemical inventiveness as he penetrated each layer of the building: frosted glass, in every internal door.

Bursting with hyperactivity and a nervous kinetic energy, the office looked like the HQ for a marathon TV fund-raising event. Though staff knew Max was not one to indulge in the usual 'Hi, how are you?' kind of shit, a few still shot him smiles, the occasional 'Hey, Max!' with a nauseous high-five ring to it. Back in the early days of Max's success, his four PRs would dash up and hold hands around him as if they were playing ring-a-ring-o'-roses. Those days were long gone, those members of staff hyping 'product' elsewhere.

The office looked like some soap opera's depiction of registration at college: neat haircuts, white teeth, self-defensive manners and budget clothes dressed up a bit. People around the room were breaking news stories to journalists, reading dates from computer screens and frantically hammering away at keyboards as if trying to avert a thermonuclear attack, or activate one. Busy busy busy. The burnout rate in the company was pretty fast. Max had witnessed bright young things arriving so curious, expectant – soon dampened, soon jaded. The parties, the pressure. The drugs.

Someone, somewhere, was busy alternately small-talking the finer details of Alexander technique and Chinese astrology. Someone else, somewhere, was bitching about a dry cleaner who had got something wrong – silk had been returned faded and bubbly. End of the world, Max thought. Maybe the same someone was the someone who had dumped the melon remnants into a bin somewhere. There was a rotten stink in the place that needed rooting out.

One wall was covered with nothing but posters of Max. Another wall was covered with framed covers Max had appeared on. There were three quite different life-sized Max cardboard cutouts.

'Punctual as ever,' Chief Pig hollered his way. 'Hey, Max, just got this review in on the new album. Kind of good, kind of weird.'

Max had always found Chief Pig *too much*. It was as if Chief Pig were always trying so hard to be some kind of 'character'. Chief Pig was someone who was acute discomfort to sit beside in the back of a limousine, hell across a restaurant table. Someone who every so often in the vast field of gratuitous, loudly enunciated philosophy sowed a few small therefores and so reached the bloody point. A right pain of a man. Max reckoned the pig had once invested in an audio programme on conversation confidence. Marek Alesky: Chief Pig. J-E-R-K.

Max leaned against a filing cabinet, acclimatising. He looked around with a sort of blank, bored, slightly pissed-off attitude. He did not want to talk to anyone but the journalist from last night. The interview was, effectively, his suicide note. He just wanted to make that final statement, then go.

Already the tape recorder was whirring away. REC and PLAY buttons had just been pushed, clockwise movement checked.

'Looking for me?' the journalist asked, taking Max by surprise.

Tattersall checks plus thunder-and-lightning tweeds formed a strong vein of Englishness: an outfit at a certain price range that compensated for its lack of originality.

Max locked eye contact, just for a second.

'Your manager says we can do the interview through here,' the journalist said, indicating a small side office. Max nodded his assent.

'What do you fancy?' Max asked, pointing towards the minibar.

'Oh, just water,' the journalist replied.

'Right. Two waters.'

There was no ice out, no lemon, no line of sparkly glasses.

'Like this okay?' Max asked, a little sheepishly, as he passed the young woman a chilled plastic bottle.

'Fine. Thanks.'

Max took in the gentle placing of the tape recorder on the table, directional microphone aimed towards the chair on which he was about to seated.

The room was set up the same as ever. Nice and cool, lighting just right: low. Both relaxed back into the soft black leather chairs. Pleasantries dispensed with, the journalist spread some notes out across the table. Max interpreted this in two ways: 1) she has done her homework and 2) she's taking control. Let her.

'Ready when you are,' Max said, putting the ball firmly in the journalist's court.

Again she smelled of something expensive out of a bottle with a snugly fitting glass stopper. Max found himself surveying the young woman's bones, that almost Celtic skin, those perfect clothes-hanger shoulders.

A tassel of hair had fallen across his forehead, half covering one eye. He suddenly looked very delicate, a little feminine.

She smiled, working those huge, wide-apart blue eyes, blinking once to – so knowingly – contrast the black of her feathery lashes with the perfect whites of her eyes. She had a china-like prettiness and she knew it. Daddy had always said she was the most beautiful little girl in the world. So had a number of the boys at school. She had always been such a lucky girl, everything had gone her way.

Great nose job, Max thought, beginning to pick – never

taken in by surface. Had her upper lip done, too. Restylane. Bet those little injections hurt.

The atmosphere felt special. Important.

'Have you seen today's papers?'

Max shook his head from left to right.

'There's a kind of bizarre review of the new album.'

Max took a look at the highlighted page being thrust his way. As he began to read, he was certain that he looked extremely sick in the head. Did he, he thought, did he look sick in the head? Extremely so?

'TO THE MAX' by MAX (Furnace)

Single-minded awkwardness sometimes pays off. 'TO THE MAX' is an album packed with all the ideas, emotional resonance and songwriting skills that many doubted Max possessed purely because of his age. The defining moment of this third, incredibly complex album by Max comes after just fifteen minutes. During one of the most understated moments, 'Goodbye', a desolate, guilt-ridden Max murmurs, 'I spiral down, sayonara, I spiral down, au revoir.' Those two lines, sitting dead centre of both song and album, provide the fulcrum by which 'TO THE MAX' revolves. 'TO THE MAX' is the sound of a man trapped in corrosive solitude. Impassioned, headstrong, menacing and often gloriously incoherent, this is an album fans will slash their wrists to out of Max's respect for martyrdom.

Rating:*****

Max folded the page, making a paper airplane out of it. Threw it across the room. It crash-landed against the wall.

'Bollocks,' he declared.

The journalist raised an eyebrow.

'All of it?'

Max smiled. Evasion would be tricky with this one. Oola Khan. A funny kind of name, Max thought, looking at the journalist. Oola.

The interrogation began. 'Track one. A song entitled 'Un-happy'.'

Max squirmed in his seat.

'Oh no, please. You're not going to recite the lyrics to me.'

Her face was set, determined.

'Uh-huh.'

Max closed his eyes. Exhaled heavily.

'I hate it when people do this.'

The woman only broke the silence when Max finally succumbed to eye contact.

'Tough,' Oola said with a smile.

She looked at the lyric sheet.

'Verse one, chorus. "I wasn't happy/I took cocaine/We slept together/I have nothing/We met again/We slept together/I cried a lot/I have nothing/Unhappy/Unhappy/Un-happy/Unhappy/Unhappy/Un-happy." And so on.' Three words Oola dragged out.

Max wondered what the approach was. Ridicule? Was she taking the piss?

'You know, the way you just read that was so shite. That song started off as a fragment that I carried around with me for quite a while. It was thrown up in the air and we juggled with it and shaped it and thudded it and kicked it off the wall and pummelled it and panel-beat it and spat on it and chewed it up and pissed on it and slept with it and loved it and licked it and . . . and then you came to interview me, Doctor, for the newspaper you do a regular bit of freelancing for, Doctor, without knowing the intonation of it, Doctor. I really should tell you to go fuck yourself, Doctor. You and your expensive mortgage repayments.'

Ah, he's waking up, Oola thought. Reading from the *Face*, she put on the voice of a crass radio DJ: 'Lauded in some quarters as a record of stealthy and slow-burning rock electronica, hailed in others as a deliberate and perverse act of commercial suicide, the new album by Max has rocketed to number one on both sides of the Atlantic and eleven other territories in this first week of release, despite the fact that he has insisted on no singles, no videos and an absolute minimum of press coverage.'

Max sniffed, hard.

'Y'know, I've often been accused of being morbid, bleak. As far as I'm concerned, that's the appropriate response, 'cos our culture is the most fucking desperate culture. Desperately avoiding anything vaguely depressing, which is alarming because what's the result? Well, we all know what that is, don't we? We're at a time when we are being presented with undeniable changes in the global climate and fundamental issues that affect every single one of us, and it's the time that we're listening to the most hokey shite on the radio and watching vacuous bullshit celebrities being bullshit celebrities and desperately trying to forget about everything. Which is fine, y'know, but – personally – I can't do that.'

Ooh, thought Oola, I can see all that in bold.

'How's your love life?' she asked, throwing the question out playfully: a gentler ice-breaker. It came like a bludgeon which floored Max, followed by three or four kicks to the ribs. 'Girlfriend? Boyfriend? Or don't you fuck? Asexual, *mm?*'

Max searched through his file of auto responses. When in doubt he always hit sound-bite mode.

'Provocation's like masturbation. Just got to be done every once in a while, *mm?*'

Max lit a cigarette. He blew the smoke up into the air and watched it disperse. That is why he smoked, to watch the white fade. Like dust, it worked best in a dark room in which there was only a thin beam or two of light.

He decided he would answer that question. 'There's never been . . . anyone . . .' He left the words hanging there.

'There's never been anyone? Or there's never been anyone *special?*' Oola asked.

Not now, Max thought. Not this.

'The latter,' Max said. A little white lie.

He stood. Changed his mind. Sat down again.

'Regarding your official website, I've been told that yesterday it was entirely *your* decision to scrap all visuals, dates and video clips to post a message reading: "I'm going for a walk in the park."'

'Yeah.'

The atmosphere, Max felt, was now that of a therapist's consulting room. Not unsurprising – the woman was a therapist. She had her column, a radio slot, the occasional television appearance. Digging deep and glamorising neurosis in a traumatic/tragic kind of way was her job – a nice little earner it was too.

'My mind is not all it should be,' Max admitted to the space between his mouth and cigarette filter. 'Everyone needs a psychic shield, otherwise too much of the world gets in and you've had it.'

The words felt theatrical, so real they felt fake. A sudden sense of pleasure surged through the nineteen-year-old. He had, he just realised, managed to cross some internal border. It was definite. The date he had made with himself would happen. What a relief.

In the comfort of the conference room, the woman's cellular phone rang. Quite unabashed, as if alone, she talked to someone about a dinner party that she would not be attending the following evening. It was as if she were cut off, as if enclosed within an old-fashioned booth.

She shrugged, smiled. 'My fan club,' she joked. 'Now, where were we?'

Max tugged his purple suede boots off. Before the odour of his feet rose up to smudge the air, he folded his legs under him, sat cross-legged.

'This is the thing that's going round,' he began. 'I read an interview with someone recently and they said, "Max is going to surprise everyone by releasing an album of knock-'em-dead pop tunes next." It's interesting that a lot of people this year have decided that there's some kind of master plan to what I do. They think I'm stuck away in some mansion in the heart of the countryside plotting and scheming, and the reality of it is that a lot of what I do happens by chance.'

Oola nodded. It was a 'go on' kind of nod.

'There won't be any singles off *To The Max* because as far as I'm concerned there aren't any singles on it. It's not that kind of thing. That wasn't my intention. There won't be any videos, either. There's no great mystique to it. I'm the one making the music, and I have it put out the way I want it put out. I may have been fifteen when I signed that contract with this record company, but it was a contract that *I* drew up. Hilarious, huh? Even at that age I knew that working within the music industry invariably entails compromise. And exploitation – of *everybody*.'

Again, Oola nodded.

'Your last single was unusual in that it was only available as a twelve-and-a-half-minute DVD epic.'

Max looked uncomfortable. He did not want to talk about that one.

'Although self-esteem's a bore, I wasn't happy with that video. It felt all wrong from the start, I should have trashed it. That was a year back. I don't want to talk about that now, though. Okay?'

Oola nodded.

'With the new album I just . . . just wanted to make a different kind of record, something more intimate. I wanted something away from the acoustic strumalongs, away from the classic verse-chorus-verse-chorus approach. One of the big things was trying to dispel all the hype, which was something I never felt comfortable with or worthy of, having started as a fifteen-year-old busker 'n' all. We live in a ridiculous time in which people in the entertainment business get stoopid amounts of coverage for what they do. It's just that there's this huge industry behind me, and it's not something that I feel necessarily comfortable with. It's a lot of responsibility, all along the line. *Especially* to the fans, believe me. There's a huge *need* out there. Some of the letters I get . . .'

Max broke off, tore the seal off his bottle of water. Took a swallow.

'Y'know, it's easy to fry your brains up in this line of work. Then again, my brains would be pretty fried if I were doing what my parents wanted me to be doing right now.'

'And what would that be exactly?'

Something happened with Max's mouth. It was as if he had just tasted something bitter. He looked as if he wanted to spit.

'Studying. I'd be at uni, fillin' my head with *shiiiiit*. Rude word, oh dear. Sorry.'

Oola smiled. Parents: sore point.

'You don't tend to do many interviews any more, do you?'

'Correct.'

'So, why me?'

Max screwed up his eyes. He was not keen to give any kind of answer to that question. That question: irrelevant.

'I come under a lot of hideous scrutiny when I'm inter-viewed. I think that's fair enough. It's the wilful misinterpreta-tion that I don't like. There's always a big-nose who knows better. There are some twisted hacks out there, believe me. The pig management here wanted to give me some "media train-ing". Can you *imagine*? Gross.'

'Last year there was an interview with Eric Nehr for *Q* in which you said, and I quote, "I believe in nothing, but it's my nothing – not yours. I've been draining this mute solitude too long, too honestly. There's nearly nothing left, and that's a comfort. It'd all be different if I were a liar."'

'Yeah, I said that. So?'

Oola looked worried.

'Last year you were on the cover of *Spin* with the words "Is this going to be the next rock 'n' roll suicide?" What do you think that was all about?'

Max lifted his hands close to his face, began to study his fingernails. That old evasion tactic. Lead, a PR once said to him, and they follow so easily.

'I just wanted to make an intense, serious statement – epic in scope and billowing with gargantuan sadness – because that's real. That's how I feel so much of the time. Sad. And that's for real.'

'Right.'

'Since day one I've tried to do everything from the heart,' Max blurted. 'I am not a *product*. Like with the videos. Those things are usually made more for the sake of the director's personal show reel rather than as an interpretation of the song. All those crap special effects, backward shit. Y'know?'

Max took another drink of water. It was something to do; he needed that distraction from the eye contact the journalist was making.

'The new album has been heralded as "intense, intriguing and enigmatic". Who do you think of as your audience and what kind of effects do you think your material and the presentation of that material has upon them?'

Max thought for a moment. Sniffed.

'Come with me, let me show you something.'

Max made for the door. Oola followed. At the far end of the open-plan office was a sectioned-off quarter, containing a dozen or so huge plastic dustbins.

'Fan mail,' Max said, pointing towards the spilling bins. 'Seems disrespectful to keep it in these things but as storage goes they're handy, or so I'm told.'

As Oola glanced at the handwriting on a few of the envelopes, Max opened one at random. He began to read it aloud.

'Dear Max, here is another letter trying to reach you among the thousands. It would take for ever to explain how I feel about you and your music . . . what you *mean* to me. Sometimes when I see you perform on telly I hold my heart because it feels as if it's going to burst. Really! Please don't laugh at this letter, thinking a foolish child wrote it, because I am not a child. You're probably thinking this is just another dumb schoolgirl crush as you read this, but I assure you it is not – I am nearly sixteen. I wish I could afford to send you whole guitars of white flowers but all I can afford is this stamp. BIG KISS. Jane Yamamoto.'

Max turned to Oola. Despite the fact that he had received letters such as this time and time again, the final line got to him. He quietened. Became more serious.

'Hey, Max,' a young black guy called out.

Max turned, a smile. A rare, genuine smile.

'Pshemko,' Max said quietly, almost tenderly.

Max's smile was pretty much mirrored by that of one Pshemko Kander. Warm, natural. A young guy wearing a combination of different-coloured leather items that were all at once twisted, textured and panelled. Some rugged, some super-soft.

He must be sweating bullets under all that buckskin, Oola thought, as she beheld the weird but not unpleasing combination of pink, grey and aquamarine.

'Got more stuff here from your favourites,' Pshemko said, pointing to a shelf marked with yellow memo stickers: A, C, I, M and Z.

Oola's forehead bunched, quizzically.

'Favourites?'

'It'd be virtually impossible for me to read all of this, but I

44

do read some. Pshemko picks out certain "regulars" for me, people who I've corresponded with when time has allowed. Sometimes I come in, plonk myself down and read through what they have to say, drop 'em a line back.'

'Right,' Oola said, estimating the number of letters surrounding her. Thousands.

'I can't answer all these, but each letter gets some kind of reply from Pshemko and his team who run the fan club. Some of them . . . well, I shouldn't be saying this but . . .'

Max decided not to say anything; he just took in a deep breath and did an impression of a blowfish.

'Some girl in Texas wrote to me every day for weeks once, same thing – over and over. "I WILL KILL MYSELF ON VALENTINE'S DAY IF YOU DON'T WRITE BACK."'

Max shook his head, shrugged.

'I didn't know about those letters until I got back from a tour. It was too late for me to do a thing to help her. Hanged herself. Occasionally some of her friends send these vile letters to the fan club, like it was all my fault.'

'Do you think you often reflect the feelings of fans considerably like yourself?'

'Yeah, but that's just me being me. What I do is me. It's . . . it's for real. When I was fourteen, fifteen, y'know, I never had a band who said anything about my life, that's why I do what I do. I say what my life was like, *is* like.'

'And what it's going to be like?'

No reply.

Oola thought for a moment. A track on the new album was entitled 'Young, Pretty & Fucked'. 'A rope around my neck/The sweetest caress/A rope around my neck/Halting breath/A rope around my neck/Dying young – leaving a good-looking corpse.' Hardly the kind of lyrics designed for casual listeners.

'Y'know, some of the fan mail is so beautifully written. I get sent the most extraordinary poems and interpretations of my songs,' Max said.

'He's got a top five,' the young black guy said. 'We sort them as they come in, see?' He pointed towards the shelf marked with yellow memo stickers. ' "A" for Angela, "C" for Chieri, "I" for lzzy . . . get the picture?'

Oola took in the 'M', the 'Z'.

'And "Z" is for Zoran.'

'Some gay guy from Macedonia,' Max added, 'who's studying film.'

Max removed the mail from these five makeshift pigeon-holes, less curious today than usual. The letters would not get read this time. Not today. He put them back, something which Pshemko found odd.

'Let's get outta here, I hate this place,' Max said to Oola Khan. 'Let's go sit in the park. There's a café there.' Then he smiled. 'I'll buy you a sandwich.'

As Max stood in line, waiting to have money taken from him, he looked directly into the CCTV camera pointing his way. A little red light next to the ever-glaring big black eye was pulsing. Maybe, Max thought, someone in an office some-where was feeling an unusual moment of job satisfaction as that face stared upward.

Oola was sitting like a good girl, under a tree. A cool, shady spot. Like a sleepwalker, Max approached with a tray. Sand-wiches, chocolate, apples, a couple of Cokes. His movements seemed controlled from some dark and unrecognised centre as he put the tray down, as if he were going through the motions of being a regular guy.

'When I was about fifteen,' he began, 'still at school, y'know, there was an unusually sweet-tempered but rather disorganised music teacher who continually mentioned suicide in a jokey way. He'd only been teaching a couple of years, someone not much older than myself.'

Oola pulled off the cellophane wrapping of her sandwich. Smoked salmon with mascarpone cheese on sun-dried tomato ciabatta.

'One day, at the end of a lesson, this teacher put a few people off their lunch by saying that anyone who considered cutting their throat as a form of self-murder should show consideration for others by putting their head in a sack first, to avoid making a terrible mess. Pretty much everyone laughed. We could never make him out, and that was part of his appeal as a teacher. While we were eating our sandwiches, he was on his mountain bike heading home. Seemingly, he put a sack over his head and dragged a blade from here to here. As a fifteen-year-old I was tremendously impressed.'

The journalist barely reacted, only conceding the lightest nod. Then came some shy little laughs, the kind generated by nervousness which evaporate the moment laughter is put in gear. Was this some kind of test? A strategy? Was she being sent up? It was not a tale he had told before. There was nothing like that in any of the clippings the record company PR had provided her with. Max had never played that anecdote before. Whatever, she felt that there was some essential horror in the story which was relevant to this young man. What exactly, she wondered, had so impressed the fifteen-year-old?

'I hope you don't mind me saying this, but whilst I feel that the technical ability of your songs is great, I feel that there is still a sense of resources and disturbances not yet tapped.'

Ouch. Max did not feel too comfortable with that.

'With "Inevitable Sunrise", for example, on the latest album, I feel that the suicidal feelings aren't fully explored.'

Max laughed, only just managing to control the oncoming

of a coughing fit. Oola had obviously started writing up her 'theory' on him. The way that statement had just come out was too formal. Just not natural.

'You convey that still-blue, almost eternal hour before the baby's cry, before the glassy music of the milkman, settling his bottles in those dead hours between night and day, but don't quite . . .'

'What? Hit the jugular?'

'Are these feelings true? That's what I want to ask. Are they . . .'

Max looked incredibly pissed off, insulted.

'For real?' he asked, practically sneering.

Oola nodded, aware that she had hit a tender point.

'Only time will tell,' Max said, with a toss of the crusts off his panini to a couple of sinister-looking crows, watching their every move.

Between his legs, crawling over crumbs that had fallen, were ants. An industrious crew that were suddenly busy with the boulders of food they had discovered. There a tasty piece of chicken. There some juicy avocado.

'Ever fed a crow grapes?' Max asked. 'They love 'em. Try it some time. Very entertaining.'

He gave good quote, no doubt about that, but Oola wanted to get beyond Max's defences. She felt miles off the mark.

'It's coming up to three,' Max said. 'We've got an hour *max.*'

Both laughed at the unintentional pun.

'Okay,' Oola said, sitting up. 'Last night you ended your set by holding a skull to your face and kissing its lifeless jaw. What was that all about?'

Max's concentration was waning. He found himself not listening to what Oola Khan was saying, not to the words, but to each inflection of her voice, the chords, the harmonies made.

Max threw his entire sandwich towards the crows. They cawed appreciatively.

'Hey, birdies,' Max sing-songed, as if those big, black-feathered hulks were the cutest sparrows he was feeding. 'Hey, any of you got a clever answer to that question for the nice young lady?'

Then he looked at Oola the way young men in advertisements step off buses before bouncing off into their glorious future.

# 3

Sitting by the window, Minty was purring. Her ears were high, her tail curled over – a sign that she was content. The last of the sun felt nice, all that food in her stomach a comfort.

She had managed to open a kitchen cupboard earlier that day. Tins of turkey and smoked-salmon cat food had fallen. All the varieties had gone tumbling, many pouch-packed in foil for easy access. Minty had managed to pierce a few packs with her nails, enjoying a sniff and lick of the 'Gourmet' varieties which had frequently made the owner's mouth water: the salmon-and-tuna, duck-and-heart, rabbit-and-lamb combinations. Breaking into that as yet unopened box of dry cat food had taken quite a while, a challenge that had been successful after much chewing at the side of the container.

She knew she had done wrong, knew that she would get a slap, but for the moment she did not give a damn. She felt wonderfully bloated, her coat was fabulously clean, and the cushion that she was now kneading, there by the window, was lovely and soft.

Despite the bliss of comfort, Minty knew that it was almost time to shimmy towards the sofa, duck her little head down, and enter the tight confinement of that dark space. Her mistress would soon be home and she would not be pleased with that mess all over the kitchen floor.

There, now, the sun was to the extreme far right of the window. Time to move, take cover. There would be the sound of the elevator shuddering to a halt, those shuffling footsteps, the rattle of keys at the door, then the sing-songy 'Hello, how's my . . . ?' There would be no kiss 'n' cuddle routine, more like a stamp of a foot. Would she throw back the sofa in one of her rages? Would she confine the cat to the bathroom for the night?

The cat let out an *oww*.

As expected, there was the sound of the elevator shuddering to a halt, those shuffling footsteps, the rattle of keys at the door.

She was back. Max's number-one fan was home. When she saw the mess on the floor, she tutted then ignored it. She was in a hurry. She had twenty minutes to drop her knickers, wash, dress and get out of there fast. It was the last night of the tour and she had a ticket.

'Silly puss!' Angela said in the direction of the sofa in an outburst of breath which had plenty of hiss to it. 'You deserve a smack.'

Facing away from Angela, the feline equivalent of 'mooning', the cat began to purr.

Waiting for the tub to fill, Angela looked in the mirror, surveyed the ruins of south face, front face, north face.

'Not a pretty sight,' she said to her reflection. 'Fat pig.'

Three hours to go, and already the fandemonium had begun outside. Obsessive fans, many of them carrying DIY Max dolls, were massed by the gates, waiting to charge in. Semi-naked schoolgirls with 'MAX' stained on their forearms in Bic ballpoint – or scarred in with the blades of box-cutters – would be the first to enter, first to get their hands on the merchandise, first at the head of the drinks queue. How many of these inappropriately dressed teens would demand the impossible of seeing Max by the stage door? How many of these panty-dampeners would be pulled from the front-row crush for mouth-to-mouth resuscitation? Answer: one fuck of a lot, that was half the *fun* of it.

There had been no problems with the sound check. It had been a quick run-through. So much so that Max found himself with time on his hands. While the backing band were chilling backstage, Max had decided to sit himself down at the grand piano on stage. It was as if he were alone, like some kid in a sitting room at home for half an hour of compulsory piano practice. Max was unaware that the sound technicians at the mixing desk had pressed REC and PLAY. Each note Max played was being recorded for a future bootleg release.

Piano lessons. He had loved/hated them. For the first year his mother was told that Max had a good ear, but that he was having a little difficulty transforming the black and white on the page to the black and ivory of the keyboard quickly enough. It was kind of the piano teacher to put it that way. Sensitive. Though his total inability to read that language of black dots and squiggles had not been discussed in any detail, for the first year of lessons it was generally accepted that staffs, semibreves, clefs, bars and crotchets were just a little tougher to pick up than ABC. They seemed so superior, the way they stared back from the page.

More than once, Max had wished that notes would make sounds the way words made pictures. Rather than cruelly expose his failing, the piano teacher had patiently encouraged. She was sure that he would get there. Eventually he did. And *there* was this concert hall in the capital city. Capacity? Twelve thousand. Every seat had been sold months back. Attending the last night of a tour had an appeal to many, as if something special would climax.

Max was also unaware that the journalist Oola Khan was out there somewhere in the auditorium, watching. She did not need a telescope to see every one of Max's changing facial expressions. Unbeknown to Max, a team of technicians were following his every move as a run-through for the show. Every blink of his eye, every private moment, was magnified hugely on those stage screens. Once again the buttons of REC and PLAY had been pressed, deviously capturing Max unawares. To Oola, Max's expression seemed to carry two opposing meanings: on the one hand there was sorrow, and on the other a calm – a precious moment of stillness amid a restless life.

Ten minutes later, Max was standing by the window of the backstage dressing room, unbuttoning the flies of those old blue jeans he was wearing. They had worn so thin, were wonderfully soft.

The heavy black cascade of all that hair which framed his face bounced as he tugged the denim off. He placed the old Levi's over the back of a chair. Sat, and looked at them. These were one of five pairs of 'trousers' he owned. He would never wear them again. So it was a goodbye glance he gave them.

Max picked up the denims and went to the window, holding the jeans in one hand, crushing them up against his chest. He looked beyond the setting sun too long, then closed his eyes. Were they cheerful little amoeba he could see swimming round his eyes? Strange and beautiful creatures, perhaps, that defied analysis. Or . . . dust particles. Whatever, they seemed to unfold in advancing somersaults and float from far to near and nearer, then past his ears. He liked them. Always had. Is this what blind people see? Max wondered. Is this what their dreams are made of?

The streetlamps came on: a silent awakening of the land-scape.

Right now, in the here and now, I can see cars cars cars. Cars as far as the eye can see. After now, soon – very soon – when I'm not around to bear witness, ice caps will melt. Norway will soon enjoy the climate of North Africa. Soon the oceans will be boiling. Soon, Max thought. Everything's out of control.

Max left the jeans by the window, half hanging out. As far as he was concerned he did not own them. By the end of the night someone would have taken possession of them, perhaps telling people 'these were *his* jeans'.

Sitting by yet another light-surrounded mirror, Max put the gold-ringed finger of his left hand to the very outside corner of his right eye, then rubbed in a tiny, delicate circle. He sighed softly, as if absolutely exhausted.

'Soon I'll be cold as this mirror.'

Max drew very close to his reflection, fogging the glass. He kissed his reflection, tonguing a taste of chemical cleaner. He thought he looked like shit, he certainly felt like shit. Not long to go, that was the comforting thought. Stay cool. Don't want you going out ungraciously, now, do we?

Although Max had been drugging himself in the direction of a mortuary slab for quite a while, to only his mild amusement, he had not taken anything since the rehearsals for the tour had started up four months back. He had made it through, all the dates. Every one of them. Now there was only himself to deal with. Last thing on the list. He had built up to the act carefully, with a blank pertinacity. His death had long been the focus of his life, making everything else irrelevant: a diversion. Each sporadic burst of success, each rare moment of calm and relaxation, seemed merely a temporary halt on his steady descent through layer after layer of his spiral – like an elevator stopping annoyingly for a moment on the way down to the basement. At no point was there any question of getting off or changing the direction of the journey.

Max took a cigarette, put it in his mouth, then thought about it. He lit up, took a pull, coughed. Then he extinguished it against the fingerplate of his guitar. His hands seemed intent on meandering exploration, the thumb and forefinger of the left occasionally touching and squeezing the silvery tuning pegs at the machine head, the middle finger of the right trailing downward, randomly tapping against the inner curve of the cutaway at the neck.

Max inhaled, held that breath, then exhaled slowly. Lowering his head towards the guitar he began fucking around with the diatonic major scale. Quickly tired of this, he tapped an arpeggio: a C6 with an added 9th. Then he played a minor 7th barre chord.

'After I'm gone they'll probably go to town on remixes, working a sample of my voice in a way that I would never have gone with when alive. But so what. Who gives a damn anyway?' he said. It was as if he were replying to a question that had not been asked. 'Just hope to God that Fat Boy Slim doesn't get his hands on my masters.'

Downstroking a G, Max then hammered on a B flat. He was feeling uncomfortable all of a sudden. Tense.

The dull, irregular pulse in Max's left eye – dull and curt – was annoying him. Every fifteen seconds or so it would go *ripriprip*, like a blade through skin. Max stood, splashed his face with some cold water, then returned to the window. The air was so clear. Car brake lights in the distance looked so vibrant. Red. Neat, controlled lines of red.

Max flat-picked at the second, fourth and sixth strings.

Why is everyone hung up on an ugly piece of wood and metal with strings? he thought, as he gazed into the dark cello-like sound holes at the side of the guitar. But he knew – the instrument was part fashion accessory, part prosthetic penis. He felt that he could not really play very well, but could fake it. He could make that guitar look lethal, totally rock 'n' roll.

It'll soon be time to be alone out there with everybody once again, Max thought. A magnesium-white flare of adrenalin coursed through him. He was surprised to be feeling so nervous. He went to the sink and vomited a torrent of browns and greens that he could not remember having eaten. He rinsed his mouth out several times with water, then put on the silver PVC jeans that he knew would cause gasps out in the sea of blank faces.

Then he sat, did nothing. His mind was blank. Eyes shut, he listened to his breath, became aware of his beating heart. It filled him with distaste. He did not want to be alive. The comforting thought was that he would not be in that condition for much longer. That was the plan. Everything had been planned, and he had always been so meticulous with any kind of plan. Disciplined, to the last.

In the half-light, Max looked like a charcoal sketch, the darkness of his eyes and hair marked crudely against his pale skin. He took in a deep breath, then downstroked an E major superimposed on the E major chord, playing a perfect fourth in the rasguado style with three fingers very quickly. The flamenco feel seemed to serve as a letting off of steam, a necessary outburst of energy.

There was a gentle double knock at the door. Max did not respond. Again, a double knock, this time harder, more insistent. Max waited for the handle to turn down, the door to be pushed open. He knew it would, knew that would happen.

What Oola Khan saw was an almost alien figure, sitting there, so alone. Staring, staring her way, the last of a vibrato still sounding.

'Hi,' she said, no more.

No response, not even the lightest nod. It was as if he were waiting for some kind of explanation from her. His gaze was inquisitive.

Same perfume as yesterday, different outfit. Lighter, younger. Something sexy, *sexier*. A combination of leather, suede and silk. Again, somehow the look was more safari than concert hall.

Max gave the sixth string of his guitar a gentle slap and pop, then put it aside.

'Hey, Oola,' he said in a voice much softer than he had intended, at a volume that surprised them both. 'Little present.'

Max removed one of the three silver bracelets from his left wrist and, with a gesture which seemed to lack motion, held the bracelet for the woman's fingers to reach out and take.

'It was nice meeting you,' he said. And he meant it. Had it not been for what he had planned, what had long been in motion, it was possible that this was somebody he would want to spend more time with. Fuck? Friend? Lover?

Oola pushed the single bracelet high up her left arm, so that it rested where many a barbed-wire tattoo decorates too many a bicep. She resisted the temptation to kiss Max on the forehead, then left the room. Once outside the dressing room, she rested her back against the wall, surprised at the rapid beating of her heart – and the fact that her eyes were flooding with unexpected, quite humiliating tears.

The crowd were more than ready. Out there, somewhere and everywhere, dried voices were whispering together. The collective sound was quiet and meaningless like wind in dry grass or rats' feet over broken glass.

A solid wall of photographers whose cameras were ready to *clickclickclick* like hundreds of electronic butterfly wings were busy making those last-second checks on a variety of settings.

A well-known radio DJ took the stage. The crowd roared. It was time.

'Every generation has its one defining moment,' the DJ began in the tone of a Bible-basher. 'Max is *it*.'

Again, right on cue, the crowd roared. The DJ went on to gild the lily.

'A musician such as Max only comes along once in a lifetime. You should be grateful that he's come along in *yours*.'

Once again, so predictably, the crowd voiced their enthusiasm. The sound made was a variation of *Phwoar*. They were ready. Already girls were close to fainting at the crush barrier.

From blue to black. Just the flashes of cameras, hundreds of them. A prolonged moment. Then the massive release as Max slouched slowly from stage right, trailing his Gibson behind him by the neck. Looking up towards the swooping camera that followed his every step, a camera that was feeding two giant screens with two different cuts at that moment, Max hoisted his instrument up over his shoulder, then plugged in. There was that familiar sound the crowd loved, the crackle and clunk of a jack being jammed into the cheap amp that Max insisted upon, its dial turned to 9.

Then, right on cue, Max assumed what many fans thought of as 'the position'. Legs wide apart, in those uncharacteristic and totally surprising silver PVC jeans, head tilted right back – the geometry of contempt – Max downstroked an E major superimposed on the E major chord. Just one slashing strum. It was a chord that could be heard a mile away. Max's guitar sound, blasting through a Marshall amp with no effects pedals whatsoever, could scarcely have been more classic.

'Okay, here's a song that I hope will be used in a car advert or something one day,' Max drily remarked to a single face he had picked out in the third row. The way he launched into that first song, 'Tomorrow's Zero', was as if a gun had been put to his head. Literally thousands of people who had seen Max perform the night before at a different, smaller venue felt that something had changed. There was a startling bizarre extremity, an unnerving *urgency*, a headlong aggression with which Max assaulted his guitar. A life-or-death feel. Anything but unit sales was on his mind as the crowd sang along.

'You see that yawning precipice?/It leads to liberty/You see that bridge curving over that river?/It leads to liberty/You see that stunted, parched and sorry tree?/From each branch liberty hangs/Your neck, your throat, your heart, every vein in your body: invitation cards/Exits are everywhere/Tomorrow's zero/ Tomorrow's ze-ro.'

By the third song, the auditorium had the way-too-small pressure-cooker feel of a low-ceilinged nightclub. Even the turnstiles were sweating. By the fourth there was mayhem at the front – barriers had crashed. The house lights came on; there was panic.

A procession of limp bodies was carried away for medical treatment. Max caught sight of one of these, a girl who had blood all down the left side of her face. At first he thought all that colour was a birthmark, then he realised. It looks worse than it is, he thought, as he strummed the opening chords of 'Family Tree'. It'll wash off, he thought. She'll live.

Pipe-cleaner thin, sweat-drenched hair hanging like seaweed pitched across his face, guitar held aloft in classic style, Max flitted from the lips of the stage to the auxiliary drumkit suspended in midair before a fearsome bank of stage lights for a head-to-head duel with drummer Sølve Sundsbø. Then he turned, the stage was flooded with dry ice, and the drumming ratcheted down, reduced to a couple of brushes against a single cymbal.

There was a great moment when a roadie ducked on to the stage to rescue a fallen mic stand, only for Max to grab it off him and throw it back to the stage floor, veering from sincere buddy to anguished foe in the blink of a beautiful, oval eye. It was a moment which made diehard fans shiver, swerving from semi-hysterical to fully alert.

Lips against the flat-top grille of the Shure Beta 57A microphone, voice slow and low, as if attempting to whisper into everyone's ear, Max began, seductively. 'Imagine you're in a cinema, sitting there. Alone. The film begins. The opening shot is of . . .' And then the usual pause, the pause that he always made before introducing the next song '. . . and the opening shot is . . .' Everybody in the audience knew what was coming. '. . . and the opening shot is of a boy walking, walking across a featureless landscape. A landscape like a grey stage. There's a hint of rain in the breeze, a breeze that tightens the boy's sad eyes. Photography: grainy black and white, which turns to colour as the boy's progress gains in interest. Aged nine, maybe ten, the boy wears nothing but a pair of white, skin-tight, thin cotton Fruit of the Loom pants. He looks up at the sky, then crouches down, knees touching chin, bottom skimming the air an inch above the sand. He carries an umbrella which looks black until the colour comes up as it does – yes, now. It's a shiny red umbrella, an item more suited to a little girl. Cheap. Cheap plastic. Bright red. Heavy rain begins to fall. The boy makes eye contact with the camera, then looks beyond the lens into the mind of the viewer. And the title comes up on to the screen, one word, and that word is . . . *'Goodbye'.'*

With make-up in meltdown, Max was dreading this one. There were too many words for each line, too many big ideas for one little song. He did not have to worry, he was on auto. His brain was barely ticking over for the duration: 168 seconds. Into the microphone stormed a shivering, impassioned vocal which occasionally hit the most unexpected and beautiful melancholic bends, working the power of a minor key. He was hurtling, breathless now, headlong towards the climax of the song. He hoped the crowd felt they had got their money's worth, got their fix. He had decided that was it. Last song.

Max unplugged, removed his guitar and began to smash it up. He had never done anything like that before, so at first there was an element of genuine shock, then the crowd cheered. Cameras went crazy as the Gibson ES175 was destroyed.

The backing band were stunned. There were still three songs to go.

Max took the microphone off the mic stand and croaked, one word at a time, almost petulantly, 'Guess this means no encore.'

He stood there a long moment, dazed by the lights which bathed him.

Then black.

The tour promoter growled through a discussion with Max's management immediately after the gig. Things had not gone quite as planned – the performance had finished pretty much fifteen minutes earlier than agreed. The merchandisers, however, were thrilled. People had left wanting more and decided on a little last-minute shopping: T-shirts, posters, CDs, DVDs . . . the lot.

Despite the shortened set, backstage was buzzing. Everyone wanted to get to Max. As usual, access was tight. Security had their work cut out for them. All four of Max's PRs were having a hard time from music journalists who were raving over what they referred to as the guitar 'stunt'. Manic, they all agreed. Totally. They were all there: Toby McFarland Pond and Marcelo Achike, chatting away with Ziad Alhaznawi and Wladyslaw Moes, the latter of whom was wolfing down sushi whilst still chewing gum as he eyed Poppy Ringrose, who was doing her best to stay cool as she sweltered under an embroidered silk robe of Qing dynasty design, a little something manufactured entirely out of viscose in Korea just one month back. Beside that little coterie, Paul Bellaart, Mats Niquet and Priska Morger were talking of this and that, of nothing, while checking out Moa Croft's Courrèges-inspired super-sheen PVC sari, circle-cut at the base to draw a focused eye upon wooden clogs which had been adapted to fit a somewhat perilous stiletto heel. Ms Croft felt a little upstaged beside the disco diva drag queen DJ Stella Stein, who was wearing an item made up of twenty-five vintage leather gloves in various styles, shapes and degrees of use in tones of white and beige, assembled to form a backless Moulin Rouge showgirl kind of halter top. Nish Vyas, MJ McGuire, Federico Gutiérrez-Schott, Wendy Ide, Abdi Ramprakash, Sabine Braeuniger and Prot Jarnuszkiewicz were all lined up against a wall as if about to be shot – they were just watching, taking it all in, every last visual detail. Sophia Szczotarska was having a spot of difficulty with Alexander Maartignani after he had been caught flirting with Georgina Hristova. All agreed, *everyone* was backstage, right down to the likes of Nicolette Santoro ('Oh, I *love* that song. I listen to it every night until the batteries run down'), Bianca Vadukul . . . and Kate Moss. A-list pigs, Max thought, each and every one of them. The collective sound made by the lot of them was akin to a jam jar full of kittens on which the lid had been firmly screwed shut.

Pulse slow, in awe of the skyline, Max tossed his cigarette from the dressing-room window. With this rain it'll be out before it hits the ground. He was right, he did not bear witness to a bouncing dot of red down below.

The photographer behind Max was asking him to turn a little to the left, give a profile. The request was ignored, as if he were not there.

The pig. Go fuck yerself, pig.

There were other people backstage, too. Against his wishes. It always happened. It was too much. Max did not want to hear what the pigs had to say. All that collective oinking.

Arms hanging, limp and heavy, he conducted a low dull tune in his head. He could have stood there for a while, it was nice to be doing nothing, but he had to turn his head. He had scented her, that distinctive perfume. That mixture of cloves and . . . herself. Soft skin. Warm, clean, soft skin.

Oola Khan was in full journalist mode, holding a small cassette recorder in front of her. The REC and PLAY buttons had been pressed. There was no question to answer, no prompt. The tape was whirring away, ready for anything that he cared to say. Max chose to say nothing but all was not wasted. The photographer snapped a picture, then another. The two of them together, as if in the middle of an *EXCLUSIVE*.

'Turn it off. You're wasting the batteries,' Max snapped.

Again, the photographer close by framed another picture, shot off more super-fine-grain Provia 100 ASA. From the cameraman's point of view it was perfect, almost a head-to-head shot. That close. Somehow lovey-dovey, somehow confrontational. It was a picture that would soon be syndicated worldwide, a picture that would seal negotiations for a major book-publishing deal by the end of the following week.

Max picked up a black dustbin bag that was by the door, swung it over his shoulder and glared at those assembled: the latest batch of pig session musicians, the latest pig producers, the pig PRs, pig management, then the pig journalist with her pig photographer. Again, the pop of a picture.

White light. Bang of the door.

A cranial trigger clicked at the back of Max's brain and, one nanosecond later, a half-thought confirmed it. This was the moment Max had been planning, the escape.

'Go-go-go,' he self-instructed.

Relieved that he had not been followed through the maze of corridors, Max located the emergency exit which backed on to an area of wasteland, far from the streams of fans making their way towards car parks and train stations.

He changed quickly, swapping silver PVC pants for black denim. Added to this was an outsized navy raincoat, baseball cap and army boots.

Max turned the collar of the raincoat up as high as it would go and set off.

The scent of rain came before the heavy drops spotted Max's raincoat. The not-unexpected rain, splashing down in seconds, soaked through the polycotton. Trickles of warm wet slid down the back of his neck, the small of his back. The material clung. Rain dripped from his nose, chin, elbows. Max liked the rain in cities, angled in headlights, backlit by advertising and silly windows. Raindrops like long silver needles.

The delight of the drenching was intensified by its just-as-sudden cessation. With the abrupt end of the downfall, Max became aware that steam was rising up off him in what had become the softest air.

Momentarily in silhouette as he ran from the streets surrounding the auditorium, momentarily in the floodlights of cars, among fans on their way home, he felt fabulous. Liberated.

Even with the hindrance of his dragging leg, he ran for ten minutes, an exertion that felt tremendously empowering. It could have been a concentration camp that he was escaping, or an earthquake zone. Fleeing for his life. But not quite.

As he came to a halt close to a bus stop, a waterdrop at the end of Max's baseball cap could not make up its mind whether to fall or not. A 48 was approaching.

'Final stop,' Max said to the driver, offering up a note that was way too much for the small fare.

'Final stop's the next stop,' the driver said, pissed off and bored. 'End of the road. Hundred metres, if that.'

Max shrugged. Stayed on.

The driver looked at Max.

'Keep your money,' the driver said. 'No change.'

By the time Max had taken a seat it was practically time to get off the bus.

Not even thirty minutes back he had been leaving the stage to thunderous applause. Now he was on a bench, at a bus stop, beginning to shiver in rain that was cold.

Max pulled out the notebook and pencil he had chosen to draft his suicide message with. He hunched over the page to keep it dry.

## *I want you to know*

That was as far as he got.

He put first one line through the five words, then another. Two neat horizontals. Then he broke the pencil in two. The two halves were gently pushed into the notebook spiral, forming one uneven horizontal. Then he wiped his knees, as if covered with dust or the juice from an orange, and stood.

The notebook looked perfect on the bench, he thought. Like that. Off-centre. A brand-new notebook. Brand-new broken pencil. Message reading like the first line of a poem. Or song.

He walked past a café. The open sign was up, but not a single customer was in there. The idea of shelter was tempting, just for a while. A coffee.

I want to die. It's not a very big thing to want, nothing too ambitious. Just a little death. That's what I want. That's all I want right now. Just not to be around.

If someone had asked, 'Is anything the matter?', Max would have chirped, 'No, I'm fine. Thanks.' But there was no one around to avoid eye contact with, never mind avoid questions from.

When he stumbled and fell he wondered whether bones would break.

It was nice, just lying there in the doorway of a barber's shop. Being a nobody. An anybody nobody body.

'No one will miss me. Heap of garbage.'

Max knew that the earth revolves at half a kilometre per second; knew the Earth orbits the sun at 30 kilometres per second. Knew, pretty much for sure, that the sun orbits the centre of the Milky Way at 300 kilometres per second. Knew, because he really did know about these things, that the Milky Way is travelling in the general direction of Virgo at 300 kilometres per second – or thereabouts. And they all had something in common with him. Everything was distancing itself. The black of all that sky looked so appealing.

When he managed to get himself up, he stared at the face reflected back at him in the black glass of a store window. There was the face he knew by heart: his face, bruised and bleeding.

Then his mood changed, like some sharp, annoying body twinge. He wasn't crying like a baby, he was crying like a man.

The sky seemed more present than ever as he walked. Black was in everything. He felt anchored to the spot. So wholly separate from everything around him. Him, there, reflected in that window, so clearly defined in that sharp, clear light. Geometric.

He was not out of his mind, he was in his mind. Too much, he felt. He wanted to erase, delete. Wipe away, wipe clean. Kill the hard disk. That was what he was thinking as he moved off. Kill.

He had somewhere to go. Had an appointment with himself. Had something he wanted to get done. Kill. Himself.

To get to that somewhere he had to go, he wanted to roll sideways through the streets. Over glass. Over hound dirt some dog owner failed to notice being shat. Over pedestrian crossings. Over the shiny boots of a policeman who would say nothing out of absolute astonishment. Max wanted to piss his pants, bang his head as he head-over-heeled down flights of stone or crudely tiled stairs. Get run over. But he would have to do it himself. He would have to do every last thing all by himself. No one was going to help him. And, he thought, why should they?

# 4

There was no one about, Max was sure of that. He had passed by the lobby entrance twice before deciding to go in. The elevator had remained at '11' for a couple of minutes. All it would take would be for one of the residents in the block to see him and word would have got around. Yesterday had been one thing, now was something different.

Awakened by a hidden electronic eye, the building's sleek metal-and-glass doors parted soundlessly. Stepping out of the rain without breaking stride, Max passed through the lobby quickly, which was softly lit by discreet spotlights, he was heading for the emergency stairs which no one ever used.

Max took the stairs slowly. Sneaking up towards his parents' apartment this way was something he had not done since he had been a kid wanting to develop his leg muscles. There were two elevators; at least one was always in service. It was a long way up and Max was no one-step aerobics fanatic.

Breathless by the fourth floor, he found each greasy step somewhat hilarious. While the exterior of the building and the lobby proclaimed an upper-middle-class respectability, the questionable cleanliness of this staircase undermined that first impression. The walls were a state. Minute yellow flowers could be seen budding on aquatic moss. Such prettiness failed to camouflage the slime.

As he rose, steps resounding, he moved farther away from iron doors stencilled with warnings and skulls, bins loaded to the brim and leaking. Behind the smell of steamed fish and floorcloths, mops and broom heads, sour sponges in plastic buckets, half-used paint pots and insecticides, were a host of frequently oozing tins, squeezy bottles and sprays containing miscellaneous supplies for patient cleaning, regular mainte-nance. Products to brighten, shine, untarnish and unblock. Bleach, beeswax, ammonia, acid and descaling liquid. To the fore of this veil of scent was the building's number-one weak spot, ignored each and every eight hours of the concierge's shift: damp. Damp was eating the walls, warping wood, rusting metal.

There were seepages. Microbes were alive and doing well. Nests were warm and growing in populace. There were blind termites with insatiable mouths, tubular hearts and massive guts, scurrying mice and Lord knows how many ants, spiders, centipedes and cockroaches on that staircase.

Standing at the door of his parents' apartment, Max re-membered returning home on other occasions. Times past, all gone and run away.

Max removed the key which he had safety-pinned to the lining of his right-hand pocket, then slid the thin steel key into the single lock.

'I'm *ho-ome*,' he sing-songed in an action replay of earlier that day, as he switched on the light. 'Just thought I'd pop by to kill myself.'

Though alone, though there to do what he had come to do, he still obeyed the household rule by removing those heavy army boots.

As he stood in what had always been his spot by the window, the look Max wore on his face was both fixed and faded. Half smiling, half mourning. What he felt was relief. He was looking at the view he knew so well, the view he had grown up into.

Max had offered to buy his parents a place far away from the city they had come to hate. His father hadn't been keen on the idea, living somewhere bought with his son's dirty money. Max stood there, doing nothing in slow motion for a full fifteen minutes, then yawned. Skin that sensed it would only be alive for a short while longer smudged up into the air. His breathing had formed a grey halo around his head. When he became aware of this he wrote his name backwards through it, then erased it with the most tender part of his left wrist.

'This has been much easier than I thought,' Max confided to the lights of an airplane going somewhere, far, far off. Maybe his parents were on that plane, anxious after a lengthy delay at the airport.

Off to Kagawa, to Tsuda again, Max thought. Their annual trip. Off again to walk the beach facing the Seto Inland Sea, taking Polaroids of each other as they had done at the end of every summer since 1982. Always the same spot, by the giant exposed roots his mother had been sitting on when their eyes first met. They would bring grains of white sand back with them in their pockets and in their grey hair. Those grains would show by the plug after a sensible hand-washing of the clothes they had worn. Those grains would show when they got round to taking a long, hot soak in the tub. They would be back soon enough, with their same old reports, same old bunch of so 'n' so's regards. Things they would be unable to tell their son. All being well, their son would be dead.

The sense of freedom that he always felt when his parents were off somewhere flooded him. It was just like old times, before he had become a different Max. The last time they had gone away, departing at five on a Wednesday in April, Max had taken the opportunity to hide out from everyone for a few days there in that apartment. They had known of his intention, had approved. Said he needed the rest. He had waved bye-bye to his parents from that same window as unnecessary luggage had been loaded into the cab. Then he had sat there for sixty-four hours until nine on a Friday evening, staring beyond the clear screen of glass at the stillness and tiny focusing movements of people and machines as if it were all a film. A light shower at one had improved the air quality for a while, then a breeze had started up.

Falling asleep was not part of the plan, it was something which just happened. When Max awoke, crumpled and cold, he felt embarrassed by dawn. The sun was lazy behind layers of mist and gauzy cloud. The sky kept changing. It was a heavily soiled white, mainly.

Among red roofs, blue roofs, neon and orange TV aerials, there were 750 variations of grey. The view he had was not old, but felt it. Most of what he saw had gone up over two previous generations. It did not look so bad in sunshine or at sunset, but in total cloud cover it was dreadful. He had somehow managed to let the greys of that view invade his soul, was filled with the fragile existence of those quickly thrown-up, quickly pulled-down structures.

Sleep was not part of the plan, but his old bed was where his body walked him, laid him down to rest. He closed his eyes at dawn, opened them again at dusk. At first he did not know where he was. He felt that he had been asleep a long time, unusually long. His pillow was wet with more tears than average for a nineteen-year-old.

By nine, the smell of coffee made only an hour ago was already fading. The walls of his room – lined with books since he had been a child – had been bared. Those precious books had been roughly bound with nylon string and dumped in the bins down in the basement; goodbye to all that. All those practice test books of old old old exam papers seemed like nothing more than a giant trivia contest compiled by impotent scholars.

Sawing the desk he had sat at doing countless hours of study in two, then four, then eight, then sixteen neat parts brought a smile to his face but no sweat to his brow. The desk had been one of those deluxe models, with a built-in alarm clock for self-imposed speed tests, a built-in calculator, high- and low-intensity lights. A special-offer buy his parents thought was a good investment, once upon a time. Dismal. During the destruction, clusters of random data had hit him. Percentages. Old exam-paper questions. School shit.

Sawing the planks of wood that had made up that sad single bed in two, then four, then more more more parts had felt good. Brilliant. If only pain could be hacked through as easily, Max thought. My thirteenth year, my fourteenth year, my fifteenth.

Holding up for inspection a rust-coloured, one hundred per cent Shetland wool jumper, fortified and waterproofed with lanolin to protect the wearer from rain, Max felt a hint of shame. His mother had done her best, had tried. The jumper, however, was a nightmare. Something he had only ever worn to please her. Just *so* not him.

Max wanted to leave things tidy, right. Getting everything right included binning all personal items from the apartment so it would seem as if he had never been there. The back-and-forth trips to the garbage had been precision-planned for years. All those junior high school paintings, the awful attempts at pottery, merit awards, Hi-8 cassettes, CD collection, clothes – all binned. Postcards off the kitchen wall, photos from the family album, floppy disks, cacti – disposed of. Binoculars, computer – dumped. In all, Max hauled the contents of two suitcases down those greasy stairs, fifteen times. Together, Max reckoned, they were the weight of six average men.

'And that's a lot of junk.'

Most of this clearing out was done mechanically. Only two things, however, twitched Max out: dumping the photos of himself and his old school uniforms. It had been a long while since he had been through the old photo album, something which his mother always referred to as 'My Son's Book'. It was an old-fashioned item, perhaps purchased at a discount store at a discounted discount price. His mother loved a bargain.

Max had laughed at many of the pictures as he ripped them out, the way everyone was always smiling in them. Ingenuous now, he thought. Those say-cheese smiles. Mom 'n' Dad, doing that 'let's pretend' kind of stuff that people turn on for the camera. Birthdays, holidays, same ol' on New Year's Eve. All that fake feeling of seriousness, joy. Tradition. What a lot of shit. No feelings for their children. No feelings for each other. No feelings. That's what Max thought. S-H-I-T.

Getting married and having me was just them having something to do. Keeping busy. Had they not been killing time replicating themselves, what would they have had to talk about? Them, Mom 'n' Dad, and all those millions of other bored, unimaginative people doing the same things over and over because they are so dumb. And, ha, look what they got: me.

Each photograph in that photo album took up an entire page to start with, a thin sheet of shiny-shiny plastic protecting the picture from dust and greasy fingers.

Eighteen hours his mother had been in labour. 'You ripped me apart. My insides were like offal.' How many times had she said that? Max thought.

After the age of three, the photographs had started to be crammed in, overlapping. By the time Max had reached his teens, the book was full. There was a scruffy envelope for years thirteen to the time he left home. Max noticed how the smiles became fewer and fewer over the years.

Max had long felt nothing for his father; he *had* to feel nothing, or he would have felt too much. Two years ago his father's right hand, clenched into a fist, had approached Max at a steady pace from across that same room – father following close behind – and dealt the householder's only child the heaviest blow he had ever felt, and all because Max had worn lip gloss and a zigzag line of glitter across his face for a television show. According to Max's mother, it had taken quite a while for the air in the room to settle that day. Even after Max had left the apartment, it went on rolling, like the surface of a swimming pool long after the shrill sound of the lifeguard's whistle.

When Max thought of his father, he saw him only as a silhouette. A profile, chopsticks raised to mouth. Chopsticks carrying too much, too quickly. Mouth chewing, open. A silhouette was ugly enough.

Max's mother had kept every one of her son's school uniforms. They were in the hall wardrobe, lined up. Ever-growing Max shells. With each new uniform she had always said he looked best dressed that way, in one of those silly suits. What she meant, of course, was that the suit(s) looked good. Nothing to do with him. She did not know that each and every one of those outfits had made her son squirm, fidget and sweat salty rivulets down his back.

The suits always did what Max could not: be strong. All those uniforms had been a disguise. All those uniforms were costumes in a performance. In the seam of each of them, Max reckoned, was a remnant of him. The old him. Max shook his head from side to side. Binning each uniform felt like laying all those boys he had been to rest. Their years of usage had reduced the wearer to feeling like a barely usable scarecrow.

The last journey down to the bins was the hardest to return from. Max had actually felt like getting in there among all that old stuff to take a nap from which he would never return. Being dumped with the garbage of his life seemed wholly appropriate.

'Nice idea,' he said to a book jutting out at an angle, calling for his attention one last time, as if to say cheerio.

Max removed the protective jacket from the book that he knew inside out. He stroked the cool surface, fingered the grooves of the embossed gold lettering, enjoying the indentations of those curves and sharp edges. With the book open, the released smell reminded him of all those exercise books solemnly distributed at the start of a new school year.

Travelling past the foreword, the contents, a list of all the countries and cities of the world, Max stopped to feel the thick white pages for a last time. Pages so thick they gave the impression of two or three stuck together. Pages that had often fooled him into thinking he had turned over one or two too many. Pages with cross-sectional globes. Outer cores, red-hot inner cores, geological timescales.

His mother used to test him, asking him the names of mountains, rivers and capital cities.

'And what,' Max said, imitating his mother, 'is the population of Peking?'

For one last time his eyes passed over the planets, from Mercury to Pluto.

Aged eleven, Max had written to a boy in Finland his parents had hand-picked through some pen pal set-up. Max had enclosed an addressed envelope with the number of the apartment, the name of the building, the street, the conurbation, the county, country, continent, hemisphere, planet – Earth. It had looked good. It had looked great. So he had continued with the train of thought, writing smaller, adding – after Earth – in capitals, for that is what he felt the latter half deserved, THE SUPERIOR PLANETS, THE SOLAR SYSTEM, Nr ALPHA CENTAURI, THE ORION SPUR, THE MILKY WAY, THE LOCAL GROUP, THE LOCAL SUPERCLUSTER, THE UNIVERSE.

'Cute,' his mother had said.

No reply.

'I liked being eleven,' Max whispered to the book as he put it in the bin.

Getting everything right included binning the curtains in what had been *his* room. The bed-sheets, too. Getting everything right involved laying down three double pages of the local paper to protect the tatami when painting those four thin bedroom walls. It had been three years since they had last been done. The Apple White emulsion spread with a lovely thickness. Glossing the doors, shelves and skirting boards was a tiring, tedious affair. Only a sense of humour helped him finish the job off. No traces of his existence were to be found in the apartment, except the body. That was the plan.

As he drank a glass of tap water by the window, his eyes scanned the apartment building opposite. He knew each window so well. Some with curtains half closed, some with blinds permanently drawn. Many with venetians turned to a precise angle. Grey ferroconcrete. That could have been him for life. Stuck there.

One day, Max thought, the demolition men will go about their work with cranes, drills and hammers, pounding through the partitions of that block, smashing down exteriors, ripping out ironwork, reducing all to piles of raw materials to be sold for scrap, recycled or dumped. The bulldozers of the site-levellers will tidy away before men with brooms appear. Housewives will wipe their windowsills free of dust, then there'll be nothing left.

Max was pleased he would not be around to see that day. He was more concerned that someone might witness him jettison the clothes he had arrived in from the eighth floor than that they should see his nakedness at the window. He waited a moment. Down below was the boy from number 608, heading home on a skateboard from the same school that Max had once attended. When the boy was gone from view,

Max dropped the black denim jeans, the raincoat, baseball cap and army boots.

Down they fell.

'Just one more thing to do: *Me*.'

The floor and walls of the bathroom, laid with glazed ochre-yellow hexagonal tiles, shone brilliantly. Every surface shone. The place was immaculate but for the plastic shower curtains which were spotted with damp. Light blue seagulls, frozen in flight – his mother's choice – went back in a whoosh. Perfect but for the drip-drip of the shower head.

Max splashed his face with double handfuls of cold water. Drops splattered his chest. He needed the water, needed to splash, rinse and wipe. More and more water. He let it splash into his hair and ears. It did not matter about the floor, not any more. The emptiness of the tiled room gave back to him all his sounds and movements, echoing like an indoor pool.

Getting everything right also meant standing still for ten minutes covered from head to toe with lemon-scented Nair. Removing the darkening patches on a body that he felt was polluted and foul was also part of the plan.

He showered carefully, rinsing off thoroughly as suggested, obediently following the step-by-step instructions. A mess of dead black was retrieved from the plug hole and flushed. The depilatory exercise was successful but for a few isolated areas that got a quick tidy-up shave with a Bic. This included eyebrows, an impulsive final touch. *Shocking*, he thought, applauding his reflection.

There was gloss paint deep under the nails of the index and middle finger of his right hand; neat semicircles of white. A careful clipping removed most of the imperfection, but not all. He was too exhausted to care at that point and let it be.

The enema seemed like a sensible thing to do. Shit was not a feature that he wanted for his scene of death. Removing the shower head, he inserted the tubing just an inch or so. It was well worth the bother. A number of small ping-pong clock-work turds bounced against the fibreglass of the toilet.

'Why did he do it?' he said to himself in the mirror, running a hand over his bald head. 'Can't imagine,' came the reply, uttered in a voice two octaves below his usual, hands on hips.

He watched the tub fill, emptying an entire bottle of shampoo into the flow. The water creamed into bubbles as it mixed. Large bubbles, peppermint scented. His eyelids grew motionless. They ceased to be focused on the rippling, furling surface. He knew what he was about to do would not be pretty.

'Bath time,' he sing-songed towards the mirror, but his reflection had become a steamed-up blur. Waving a hand from side to side over the glass, Max half laughed at himself. To him it looked as if he were waving a giant, desperate bye-bye.

'Ciao,' he said with a wink, 'and good riddance to bad rubbish' – a stock expression heard so often in that household, usually when removal men were doing one-way-only carrying: people moving on. Then he switched off the shuddering brightness of the fluorescent.

It was as he lit a candle by the mirror that Max surprised himself with tears. Grief came like a big pull-out drawer which had not been opened in ages. There was a small part of himself, deep inside, that Max had shielded from the touch of his parents, and from the scratching nails of fame. No one had ever managed to brush it with their hands, no one had ever managed to use it for their own ends. That speck was longing to spark, preventing the planned self-murder. It was there, and Max could feel it, but the feeling was faint. Too faint. It gave no impetus to stop, no comfort. The only comfort the preceding months had held for Max was the intelligent planning of these last days. The highlight of the day had come and he was surprised to be feeling nothing but a modest trace of determination.

When he bent to elbow-check the temperature of the water, muscles in his back, particularly the shoulders, rippled beneath his smooth, taut skin. Momentary flexings like sparks. Musculature as natural and effortless as the structure of a flower, not studied and built with rapid-grow drinks and Nautilus pumping.

Only head, knees and shoulders emerged above the level of the water, like something severed, set there for viewing. The temperature was a bit too high; perfect. No vodka, no gin, no bottle of Suntory beer. Max had not had a drink inside him for the last six months. Alcoholism would not be a cover-up excuse his parents, management or the media could use when questions started to be asked. Same for drugs. Those tests would come back as negative. The HIV test, too. There had been all kinds of rumours about Max's recent weight loss. The tabloids had printed anything and everything, as tabloids do.

Max looked at the point of the ten-centimetre, spear-point paring knife which his mother had bought from a catalogue as part of a set, colourfully advertised as 'The Ultimate Kitchen Knives'. He practically went cross-eyed looking at the zirconium point. Now was the time to follow the plan. The first cut was to be taken slowly, tentatively – a vertical, up the vein. All he had to do was slowly push the blade through the skin of that raised, waiting arm.

'That's all you've got to do.'

Dragging the knife firmly up from the palest part of his left wrist in a perfect and deep straight line was all he had to administer upon himself. *Now* was the time. This was what he had been planning. This now.

'*Here we go*,' he said, gearing himself up for the moment.

The flesh would kind of peel back in that moment, opening up quickly, blood type A jetting out to pink the water in a tropical way. He knew that.

Max squinted against the pain he was about to feel.

The knife moved down to the spot that was awaiting the cold touch of metal. The ligaments were ready to be shredded.

The plan was that he would slice the underside of that pale forearm three times, then lower it to his side. The plan was that he would rock on to his left buttock to tidy the knife away in his rectum, black plastic handle first. Would the media ever get to know of the surprise Max had in mind for the pathologist?

Max relaxed, resting the knife across his collar bone. His eyes wandered over the perspex towel holders, the neatly folded pale blue cotton. A paring knife, albeit one made of zirconium – second in hardness only to diamond and originally developed for use in the space programme – seemed such a mundane thing to end his life with. He would have preferred a sword, something decorative, inlaid with agate and jade, though such an item is difficult to dispose of in the depths of an average teenage dirtbag.

He wondered what shade of opalescent yellow his skin would fade to, how dark the water would become, how long it might take the concierge to make use of the emergency key if a nasty smell were noticed, permeating the corridor just a little more each day. Max was sure of one thing – the person who would pull the plug, revealing more of his remains inch by inch, would do it not in the style of a galloping chicken with its head cut off, unsure of its direction, but with a cold, professional detachment – careful not to get their fingers wet.

Stretching his neck, resting his head back, gave him –

weight-wise – balance. The ribcage also became nicely elongated; suds held him sweetly at the waist.

All he had to do was complete the final stage of the plan, just that slashing, one, two, three. A minute from now, he thought, and it could all be over with. A minute from now my blood could be gently pumping away, curling out of me with the consistency of a barber's turning candy stick.

The bubbles popped one by one. Sometimes, a few together at once. He liked the irregularity of both tempo and volume. It was all quite musical with his eyes closed. Behind those eyelids was a whole galaxy of red stars.

He felt wonderful. Just fine. Perhaps the way an imago feels cracking out of the chrysalis or how a snake feels when a skin is shed. It was the kind of experience he used to take drugs to have.

Tears, not sweat, rolled down his cheeks. It felt so good to have completed the tour, walked away from all that. Getting soaked in the rain had even felt right, part of the shedding. Somehow cleansing.

Emptying out that room had felt great. Everything had gone. Everything. All that stuff. Max felt freer. He had not been expecting that elation. He thought that there would be no feeling, that – if anything – there would be an angry sadness which would fuel him.

Max wiped the tears away from his face, picked up the knife and held it to his throat. For some, he thought, this would be a braver way. This would be the way to do it.

Just like my ol' music teacher.

Max sniffed. Tutted, as he imagined the view of himself from above, as if viewed from a CCTV camera.

Reluctantly, but relieved, Max put the knife down to one side, then knew what he had to do. And quickly. He pulled the plug, switched the light on, then – shivering – began to dry himself with a towel he thought he would never touch.

It was not long before the tub held the same absent presence of a deserted bird's nest, and Max was sleeping like a child in his parents' bed.

# 5

When Max opened his eyes he felt like a kid who has just got off a fairground ride that he was not quite prepared for. Not just a bit dizzy, not just a little in shock, but disoriented.

Noon.

The fact that he was alive was a stubborn fact, something Max was still unsure about. Continuing to live meant too much. Bad thoughts approached stealthily, like fog invading fields. Unhurried and regular, to the beat of his pulse. Lying there, in the middle of his parents' bed, Max realised that he felt clean, at least. The shaved body, shaved head. At least the exterior felt good.

Then he smiled. I can do whatever I want. Sleep all day? Do it. Take a cab, take a train, take a plane to anywhere. Can do it. But wearing what? The thought made him almost laugh out loud. He would, he decided, have to go through his father's wardrobe to find something to wear. He would have to do a bit of shopping.

Unless I . . .

There was the option of hunting through the bins, salvaging an old T-shirt and jeans, at least. Then it hit him: today was trash day. Already the contents of those bins would have been crushed, perhaps now piled high on some dump. On that thought Max closed his eyes. He soon felt a sinking sensation, then his body seemed to be turning, swerving into black.

When Max opened his eyes at around two o'clock, he did not get up with a leap – full of vigour – but gazed for one long hour at a space between lampshade and ceiling and thought of nothing. Then nothing got budged sideways.

'Mum's peppermint foot lotion,' he said aloud, 'that was best.' He smiled. 'Better than spit, Vaseline or face cream.'

He remembered how he used to lie there in the room next door, in that room which was now as vacant as an unoccupied car space. A panting teenager, jerking off.

Thoughts of self-comforting masturbation got tossed aside. Nobody loves me – that was the single thought now running through his mind. Sometimes the thought took a break, and just the first word of it plagued him. Nobody. Like something sampled, the word rat-a-tatted at him. Nobody. Nobody. Nobody.

After much self-coaxing, just as the digital alarm clock beside his parents' bed was about to turn from 15.29 to 15.30, Max shifted himself sideways.

Standing by the bedroom window, he listened to the symphony of the washing up coming from next door: a cacophony of percussive cutlery, deep bass stoneware and ringing glass. The occasional wood sound.

'Are you going to come and dry up or what?' the old lady next door shouted to her husband. It was a question she repeated a moment later at increased volume. The old man was quite deaf; so was she.

Down below, out there, a gang of women, pushing prams. Ever onward, the caravan of prams.

Max opened his father's side of the double wardrobe, picked out an old navy shirt which he threw on to the bed. A pair of pale chinos followed, then blue-and-white gingham boxers, black socks.

With a sighing effort, Max switched on the television, to be told that the humidity levels were 'sky high'.

The bathroom had all the atmosphere of a stage set after a failed performance. Everything was as he had left it twelve hours back. There was the knife, on the side of the tub. Still ready.

Max did what he was doing – what he needed to do – in a polished, actorly way. It felt good. It felt stupid. It felt out of control yet methodical and calm. He picked up the knife, went to the living-room window, slid the glass partition aside, and then threw that knife in the direction of a clump of massive rhododendron bushes. Once he had done that he felt completely different.

Hungry, Max opened first one tin of peaches, then another. Halfway through the second tin, Max wondered whether there was any tinned cream. There was. He emptied the contents of another two tins of peaches into a cereal bowl, then splashed them with cream.

'Yum.'

It had been a while since he had eaten peaches; he had always loved them.

'Ah, shit,' Max exclaimed when he took in the sight of his father's wallet beside a paperback and a small container of travel sickness tablets. 'Always forgets something.'

He glanced through the wallet. Cash. Lots of cash. He sighed with relief.

Oh, he'll be okay. Mom'll have her Visa card 'n' all. They'll cope. Meanwhile, I'm gonna have to borrow a bit of the ol' man's spending money.

Sitting himself down by the balcony doors, Max watched sparrows hop from terracotta pots and fly. When he closed his eyes, savouring the flavour of the peaches, he could see the outstretched wings, frozen in flight. The afternoon sun was warming his face. It felt lovely. Everything was so quiet. Just the hum of the traffic down below. Just that. Then the sparrows were back.

Those little feathered friends were wondering where the seed was. Max's mother fed them twice daily. First thing in the morning and around five. She liked to sit on the balcony, sipping a cup of Twining's Lemon & Ginger, watching.

Max looked about. There was the seed packet, close by. He rattled it, gaining the attention of first two birds, then four. He laid out one long neat line of seed. Four became eight, then sixteen.

The shirt looked okay, but the trousers were a joke, way too short. The selection was limited. Max had opted for a raggedy pair of old flip-flops. The finishing touch to the look was a pair of his father's sunglasses, fake Ray-Bans.

Taking the elevator down felt like a gamble. His height was against him – someone was bound to recognise him because of that. The shocking lack of hair, however, made him look so different.

Kind of like a basketball player, Max thought. Mm. And that was how his shopping spree started. First stop was a sports shop. Without hesitation Max picked out an XL steel-grey tracksuit, some long black baggy basketball shorts, a navy blue hooded top, a pack of tube socks and two pairs of Reeboks.

'Dressing room this way?' Max asked a yawning sales assistant.

'Uh-huh,' the girl replied, bored. Desperate for home time.

There were so many disparities between that reflection in the dusty changing-room mirror and the smiling Campagnolo team in the poster taped to the back of the door. Sharp, defined, glowing, with shining smooth skin glistening in the sunlight, the athletes in the picture were a total contrast to the pale, gaunt youth dragging off his father's worn-thin boxers.

Max took a look at himself. He felt like some kind of cheap impersonator. The combination of man-made fibres was such a contrast to what he was used to: satin, leather and suede. For a moment he thought of Oola Khan.

En route to the checkout, Max selected a pair of Oakley 'M Frames' reflective cycle glasses. The unobtanium earsocks worked so neatly in conjunction with the nosepiece, gripping Max's head tenaciously yet comfortably, at nose and temples. He was transformed, and everything had gone yellow.

'Got a bag for these too?' Max asked the cashier, indicating the clothes he had entered the shop in just ten minutes ago.

'Sure. No problem.'

The cashier looked at Max quizzically. There was something familiar about him. Very. The zero crop, however, was throwing her.

'How would you like to pay, sir?'

'Cash.'

It was close to dark when the itch to go walking began. The bell in his head went *ding* and Max raised himself off the sofa, wiped the sleep from his eyes. A wave of exhaustion moved through him, an irresistible fatigue.

Didn't realise I was this tired. This time yesterday, Max thought as he headed towards the balcony, I was backstage. Ready to go on. How was I? Did I do okay?

In the last of the bright, flat light, the city looked so toyish. Max glanced down, then up. Sniffed the air. It was close, so muggy. The Beaufort scale was on zero, not the slightest breeze. Max knew a storm was brewing, could feel it coming. When he realised the fingers of his right hand were sculpting a teeny clown hat out of his left nipple, he put his hand down by his side quickly.

Barely conscious, yet perfect in motion, Max got naked. First he showered, then pulled on the new big black baggy basketball shorts. The first spots of rain were falling as he began to lace up the Reeboks. He decided against wearing anything up top except the light disguise of the cycle glasses. With enough cash for a bite to eat and a cab tucked into his right shoe, the front door key into the left, Max set off.

The best kind of walk made him feel nowhere. The walks he had always set off on from that apartment building, however, were controlled. They would last three, five or seven hours. They would adhere to unconscious designs. He kept to a narrowly circumscribed area. The itinerary was always different, haphazard, but somehow shaped. The meandering was like a stalking, of what he did not know. A mystery tour of . . . a territory. A mystery tour which, if mapped, might have formed an almost perfect circle one day, a rectangle the next. Then a triangle. Maybe more lively shapes, like the shape of the letter 'E'. The curl of a snail's shell. Whatever, each walk brought back some kind of point.

Hondas and Toyotas, bumper to bumper. Lights, faces, doughnut shops. Gleaming steel and glass. Neon chaos.

Max had first felt the need to go off walking at just seven years of age. Escaping the confines of his parents' apartment during the unstructured time of weekends and holidays meant walking. Every day, rain or shine, hot or cold, he would leave that apartment building and set off with no set plan. Never being sure of where his legs would take him was part of the thrill.

The city, like all cities, was a labyrinth of endless turnings, steps galore. He enjoyed getting lost, he made sure of that. He knew his own neighbourhood too well. He had always fled it, zigzagging up side streets. Bumping into people he knew or half knew was not what he wanted to happen. He wanted to be a nobody. Invisible. Lost: in a city. Lost: within himself. That was what he wanted. When he got lost he became absorbed with the new surroundings, ideally. When he got lost he forgot about himself. Left himself behind.

Max often wished he had the memory of a fish, which is reckoned to be two seconds. He would never get bored that way. Or melancholic. Reduced to a seeing eye: fab. No depth of thought: the perfect tonic. Peace. Being caught up in the movement of the streets, all those unconscious dynamics at play, brought him a measure of tranquillity. Caught up, yet still outside. Not participating. No participation. Again, like a fish. Just passing through.

The simple act of putting one foot in front of the other and moving at a pace that would not draw attention was all he had to do. Sometimes he wanted to run. Close to impossible without inflicting a degree of discomfort, however, since the motorbike accident. Sometimes, when tired, he wanted to roll along the streets. Sometimes crawl. But he walked. One step in front of the other.

A good walk had nobody. A bad walk had barking dogs and spoiled-brat kids screaming. A good walk meant lots of sky. The reds, the pinks, purples and vermilions. Sky. Feathery persimmons, oranges, golds. Colours merging. Colours fading. Dawns. Dusks. Midday transformations. Night-time black.

The usual walk meant concrete, gum-spotted sidewalks. Eyes down. Concrete, gutter, phone boxes, shoes. Broken plant pots housing broken plants, grouped together, tied with string. The need to piss up an alley. The best walk left him exhausted. Although he had not been walking long, he was already thinking of the return journey.

Splashing past Max, towards traffic lights, was a perfect, doll-like little girl carrying a tiny transparent umbrella. Trotting along beside her was a long-eared, long-nosed Artois beagle wagging its tail. The dog was doing what it liked to do best: going walkies.

In a narrow side street flagged with cloth signs in vertical folds and hoardings rampant with black ink, the perfect, doll-like little girl out walking her dog paused to attach clip-on earrings. Then lipstick.

When she lit up a cigarette, Max slowed up. Curious. The little girl took in two quick lungfuls of soothing smoke. Instantly she appeared different. Older. Max wondered where she was going, what she was up to. Off they went, her little dog ready to dodge the particularly heavy foot traffic ahead. Would she become a girl like this, Max wondered, taking in the sight of a fifteen-year-old schoolgirl with a big, illegitimate belly as she crossed the road.

A manic, born-again megaphone nut was blurting blind wisdom the girl's way all of a sudden. Some mad-eyed screamer on a mission. Max moved on, fast.

There was a huddle of lithe figures hovering by the chrome entrance of a pizzeria. They had found a spot that was dry, under the pink-and-blue canopy. Each stood clutching flat black folders. A couple checked their watches at exactly the same moment, cool in their linen suits and silk dresses. Max guessed they were models. Acquirable youth and energy, probably awaiting some manager to escort them to a casting. Some of the huddled group looked Max's way.

I probably look weird. Shaved head, these shorts. The skin and bone of me. A nutter, a right nutter.

He wanted to eat. He wanted to eat lots. Wanted to slurp hot noodles, chew chicken. Wanted the fizz of a soda in him, through him, out of him. Wanted to ingest a long long long red silk scarf which he would be shitting as the end of that long long long red silk scarf was still going into his mouth. Wanted to lie down, to have two tug-of-war enthusiasts pull at that long long long red silk scarf in him, scouring his insides, cleaning the tubes. The winner would be at the rear end. That long long long red silk scarf, metres and metres of the material, would finally *whoosh* out of his ass.

Max entered a Seven Eleven. Despite all the free water

falling from the sky, he bought a bottle of the bottled variety. He felt the need to drink. Then eat. That feeling felt good.

On the way back to his parents' apartment, Max sat on a wall by a car wash, mesmerised by the soap jets, the action of the brushes. All that whirring round. What would it feel like to walk through that machine? Would I feel clean? Would I feel renewed?

The petrol pump attendants stood in a line as they watched the naked man emerge from the car wash.

'That boy needs therapy,' one said to another.

'Yeah,' his colleague agreed, 'sure looks that way.'

# 6

*I wanna die, die in the summertime* was how the first letter began, words which had been scribbled on a page torn from a school maths exercise book. No *Dear Max*, no *Hi There!* or *My Darling*. Straight from the heart and down on to the page in green felt-tip, the intimate and disturbing picture of the psychological mechanisms set in motion by the Max machine began to unfold before the journalist's eyes.

Oh Max, I am really DESPERATE to meet you. I have actually considered getting myself knocked over just so that I would be hurt badly enough to be put in a coma. I know this probably sounds totally sicko but if I was in a coma my mother would write to you asking you to come and visit me in the hospital. To everyone's surprise you would appear by my bedside to hold my hand and talk to me, then sing 'Hidden Bruises' or 'Deep Love Scar'. And I would open my eyes and everything would be all right. It would be like a miracle. Then you would kiss me. Your saliva would be like the sweetest wine.

I love you, Max, but you should know that by now, this is LETTER #156. I'll write again tomorrow.

You fascinate me.

MAXIMUM LOVE

Shelby W

'Wooh!' Oola exclaimed in a whisper against the page. She checked the address. Charlotte, North Carolina.

Oola put the letter down and began typing on to her laptop computer.

The kind of fan mail Max receives takes you right inside the minds of his fans, blowing away the cosy clichés of pop fanhood. The full and shocking extent of his fans' sexual obsession, delirium and quasi-religious ecstasy reveals itself with each postal delivery. Many stars are entirely unaware of the kind of letters they are sent, the kind of emotions and actions they inspire. Not Max. Despite a hectic schedule, Max actually responds to many of the letters personally. In a recent interview with the nineteen-year-old rock phenomenon, Max showed me . . .

Oola took a sip of her coffee, a drag on her cigarette.

'Such a load of emotional discharge,' she said to herself as she glanced at the letters beside her.

Wearing a luxuriously soft white towelling bathrobe, hair still wet from a shower just ten minutes earlier, Oola was longing for bed. Bed, she had decided, was going to have to wait. She was itching to make a start on the piece she was to write on Max, even if it was a bad start.

A letter from a girl named Jutta in Elz, Germany:

DEAR MAX.
YOU PROBABLY HEAR THIS EVERY DAY,
BUT I'M YOUR GREATEST FAN.
YOU ARE THE CLEANLINESS AMONG THE DIRT.
IF A NUCLEAR WAR HAPPENED I'D BE THINKING,
IS MAX SAFE?
PLEASE, PLEASE, PLEASE TAKE GOOD CARE OF
YOURSELF.
XX
JUTTA

From inside a plain white envelope came one hell of an A4. Much of the large, forcefully written page was smudged. A letter from a girl named Ella in Barcelona, Spain:

> Max, mi querido,
> The night you here play concert in Barcelona, after I lie in my bed SHIVERING and SHUDDERING and keep thinking OH MY GOD. And, Max, I orgasm with no touch, just thinking you. Love you so much, Max. Too much, I sometime think.
> Besos x 1,000,000
> Ella

Oola took another drag on her cigarette. She did not know what she was going to write as her fingers hovered above the computer keyboard.

'If . . .' she said, summoning up a sentence, perhaps a sentence which would become the start of paragraph one or the punch line of her conclusion.

'If . . .'

If celebrity is the religion of our consumer society, then Max is God.

'Too much?' she thought aloud. 'Would that freak the religious freaks?'

Oola decided to keep the line, building on it.

If celebrity is the religion of our consumer society, then Max is God and the fans his disciples.

Oola breathed in through her mouth, out through her nostrils.

'Uh-oh,' she groaned Tellytubby style at the screaming error. 'It was *Jesus* who had the disciples, you fool, not God.'

If celebrity is the religion of our consumer society, then Max is Jesus Christ and the fans his disciples.

'Mm, that's more like it,' Oola congratulated herself, remembering how she felt when first meeting Max. She had been surprised that she had been unable to suppress a slight blush, a touch of tremor and a giddy sense of déjà vu in the presence of that perfectly ordinary mortal.

An exploratory finger moved beneath Oola's bathrobe to her left breast as she remembered being alone with Max. She felt that what she had just thought to herself was untrue. Max was no perfectly ordinary mortal. He was . . .

Oola closed her eyes as the finger circled the nipple, wanting a hot mouth there. Max's mouth. Her fingers began to gently pluck at the long, narrow stainless-steel bar piercing that many might have thought a little out of character for her.

Hey, girl, Oola prompted herself. Reality check. Come on. Back to the job in hand.

The music industry has been a frustration machine since Elvis started gyrating his hips and Jagger got licking his lips. Icons such as Madonna and Max have been offered so lavishly for consumption via all that jolly talk by radio DJs, the rotational videos, all those glossy pix, that they incite a massive and systematic social and cultural provocation. They cast an international spell, catalysing a fan culture which exists in isolation.

Oola was scratching about, unsure of her use of the verb 'incite' but not too fussed at that moment. She decided to scroll down, move on fast. This was how she worked, jigsaw fashion. After a while it usually started to glue together.

'Thank the Lord for cut 'n' paste.'

What is the acceptable norm of fanhood? Buying every record, whatever the quality? Wallpapering a bedroom with posters and magazine cuttings? Logging on to the virtual altar of an official website for hours every day?

That was not the angle the editor wanted. He was more

interested in two things and two things only. One, Max. What made him tick. Two, the depth and involvement of his fans, with a particular focus upon the behaviour of the more obsessive Maxettes – the droves of Baby Nothings who carried the Max dolls, the self-mutilators who carved M-A-X on their forearms for all the world to see, the extreme deviants in the T-shirts featuring slogans such as 'THEY FUCK YOU UP, YOUR MOM 'N' DAD' and 'YOUNG, PRETTY AND FUCKED'.

Oola had been given contact details of fans who were more than willing to admit their breaking into Max's hotel room, dressing in his clothes, drinking from his stale coffee cup, stealing his used bars of soap – even rolling around in the bed he slept in.

Her mind rewound to the last night of the tour. As she watched from the wings, her focus had been more upon the fans packed like sardines at the crush barrier than on Max. She had seen how much he mattered to that army of partisan obsessives gathered there by the dotting of glazed, staring eyes. Tiered faces, mouthing each line as if they were praying. That kind of intensity.

From the first fan suicide of Peggy Scott above a London hat shop for Rudolph Valentino to Mark Chapman's grisly *Hawaii Five-O*-style execution of former Beatle John Lennon, there has always been a dark side to starlust, and it comes no darker than within the minds of Max's fans.

Too tabloid, Oola decided, tutting aloud. And where's the evidence for such a statement?

'Ooh, I could do with a shag,' Oola half groaned as she highlighted what she had just tapped in before again hitting the marvellous vanishing trick of the delete button.

'Question: What do I want?' Oola asked herself. 'Answer: A sniff of all that masturbation going on behind locked doors, all those nights of weeping. All the usually concealed aspects of adulation, all that unconsummated, unconsumable passion.'

A postcard from Maidenhead, England:

When I make love with my husband I imagine it's you, Max. Every time. You are my astronaut, my alien, my dancer, singer, my main man.
XXXXXXXXXXXXXXXXXXXXXXXXXXXXXXXXXXXXXX
Love Judy V

Oola cast her eyes over a stack of releases by Max. Her eyes rested on the cover of the third single – 'Come, Hear Us Rage'. A sleeve design featuring Max's chest. Just that. The line of his shoulders, wisps of underarm hair, popped-up nipples. Certainly eye catching, Oola thought. A graphic that was probably on literally thousands of walls, provoking all kinds of imaginings.

Fanhood can be quite a frightening kind of possession. I spoke to . . .

Oola scanned the handful of letters which she had stolen from the offices of the record company. The corners of her mouth turned up in a smirk.

'Names, addresses, phone numbers, e-mail details, the lot.'

'Distance is no object,' wrote Deborah from Waterford, Ireland, in neat cursive on scented paper of palest blue. 'Last year a small posse of us hitch-hiked the fifty miles to Dublin to see you, Max. We all love you to death, we really do.'

Oola skimmed. Moved on to a sharp A4 print-out from a student at Keio University, Japan. The type and size of font seemed ideally suited to the design of a story book aimed at the five-to-seven age range:

My Hero Max,
    Over the last year I have spent about Y150,000 on Max memorabilia. It is with pride that I write that I was third in

the queue in the freezing weather on 15 January of this year, waiting to stake my place at the crush barrier in Shibuya. You are my sunshine, you are my inspiration. When I get down I think of you and it pulls me through. I'd like to be with you, Max, we could be together. Yeah man, you arouse such feelings, though I have a girlfriend and do not consider myself 'queer'. Kind of like that song 'Stan' by Eminem, huh? But hey, don't worry, I'm not insane.

Yours,

Masahiko K

Not all the fans were girls, and not all the fans were young, pretty and fucked. The mail from students attending universities in Kyoto, Osaka, Hitotsubashi, Waseda, Kobe, Tohuku and Yokohama alone amounted to an estimated one-fifteenth of Max's fan base. According to recent figures, sales had quadrupled throughout Japan after the screening of a NHK documentary directed by Herbie Yamaguchi.

Oola could picture them all out there, busy behind piles of stationery, seated at their computers. Handwriting carefully or scribbling away. Printing out. Page after page. Folding, tucking in, moistening stamps, pressing down, licking envelopes carefully, sealing down, sealing themselves in. Ages (if they were to be believed) ranged from a two-year-old girl in São Paulo to a fifty-seven-year-old barrister's clerk recovering from a heart bypass op in Bugibba, Malta.

Skimming through the letters, Oola felt like someone conducting market research. The repetition of desire had already become boring, and she had only looked through thirty or so letters.

She had never thought much of the fine art of graphology, but confronted by all those letters she began to look at the slant, slope, pressure, spacing and choice of writing implement. All gave an impression. Even the final signature to a word-processed piece held a message as it diminished into threadlike strokes or pierced a page with fierce triangular loops and stabbing 'i' dots.

Even got a picture of one here, Oola sneered, as she opened another envelope. 'Hello, my dear, and who are you? Ah, Laura Baby Nothing. From San Diego.'

Oola checked her watch, counted backward. Still early West Coast, she thought. Oola punched in the telephone number, waited.

'Hi, this is Laura.'

'Hey, Laura,' Oola began, all chummy, very girl to girl, 'my name's Oola Khan. I'm writing a major newspaper feature on the rock star Max and I was wondering if you could help me by answering just a few questions about what Max means to you.'

Oola could hear how excited the young girl down the line was by her breathing, all those ragged little breaths. Come on, Laura, Oola thought, give me something juicy now. Let's talk media penetration.

# 7

Max had woken up feeling like a crumpled piece of origami. A look in the mirror had confirmed that the feeling was a visible condition.

The sky was bright and clear. Max stuck his head out of the bedroom window and sniffed. He did not breathe in, but sniffed. He could tell the temperature better that way, estimate what kind of a day it was going to be. The morning air, he decided, was warm enough for him to stand there a while and scratch himself awake.

'Tell me why I don't like Mondays,' Max said to the horizon.

Already his hair was growing, spotting his head like lots of black pepper. His scalp was assuming a blue/grey look. Though tempted to shave it back to zero, he could not be bothered. It would take too much effort.

Barely conscious, yet perfect in motion, Max showered like a man just rescued from a week in the desert. He dressed himself reluctantly. It was a loincloth and wings he would have liked to be attaching, not a tracksuit, Reeboks, that big raincoat and shades. As before, with his father's Visa card and a few notes tucked into his right shoe, Max set off. Destination unknown.

That morning's journey was a figure of eight. After the meandering, his feet took him to a destination that felt right. And so wrong.

Walking into his old school, Max felt like a thief. He had been expecting a CCTV camera to point his way before he got buzzed in, but the main gate had been open. The school secretary was not behind her little window, the school guard not at his desk.

As Max ambled along the corridors he was expecting someone to stop him, or come up to him, pat him on the back – crank up the old-boy routine. No one did. Maybe he looked like a responsible adult, he thought, come to collect a brother who had just chipped a front incisor in an over-zealous playground game. Or a nervously excited student teacher trying to remember where he had left his all-important file of lesson plans. Or, Max thought, maybe I'm still as invisibly anonymous as I was when I was a kid here – a bonsai among bamboo.

Through one window he saw a teacher whose name he could not remember. She had never taught his class but had been part of the school fittings each and every day Max had been a student in that big aeroplane hangar of a place. Her hair was not how he remembered it. She had changed her style. It had been bobbed by someone who'd probably told her that it would suit her that way. It had been cut in sharply to merge with her jawline. She probably thought it a vast improvement that way, too. The grey had been done away with. Back to black. It made her look much older. Even from that distance, the pockmarks made her face look like a used dartboard.

Same old bulletin boards. Only the laminated faces of team members performing on the track, in the pool, on the horse, asymmetric bars, beam and mats had changed. Max stopped to look at the display illustrating all manner of hops, skips, jumps, dives, handstands, headstands, fly springs, backward rolls, cartwheels, splits and flips. Mr Robinski, the old Polish teacher and long-serving head of games, had always documented the boys he taught so rigorously. With a relish, Max thought. And always with a somewhat compulsive bias towards the cute ones. Funny, that. As a teacher, particularly as a PE teacher, Mr Robinski had always enjoyed that close proximity to literally thousands of boys of all shapes and sizes, many riddled with acne from waist to skull. Boys springing out of podgy childhood into clean-limbed, tumultuous adolescence. A ringside view of hormones smashing many a sweet soprano to a painful squawk.

'Pervert,' Max muttered as he headed towards the boys' toilets. He felt he was going to be sick – and he was. Colourfully.

Max flushed. He wished he could fit in the voracious, world-swallowing flush of the old school toilet. Whoosh. Round the bend. Sorted. Away.

He stared at himself in the speckled mirror. 'Have you been crying, boy?' Max asked his reflection, imitating the voice of his old music teacher. His head nodded.

Stepping quietly along the top-floor corridor, sedate as a kerb-crawler, Max sneaked an occasional peek through classroom doors. Unlike the bodies that filled each room, the classrooms themselves were old and anything but genteel, with raised lectern, large blackboard and a bank of windows to one side. The school had the feel of nineteenth-century one-room schoolhouses – hardly twenty-first century.

Caricatures of classroom virtue, faces ever alert and serious, shot up their arms to a question in one room. Obviously knowing the material inside out. In another, the drone of a teacher within changed to a sudden bark as he spotted a note being passed from one hand to another. The majority of classes just sat, staring forward passively. Waiting for the next instruction, the next fact to note, obediently following the teacher-centred approach, resigned to the boredom verging on mental cruelty.

Twelve hundred students in the one plain, three-storey collection of standard-size rectangular classrooms linked by hallways devoid of anything except signs and room numbers.

Barren. Walls painted a serviceable grey. Like being below decks in an economy-line ship.

'What a shithole.'

No maps or travel displays. No items of curiosity prettily displayed. Not a single potted plant. Such a contrast to the principal's surprisingly large and ornate office filled with framed photographs, plaques, trophies, inspirational messages, pottery and the occasional painting neatly demonstrating an exercise in perspective.

Max had reached his destination. When he had set out on his walk an hour ago, the last place he would have expected to end up was here, back at his old school. The form room Max had been unhappiest in was empty. He sat in the same straight column of sunlight at the same chair and table that he had sat at aged fourteen to fifteen, when he had the whole world in front of him. When people were saying crap like 'The whole world is your oyster'. Shit, Max thought. People are so full of it.

The atom of a ghost was there, by the wastepaper basket. And there, on that pin board. And beyond the window, out there, over by the swings. And there, on that low wall where he used to sit alone, with only his guitar for company. Within a minute he could feel each ticking second of the mood of his bored, expectant, uneventful adolescence.

Max looked at the board, recognised the handwriting immediately – old Mr Burston's. He resented the fact that he had the same handwriting as his English teacher: flowing cursive. All letters joined without evidence of a break. His English teacher's writing had been the acme of handwriting to so many boys over the years. Handwriting with a perfect lean, consistent spacing.

'Dot above the 'i', not to the left or right. Exactly above, just so . . . if you please,' Max mimicked.

It was at this table that he had noticed, a week before his

fifteenth birthday, a change in the smoothness of the skin halfway down the little finger of his right hand. A change that started with the appearance of an opaque, hardening mound. The wart he still had. The wart that did not want to leave, whatever.

Max sniffed.

'Whole world your oyster. *Shiiit.*'

Max briefly considered picking at his wart, the way he used to in that seat – pinching the thing between the thumb and index finger of his left hand. Pinching harder when it began to whiten and hurt. When it whitened and hurt it was close to coming away. Then there would be blood. Bleeding which sometimes did not want to stop. No, he thought, and let it be.

Up until about sixteen, Max had always thought his biology textbook was the best, the one with a see-through man on the cover. This book showed how everything worked. Detailed diagram after detailed diagram of perfect symmetry. Everything. Every bit of you. Functioning healthily. But it did not show how it went wrong. How blood thickens, muscles atrophy, bones crumble. How those nerves become miswired and fused. How people went round the bend.

The straight column of sunlight highlighted dust and other usually unseen dead matter that gets breathed in. That sunlight warmed Max's neck as he put his head down on the table to sleep for three full minutes.

The buzzer was about to sound any minute, marking the end of classes. Lunch-time. Max woke with a start, recognising that sudden rumble of hundreds of feet standing, packing bags, lining up. He felt that old adrenalin rush, those big black butterflies in his stomach beginning to rise up, about to beat their wings *hard*.

An hour from now, Max thought, that buzzer will sound again, and students would begin moving with reluctance towards the next set of tasks laid out before them.

He sat in the chair until the corridor stirred, then he walked through hundreds of identically dressed boys, who stared.

'Are you *Max*?' asked a boy by the old science lab Max had always detested the sour stink of.

'Who, me?' Max replied to the boy, who was bearing his over-the-shoulders satchel like a hunchback. He ran the palm of his cool hand across the crown of his head. 'Nah, not me, mate,' he said with a smile.

Max could hear books sliding up and down together as the boy moved off, pencils shaking. A noise like galloping horses right there on his back.

The man-made lake by which Max was seated had turned green and slimy over recent months.

'The powers that be decided to put two thousand fish in it,' a groundsman stopped by to say for the millionth time, 'but they died.' Having shared that, the little man moved off. Began a bit of sweeping.

Had I stayed on at school for another two years, I'd be in my second year at uni now, Max thought. Here. That was the plan.

'Once you get into university, everything will be just fine.' Max's father had been forever saying that through his son's early teen years. They had wanted him to study medicine. That was the plan, *their* plan.

Sitting there, on that bench, Max shook his head in weary disbelief. At that, the bullshit curse of education, and at a lanky six-foot pale boy with an overactive Adam's apple as he walked by. So proudly. A stack of books under his right arm. As if he really did go to that famous college whose name arched across the front of his sweatshirt.

'Clean cut, glossy haired, shifty eyed and stupid,' Max thought aloud.

It was a very weary fly that was bumping and weakly buzzing around Max's knees. It would land on one knee, then fly off to the other. Back and forth. Some kind of game of its own making, Max thought.

They'd have been delighted if I'd come here, slogging my way through the thesaurus of fatigue. Yeah. Coming home bushed, whacked, shattered and knackered. Completely. Zonked, zapped and shitted. Night after night.

All those long hours in the library, slowly killing myself. Back and forth to the Institute of Applied Microbiology, the Radioisotope Centre, the Molecular Genetics Research lab. I'd rather cut my heart out.

Max became aware of two figures in black, down by the edge of the water. Two guys, late teens/early twenties. Whatever. Holding hands. Speaking little. Broad daylight, 4 p.m. One said something to make the other laugh, then they moved off.

Max looked at the palms of his hands. He had never held hands with anybody, with the exception of three women who did not really count: his mother, his mother's sister, his father's mother.

I am one completely fucked virgin, he thought. Completely fucked.

Max removed his father's Visa card and cash from inside his Reeboks. Looked at the damp notes, the shiny plastic. Thrust both hands into the pockets of that outsized raincoat.

The tears felt hot as they rolled down his face, but they were welcome. They calmed him. Those tears needed to be released. Needed to dot his chest.

It was all so natural, inevitable. A massive thought bubble was forming in his head: Why oh why did you back out?

Max left the shades he had been wearing on the bench.

Modern art and display techniques have a lot in common, Max thought, as he left his Reeboks beside them, there on the bench. Standing back, wearing nothing but the tracksuit bottoms and outsized raincoat, Max viewed the arrangement.

Brand-new shades, brand-new Reeboks. There. Abandoned.

Dusk. The air was cooling. The fact that his feet were both blistered and bleeding did not bother Max, not in the least. What pain he was aware of felt good. He was feeling *something*.

Clutched in his right hand was one key, one Visa card, one hell of a lot of cash. He was in the mood to drop all that into a bin. Didn't.

Max was aware that he had three principal assets as he came to a halt in the middle of the bridge: his musical talent, his writing talent and his body. Oh, and number four, a lot of money in the bank.

It was as though his brain had switched to autopilot, as if his fate had been added to that part of the cerebral hemisphere which handles the heart, lungs and coordination in tap dancing. His mind was elsewhere and that elsewhere was centre-stage. The feeling had come suddenly. The transition, a power-cut effect which drained him then filled him with energy. It felt as if it were going to be there for a while so he decided he might as well enjoy it.

The sky had turned from blue to a deep dark violet. Up there was Jupiter with its four moons, all in a line, and with the bands across its face. Saturn with its rings, Alpha Centauri, which he knew to be not one star but two. A star like all stars, a cascade of light ages off. Constellations he had known since childhood as points of light joined up in his mind like a picture puzzle, scattered dots forming a butterfly, or bird of prey. Stargazing at that moment, Max felt catapulted twenty thousand years into the near past.

A breeze swerved into the delicate machinery of his ear – chilling the lobe, whizzing around the cochlea, thumping the Eustachian tube.

Suspended in the cold nothingness of infinite space, Max thought, beyond the warm, lush, spinning world of Earth, with its own innumerable life forms, are other planets, stars, comets. Meteors.

Under him ran water, miles of it. A whole world of water, polluted and fresh, stagnant and prehistoric. In this water Max saw a downward-looking self reflected back in black and white.

The river with its rattling murmur looked so inviting. It seemed to be daring him to jump.

Come on in, the water's . . .

That rattling murmur was a sound which exuded fair length, and a treacherous depth. Slow paced, with the occasional fast current to take trash by surprise. A sound invoking quiet flux. Cool. Cold under the cool. Impassive. Violent under that disguise. Minimal tempo, basic colour.

Currents whose motions were invisible to the eye drew occasional debris from the surface and, mysteriously, relinquished it again downriver into the central flow. Back into the all-accepting sea, back into deep-water currents, cold-water layers.

Max was both in a trance and sharply conscious. It wasn't as if it was *him* standing there. It was as if . . . as if someone else had walked into his body and was standing there on that bridge in the centre of the city.

Viewing himself from a distance, Max found the detachment thrilling and strangely romantic. His reflection was so real to him; it had starred in the dusty mirrors of his secret world of make-believe ever since he could remember.

Just for a moment, Max stopped breathing. No inhalation/exhalation at all. Then a tremendous stillness filled him out of the queer blue sky. Grave, quiet. He felt that he was invisible. He was floating. Something inside him had been put on PAUSE, something else on REC and PLAY. He felt suddenly sad, in a wonderful way.

Floating in the insidious drag of that river were blobs of toxic froth. Max could not detect what lay beneath the surface. Silted mud had been churned up further along. He found it hard to believe that below, in that water, anything could be alive.

The water did not smell rivery; beyond that faint smell of mud there was something poisonously chemical, something metallic.

Max had always liked the idea of disappearing. Justlikethat. Gone. Vanished. There's something magical about a disappearance, Max thought. Disappearing completely.

He found himself dully contemplating the ebb and flow on the surface of the water. He was the only person on the bridge but for those in cars passing by. His shoulders were sagging a little, something his former PE teacher would have picked him up on.

The rattling murmur of the river was promising to hold Max to itself without judgment or question, letting him become a part of it. All he had to do was jump. Fall fall fall.

Come on in, the water's . . .

Imagine falling, a voice teased Max internally. Imagine falling falling falling all the way down from up here. Just one little step up to here, one little step up to here. Jumping would feel like a Disneyland ride. Ready?

Max had always liked Disneyland rides. Very much. Loved the rush of air against his face, through his hair, up his sleeves as he rocketed up up up and – white knuckled – as he plummeted down down down.

A solitary black fin, gliding under the water, could not be seen from above. The fish was staring up at the high, lonesome figure with wide-awake black eyes. Below the fish, in apparent panic, dozens of grey, slimy eels writhed about in a squirming tangled ball on the riverbed. From pointed heads, cold little snakes' eyes stared up.

Fall was coming and soon the trees would be schizophrenic, losing control of colour up and down the riverside, ready to shed leaves from criss-cross branches before standing naked for long months.

Beneath the bridge, on the embankment, an old man crouched in the shadows playing a game with cardboard boxes; whatever the game, every once in a while he let rip an aria of profanities, then picked leaves out of the water with, to Max's astonishment, a violin bow. At least a dozen pigeons were regularly fed by the man – he only fed the regulars, that was why they were regular. His little friends. Binned McDonald's baps soaked in a tiny drop of river brought their little breasts close to him. One in particular cooed most neurotically by his side most days. Cooed, there by the side of the man's stinking, sore feet. Sometimes, almost as if to give him a treat, the bird settled on his shoulder, stretching forward to natter into the man's ear. He could feel the warmth of the bird's chest against his cheek, smelling of age and fragility. He was glad autumn was coming – at least six swarms of midges had feasted on him throughout the summer.

Secret layers of Max's personality had contradictory itches. So much of him wanted to jump, so much of that body was begging, pleading for all bodily functions to cease asap. Whilst, inwardly, he was falling, with no one to catch him, other instincts kept him standing. Still. Not belonging to anyone, being only his own.

This is me, Max thought. Here am I.

Bad thoughts which drive to overwhelming misery, deep brooding sadness, approach stealthily, almost unperceived, active like a virus. Unhurried, regular as the beat of a pulse.

'Er, excuse me,' the passer-by asked, wanting to get a better look at this tall, shaven-headed figure. As eye contact was made, the face of the passer-by changed. 'Aren't you . . . *Max?*'

Max had been recognised, but all the passer-by could think of was to scramble through his seventies BOAC bag for a piece of paper and a pen. An autograph. That was what he wanted. Above the desire to ask about the radical change of hairstyle and clothing, the lack of shoes, there was the standard desire for an autograph.

A shaky hand passed Max a file scrawled over with three different markers, the unmistakable calligraphy of a brakes-disconnected psychopath. Might be fun to frisbee the thing towards the horizon, Max thought, just to see all those pages going *flssch* in shock. Then *splash*. Oh, the look on his face. Such a temptation.

Despite the temptation, Max wrote 'DIE HAPPY' in capitals. Then, with his hand moving deliberately as if he were trying to fake his own signature, he signed his name.

Handing the piece of paper and Biro back to the young passer-by, Max smiled but was careful not to instigate any form of verbal communication.

The fan took a few steps backward. Nodding too much, smiling. With the energy born of uncertainty, the fan set off for his destination with a bounce in his step.

'Aren't you . . . *Max?*' Max said to himself, low. Repeating the question put to him just a minute ago. His nickname had never sounded so strange. Like the name of a place. Nothing to do with him.

Running the cool palm of his right hand over his ears, scalp, then back along his neck, into the collar of his tracksuit top, Max groaned.

'Max,' he said, slow and low. 'The name they gave me aged four.'

Fingers attached to wrists attached to forearms went on a journey back up, feeling the roughness of his head, the sandpapery fuzz. He liked it. The dead part of him, growing. Hair and nails, he thought, funny stuff.

'Max,' he repeated, trying to see his face in that name. All he could feel were the contours of his skull.

Max van Lieshout, that's what he was sometimes referred to as, but Max was not his real name, it was Joep. At the age of two, little Joep had discovered the power of the volume dial on the family hi-fi. He had always liked to turn the dial to MAX. Hence the nickname. A nickname which stuck.

Something about the sky was changing. A trail of low cloud was determined to make the skyline toytown.

'Joep,' Max said. 'Joep van Lieshout.'

He could feel his heartbeat increase as he left the bridge. Could feel himself begin to warm as he resumed walking.

Max did not know what time it was – some time after ten. Felt much later.

Standing in the frame of the door of his old room, he thought it looked like an icebox. A blank, cool container.

Total cloud cover: no view from the windows. Nothing worth watching on TV. Not in the mood for music, radio. Max was bored. He was tempted to phone for a cab, take a ride. Nowhere in particular, just take a ride around the city. Just to be out of that apartment.

Uncertain as to whether he would or would not spend a few hours in this way, Max decided to look through his father's wardrobe again, in search of clothes, but it was his mother's side that he opened, accidentally. Seeing all those neatly lined boxes stacked at the bottom of the wardrobe, he felt tempted to do something he had not done in many years: snoop.

Same old junk jewellery, same old collection of scarves she never wore.

'Poor ol' Mom.'

Cassettes she had stopped listening to, seashells and pebbles that only looked good when wet. A prayer book she no longer used.

Stashed at the bottom of one of the newer boxes were a dozen or so letters, all addressed to Max. At first he was puzzled, then he remembered having read them there at his parents' apartment many months ago. He thought he had lost them. These were letters that he had read but never replied to. Letters from Angela, Izzy and Zoran – among others. His *special* fans.

The replies he had written had always been minimal. Three lines, that was all. It was a rule he had made for himself and a rule that he had kept to. He knew that one day he would get around to phoning a few of these fans, that one day he would set aside time to meet them.

'And this is that day,' Max said to the three sheets of pink A5 that Izzy had sent him. 'Wonder what Izzy is short for,' he thought aloud as he began punching in the telephone number of a phone that would ring in five seconds, just four miles away.

'Hello?' a voice sing-songed. Loud. Bit hyper.

'Hi,' Max said. 'This is Max.'

'Yeah, right,' the young girl's voice snapped, fast as anything. 'And I'm Major Tom.'

Max smiled at that. A little hoot of air shot out through his nostrils. Pressing his lips close to the phone, Max said, 'Hey, Izzy, it *is*.'

He left a pause, which felt a little too serious, but that was unintended. He had just wanted to come across as real. Normal. Just a normal guy saying hi.

The line went quiet.

'I was just phoning to say thanks for your letters. They've always meant a lot to me.'

The line was now too quiet. Izzy had recognised that voice. 'You still there?'

Izzy breathed in, held that breath for a second, exhaled slowly.

'Yeah, I'm here.'

Then she gave a little laugh. Her eyes were closed, her brow furrowed, hands shaking. Slowly, very slowly, she assumed a kneeling position. She felt light headed, dry mouthed. Hot.

'Listen, and I know this might sound odd . . .' Max was suddenly very close to tears. '. . . and this *is* genuine . . .'

'Mm?'

'Can I . . . I was just wondering if . . .' You jerk, Max thought, just say it. 'I was just wondering if I could pop by some time, to say hello.'

'Oh,' Izzy almost exploded into the mouthpiece. '*Sure.*'

Then Max felt awkward, challenged. He was breaking two of the golden rules both at once: phoning a fan and arranging to meet.

'Say, what are you doing tomorrow? Early.'

'Oh . . .' Izzy shook her head in disbelief. Was Max coming on to her? Would she fuck him? Oh, yes. Even if it was just a oncer? Yesyesyes. Even though she had been with the same guy for nearly a year now? Oh, come on, Y-E-S. 'Oh, just uni. Nothing special. I can skip a class.'

'Meeting out can be kind of tricky, you understand?'

'Right.'

'Can I pop by?'

Izzy took a look around the kitchen of the apartment she shared with two other fashion design students. It was a tip.

'Sure.'

'How about early, mm?' Max asked. 'I'll bring something for breakfast.'

Max checked the address, got a few directions, then put the phone down. As he began to dial another number, an eighteen-year-old girl nicknamed Izzy was screaming at her friends to help get the place tidied, scrubbed clean and made to feel as *cool* as possible.

Zoran, the film student, thought it was his friend Emy phoning at first. After Max had been called a cocksucking fat liar a dozen times, he began to read from the letter Zoran had mailed many months ago. He soon shut up.

Angela was not in. The phone just rang and rang. Max was disappointed about that. Angela's letters had always been far more interesting than the standard fan mail. No bizarre requests, no lengthy accounts of recent dreams, no emotional blackmailing. Angela tended to write about what her life was like on a day-to-day basis. To Max this was anything but mundane. This was real.

'Angela, the one with a cat.'

# 8

Max wondered what he was doing in that side street at nine in the morning as he got out of the cab.

A pigeon was having great fun eating vomited pasta at the base of a lamp-post. Shaking its head, breaking the vermicelli. Gobbling down. Breakfast.

Max had been buzzed in within just three seconds of ringing Izzy's bell.

'Bad sign,' he said to himself.

This kind of feels like doing a scene for a pilot, he thought. Yeah, for a show that'd be scrapped.

And there she was, at the door. Ready for him.

'Oh,' she said, sounding just a little bit disappointed that he was not in satin and leather, hair hanging down past his shoulders, with a guitar slung low.

'Hey,' Max said. Then he smiled, gave her a kiss on her right cheek, then the left.

For a moment she stared at Max with a look of acute disbelief. Her body had gone rigid, absolutely stiff. Her eyes were fixed and bulging, almost as hotly as the raised purple-pink swelling on the top of her left shoulder, the work of a thirsty mosquito.

Her hair was kind of piled up false carelessly. A look that had taken ages to get cutely wrong. Her eyes . . . Her eyes were on Max's feet, which were bare, toes on display. It took more than a little self-control for Izzy not to fall to her hands and knees and lap at them, cat-licking them clean. So that there would be nothing in between toes;

surface scoured by her tongue, wrinkles bleached with her saliva.

Her lips were winter children's lips, just that little bit sore. Like the lips of trumpeters after the second set. Lips that needed a dab of Vaseline or one of those things that relieves, protects & moisturises WITH SUNSCREEN.

So this is Izzy, Max thought. Now I know.

Her well-built, conscientiously exercised body was squeezed into an outfit that fitted her better than it had the day she bought it – a white wrap affair that made absolutely no attempt to hide the fact that her teenage breasts were very much there and well worth looking at. When she giggled about what a state the apartment was in (it wasn't) those breasts jiggled and her nipples became the point(s) of focus.

She had not slept a wink, unsure as to whether or not Max would actually come by. This has to be a wind-up, a line Izzy had tormented herself with all night long. She and her room-mates were delighted that the call had not been her cruel kid brother playing one of his tricks.

The previous week, Izzy and two room-mates had painted the walls of the rented three-bedroomed apartment pale pink, tan and a nicotine yellow. An attempt to create the atmosphere of tinted photographs. Photos in which skin is light green, lips tangerine. She had always had an eye for colour, particularly as a child. She knew how to combine the unexpected.

Everything in the personal world of her bedroom was in coordinated earth tones. She obviously admired simplicity in the arts and crafts. Functional, stripped to essentials. On the shelves there were figures made from stone, wood, clay, paper and bamboo. She enjoyed these trinkets, often given as thoughtful presents by family and friends. Fine and unusual gifts, inspired by the past – but fake. All this *stuff*, Max thought, is mass-produced crap. Nice enough as replicas go, but not authentic. Reproductions.

'Oh, nearly forgot,' Max said, handing over a carrier bag containing good-quality freshly ground coffee, fruit, hot cross buns and yoghurt.

'Oh, *hey*,' Izzy said, in a voice that even Britney Spears would have thought treacly.

Izzy blinked at Max excitedly as she began to exercise a little bladder control.

Uh-oh. This is a big mistake, Max thought. *Her-yuge*.

That girl, that Izzy creature, was intent on taking Max on a guided tour of the apartment. When he had arrived, all three had been playing so hard to be cool. The other two room-mates left after a few minutes, following some kind of agreed plan. Obviously. Then Izzy and Max were alone.

There was a double bed, a mirror, a double bed in the mirror.

There were posters of Max all over the walls. Framed pictures by her bed. Oh, Max thought, this is agony. Increasingly flirty, Izzy seemed in a state of strange anticipation, as if things were about to happen. Destined. Self-defensively, Max kept his arms tightly folded.

On the shelves of a vintage glass display cabinet sat dolls in neat lines, awaiting inspection. Dolls with composition head and limbs, moulded hair with one lock down the forehead, orange hair, black yarn hair, feathered eyebrows, deep-set flirty green sleep eyes with radiating irises, puckered crying faces, moulded-on shoes and socks, pretty little things with smiling mouths and deep dimples, some with lower lip sucked under upper lip (many with jointed wrists with gauntlet hands and widespread fingers, polished fingernails – little hands that really want to hold your thumb) lined up obediently alongside cute, cute, cutest dolls in original velvet dance outfits, adorable sweethearts with dark suntan colours and white hair. Some with bean-bag-style bodies, some with bent baby legs (with all those special little wrinkles), some with those ever-popular pre-teen bodies in Victorian hand-me-downs of finest cottons (often with wide-spread legs and human-hair wigs), deep-throated pull-string talkers. Many with hard moulded tongues, one or two with soft felt tongues, occasionally much-fingered treasures with non-removable shirts and shorts, glued-on pants (vest removable only), many with bottoms which took batteries, ready to crawl. Dolls like dreams. Reflex smiles. Built-in whimpers. Some sudden shocking cryers. Dolls so proud of their two front teeth and fancy bows. Lined up like little orphans, each one needing loving care. Occasionally one or two with a button in the back that made the head nod *Yes*.

'Hey,' Max said, 'this is really somethin'.'

Perhaps the pride of the collection was a Barbie doll, an unbelievably rare 1965 developmental prototype. Charcoal brunette hair, severest parting, minuscule fringe. The cutest nostril dotting, in perfect condition. Shiny, shiny plastic. So skinny.

Tour over, Izzy began to rustle up something to eat. After the rapid chopping of a banana, she fizzed with adrenalin. She had nearly forgotten.

'Don't mind, do you?' Izzy asked as she switched the flash on, about to point the lens of a Fuji disposable camera Max's way.

The laughter came spewing out of him like a mouthful of sick. It was a have-to-laugh-or-you-cry moment. He gulped for air and came near to palpitating. His eyes watered then shone. Had Izzy not been such an ardent fan, she might have recognised that she not only had a rock star sitting there in her kitchen, but also a medical condition.

'No,' he said, 'that's fine. Just the one, though.'

His face, the controlled expression, was more deliberate than ever before. He felt that he had to adopt some kind of Max mask for this fan. He was really working at it. Unsure of its reliability. Now was not the time for that mask to slip. The last thing he wanted was for her to see him as vulnerable. Despite this, his mouth said, 'This is Max unplugged.'

Flash, and it was done. Got him. Captured.

Izzy did not have a clue as to what he meant. She smiled, wishing he had not cut off all his lovely hair, yet wondering what that head might feel like against her tender fingertips. Since the release of his first single, not a day had gone by when Izzy had not hugged herself, imagining it was Max's arms around her.

She wanted to know all about what it was like being discovered. *She* wanted to be discovered. And what it was like being 'developed' by a record company before the release of his first single. *She* wanted to be discovered as a fashion designer by Gucci or Galliano in her first year at design school. And she wanted to know . . .

All the usual fan shit. And while Max talked away their hour together, he was elsewhere. He hoped that she would not be hurt that he would never reply to any of her letters again. She would get a thank-you card, probably. And that would be it.

Max had felt an instant rush of relief as he had walked away from Izzy's apartment building.

'Moron,' was his whispered, one-word judgment.

Nothing to do until four, Max thought to himself, then off to meet fan number two.

He wanted to do five hours of nothing. Just nothing.

Maybe just lie down in a park somewhere and take some sun. Having decided on that, he hailed a cab.

Two years back, Max had been photographed at the edge of a park in the north of the city. Although he could not remember its name, he knew it was close to a railway station, and that was where the cab was now heading.

Max stopped off en route to buy a couple of cans of beer. Why not, he had thought, why ever not? Get a bit pissed in the sunshine. Yeah.

With his tracksuit top tied around his waist, shoulders reddening after just ten minutes of exposure, Max was unaware that the section of parkland he was walking through was popular with the city's mutual masturbators. At night the glowing butts of cigarettes hovered like votive candles among the congregation. In silent slow motion, faceless fucks walked round and round in circles, stamping down the growing green. Bachelor ramblers, taking a risk.

Morning constitutionals were often interrupted by the sight of condoms and rubber gloves hanging from branches. A fact Max was unaware of. He was totally oblivious to the fact that the area was a twenty-four-hour free-for-all where every excess of the flesh was admissible.

Many international gay guides had that wild area of parkland listed under *Cruising* sections. Enter AYOR (At Your Own Risk). Again, a fact that Max was unaware of. All he knew was that he had enjoyed the late afternoon he had been photographed there, posing up a tree with an acoustic guitar, with a semi-naked pair of unidentical twins by his side. A boy, a girl. Blond. Sweet thirteen-year-olds.

The cool edges of the undergrowth invited Max to walk off the trampled paths, insisted he enter. Beyond the perimeter of black branches, Max came into the zone frequented by so many of the city's married and unmarried men. A spot which reeked of sex. All that groaning, groining. Grunting. Full of discontent, disease and despair.

Max's innocence of what went on in that neck of the woods was quickly dispelled. There, kneeling beside the trunk of a fallen tree, was a weary cruiser, dressed in nothing but a pair of cut-down Levis. A man ready for anything on bended knees. All the signs of a homo, Max thought. Those tattoos, the piercings through left and right nipples, plus eyebrow. That shaved head.

Max laughed inwardly. And what do *you* look like? Body shaved, head shaved down to the length of a number one. No eyebrows.

Instead of feeling uncomfortable, Max thrilled in this atmosphere of lunatic hide-and-seek. At least there would not be any screaming children about, playing their monotonous games, pretending to be airplanes or cartoon monsters.

The cruiser withdrew a small brown bottle from his pocket. He unscrewed the white cap carefully, reverentially. Then he inhaled deeply through one nostril, paused, then through the other nostril. As he held that breath, the cruiser returned the cap to the little bottle with nimble fingers, all the while staring Max's way. Max was not attracted, but he was intrigued.

As the amyl nitrate began to take effect, slowly reddening the chest and face of the man with the blood rush, he began to unbutton the flies of those cut-down Levis. Then his expression shifted from hopeful to hopeless, then one of anxiety. He could see that the tall young guy was not interested. Was strolling away.

A wave of humidity rolled over Max's body as he walked. Pores opened up to the air. He felt weird, he felt wonderful. He wanted to get away from that scene back there, which was a scene that had nothing to do with him. He wanted to get to a spot where there would be no one. Just him.

At a spot where autumn had already got going, Max lay down on his outstretched tracksuit top and bottoms. He had no reservations about being naked there, none at all.

He heard something, it made him jump. There were two just-dropped leaves beside him.

Swallowing down the last of the beer, he knew he would be able to hear if anyone approached. The ground, covered by dry leaves as it was, would alert him to any advancing foot-steps.

And so what if someone sees me, Max thought, what's the big deal? A naked nineteen-year-old taking some sun. So fuckin' what.

As he stretched back, with a hand cupped beneath his head, the sprouted wisps of hair under his arms unfurled slowly. What little sweat had been there made the air fragrant. The scent rose up, colouring the air.

There was a rich smell of rot and growth in that location, something Max found powerfully sexual. It was this which gave him an erection, not the bizarre contact he had made with the cruiser in the midst of all that lush green out there.

I've never been kissed, Max thought, not once.

Then he groaned.

Oh, I get so pissed off with life. My life. Your life. The whole thing. Everything.

He rolled over, pressed his face into the comforting space of his cool, cupped hands.

I'm always thinking. There's always this commentary going on in my head. I wish I could turn myself off sometimes.

The glare in the sky cast no shadows. Windless, the day was now hot but grey. Growing gradually behind blocks of sooty-windowed factories in the streets Max was being driven through were the screams of children and the gossip of women in a dozen different languages, the smell of straw and onions and urine and chicory, faces that primarily revealed exhaus-tion. Grey, stamped on everybody.

Before the final swerve the cab was to make, Max glimpsed two little girls, happy with their graffiti. A wall, covered with chalked penises whose erections would dissolve with the next rain, made the girls giggle and compare.

'Here will be fine,' Max said, as he thrust a note at the driver.

In the small tree-lined street of undesirable residences of six to seven floors lived a film student named Zoran Agius. Towering up beside him as he walked, these were just the kind of buildings that Max had always thought of as filing cabinets. The street had a Sunday lunch stink to it.

Max inspected himself in the reflection of a well-wiped neo-Georgian window before pressing the buzzer for number 759. For a moment he thought the best thing he could do was run. Away.

There was a splotch of vomit by the front doorstep. Someone had either just made it out of the house in time or failed to get in to the toilet in time. It looked like insistent vomit. Like something that had been going bad in the stomach long before it was upchucked.

Max heard the footsteps approaching. How will I be greeted, he wondered. As rock star or person? Place your bets.

Zoran arched an eyebrow, taken aback that this was a different-looking Max to the one he had been expecting, then his face just flew open. Eyes glittering, he was teeth, gums, tongue. Wet, blackcurrant tongue. Hot blackcurrant breath.

'Hey,' Zoran said too loudly.

It felt like someone's big moment in a play, the bit everyone has been waiting for, the bit where it goes so quiet all the audience can hear is the buzz of the spotlight that bathes the lone performer. And that lone performer had suddenly been seized by an attack of stage fright. He'd forgotten his lines.

'You're Zoran, right?' Max prompted.

'Yeah, and you pronounced it just right too.'

It was as though he were continuing a conversation accidentally interrupted a few minutes ago.

Zoran was blond, almost albino, with long white eyelashes and large, almost transparent ears.

'No elevator, I'm afraid.'

Only his clothes had colour, and the amber pustules on his forehead.

'Can't believe you're here,' he gushed in a voice that came from a throat which was not just sore but damaged. Too old for the body it came from. An old man's voice.

There was something about him that stank of gang rape queue: the outsized army boots, the unwashed black jeans, that XL Slipknot T-shirt.

Home was one room.

'There's a bathroom on every floor so it's not so bad,' Zoran explained. 'I'm currently looking for something better, but . . . Well, you know how it is.'

Nothing about the guy seemed real to Max. He seemed echoed, overdubbed.

'Like a drink?'

Zoran did not mean tea or coffee. Holding a bottle of supermarket-brand vodka up high, he was acting tough. Rock 'n' roll. Shy and determined, a troublesome combination.

'Just a small one,' Max said quietly.

Max sat on the floor – it was the only place to sit. No effort at tidying up had been attempted, something which Max felt comfortable with.

Zoran knocked a shot back, then poured another.

'Looks like you needed that,' Max said.

'I need something to soothe my nerves. I've been in a bit of a state since you called. Didn't get a wink of sleep.'

Zoran knocked back the second shot.

'Good stuff,' he said to Max. 'Can be a bit of a problem. I spend more on booze than food.'

He began to laugh.

'Blind fucking drunk. Paralytic, practically every day – that's me. Beer, shorts, anything wet. I'm a mess.'

Zoran shrugged as he began to pour a third shot.

'I like drinking, and I love being drunk.'

That third shot went down the hatch, then Zoran opened a pack of sugar-free gum.

'Like some?'

Max shook his head. 'No, thanks. I'm fine with this,' he said, raising his glass before taking a sip.

There was a running hint of kohl under Zoran's left eye, a blotch of spot-stick on a blister that he really should have let get some air.

Nightmare, Max thought. This guy's a nightmare.

# 9

Max lay there, in the centre of his parents' bed, glistening in a film of salty sweat. Still. Slipper warmth had filled the room for hours.

It's the hottest morning of the year, he thought. Has to be some kind of record.

Max remained perfectly still. He felt that if he did not move, the heat inside him might build and build and something extraordinary would happen.

'Like some densely packed bomb in the depth of me might go off,' he said to the ceiling light.

Max imagined detonation. Could see his parents on their hands and knees, collecting brilliant, steaming shards of their robotic son.

A screech of car brakes down in the street below aroused Max's curiosity. Sounded like a cab had just skidded to a halt because of a dog, cyclist or . . .

Max got himself out of bed, walked over to the window.

'Small child,' he said quietly, looking down. His baseball cap had blown off and he had run back to get it. The boy's mother had got such a shock that she was semi-hysterical. Boy of four, perhaps. Maybe five. After they had walked up the road a minute the woman slapped the back of the boy's legs. Twice. Pretty damn hard. The boy roared. He had just learned a little road safety the painful way.

Max swallowed. Growing up: so much shit.

Falling from this window, Max thought. It wouldn't take long. Just down. Just *wa-wa-wa-wa-wa*, then splat.

Burning alive, Max thought. That would hurt. Like mad.

'Swivelling and rocking in the eddies, arms splayed, bent at the elbow,' he whispered dreamily.

'Face down – like someone quietly, pronely asleep. Same sort of position.'

He breathed against the glass, fogging it. Began to write a word.

'But bodies don't sleep when they are lying face down in water.'

'DROWNING' was the word Max had written. A word that was smudged out with an anticlockwise finger before it had started to fade.

What he fancied right that moment was a tall glass of very cold milk. His father was very particular about milk. It had to be fresh, semi-skimmed organic milk. Straight from the cow. Unfortunately there was none in the fridge. There was nothing in the refrigerator. It had been emptied of all contents, defrosted and cleaned.

'A spotless train arrives at a spotless platform, spot on time,' Max said under his breath. He was impersonating a man who had been his English teacher once upon a time. He had never liked the man. He had been a mediocre teacher and a mammoth bore. Peter Burston. Mr Burston, all the way from sunny Brighton, England. Mr Burston, full of opinions no one wanted to hear. 'The jerk.'

The doors opened. On the floor was a man having a lavish epileptic fit. The compartment was empty. He needed help. Max was the only person to get on. He took a seat, and watched. The man soon righted himself. Had not bitten his tongue off, had not wet himself. Seemed okay. He stood, dusted himself down and casually glanced at his watch. He got off at the next stop.

Three stops on, Max realised that he had got on the wrong train and had to change. It was a mistake that really pissed him off.

At first the platform was quiet, then there was a surge of people.

Max boarded the train after a family of six. Parents, and their gang of four boys. They sat opposite. The boys all looked like variations of the same model, spaced apart at one-year intervals. The eldest had encroaching puberty written all over his face. The youngest was, perhaps, nine: the one who would learn so much from his brothers. With the exception of the youngest child, brains and eyelids soon grew sluggish, and Max watched their heads nod.

The youngest boy was wide awake, eyes everywhere. He was enjoying the journey until he sniffed and was offered a tissue which he was expected to take to sort himself out. The little boy shook his head and then sniffed a green snot bubble back up his nostril. The father tutted loudly.

For a while Max read a newspaper that someone had left behind. For ten minutes his face was concealed like a cornered hubbie in a farce, then he put it down and closed his eyes. Slept a while.

The snotty little boy opposite had turned into a beautifully pale foreign girl with yard-long blonde hair. She was brushing it. That was what woke him, a really soft caressing sound. She was careful not to break it.

There was no one else in the carriage. She had obviously felt confident enough to do that kind of private thing with just a sleeping guy present. But now that sleeper was awake and she smiled as her hair turned into billowing light as it went (expertly) up to be swirled into half a dozen different shapes before she decided on wearing it down in a single plait.

Suits you that way, Max thought as he closed his eyes again. Pretty girl.

The train went overground a while. Max could feel the sun on his face, the change in the air.

When he opened his eyes again there was a different girl sitting in the seat opposite him – a fifteen-year-old delicious coy flirt with her boyfy and dog. This girl had fussed with a ponytail, weighty as old navy rope. She had spent the morning getting it systematically wrong and lover boy beside her had not said a word to her about it. She would not be the girl in his life for much longer, he had decided. Dumb bitch. A couple more fucks then sayonara.

Flick. He was not looking. Flick. Nothing. She repositioned her ponytail by the side of her neck, gave it two little pats then one long sensuous stroke. Nothing. Didn't he like it? She was close to sobbing. The individual and uncoordinated strands of her bangs had taken ages to bend, twist and frizz.

That dog of hers sat erectly between them, keeping still but its scarf of a tongue out – panting as if in great lust. Each time the train came to a standstill and the doors opened, the dog began to pine.

'You shut up, or I'll give you a kick up the ass that'll leave a mark,' the girl said, before releasing a laugh grenade which seemed to really piss the boyfy off.

Looking deep into the reflection of his eyes bored/saddened/ tired Max. The *dackadacka* of the train eventually lulled him back into a nap. He did not want to sleep, but the moment he shut his eyes he took that first drop which led to the next, then the next. In no time at all his forehead was almost touching his knees. In his head he was rehearsing a conversation that he would never have with his mother about citrus fruits.

Max was woken by a tearing sound. He opened his eyes. Some girl who obviously knew all there was to know about bargain shopping. She had one of those plum, glossy, big

Eskimo faces. The nose of that guinea-pig face was stuck in a paperback. As she read, her fingers began rolling up the page from the book. She got through a fresh page, read the other side, then tore that page out, too.

'Why do you do that?' Max asked.

Big eyes stared his way. Lashes had been stiffened with a couple of coats of silver mascara.

'When I'm done with both sides I tear the page out so I won't lose my place,' she said, quite probably not for the first time.

Hazel-green contacts, with flecks of blue and gold.

'Guess it makes carrying lighter as well.'

'Yes,' came her reply. She had never thought of that before. Next time someone asked her the Why question, she would add that to her answer.

Max closed his eyes. She wouldn't have that option with a computer book, he thought. There'd be the weight of that laptop, always that same weight. Always that same feel. Same nothing smell.

A man born too late for success in freak shows wobbled from platform edge to seat. A stain of coffee, curry sauce or blood was on his tie, running from just below the neat knot to just above the head of an embroidered Mickey Mouse. This man was accompanied by a younger man who resembled the older man too much not to be linked to him by blood. Both had hair that was scattered over the crowns of their heads in assorted folds and clumps. Eyes half closed for aesthetic purposes, Max thought that some weird genetic characteristic had created this hairdo, which looked like a bar code that had been badly printed. All shades of black on white gone horribly wrong. What amazed Max was that as they exchanged a comment or two about the delay between stations, they seemed to actually get on. As if they liked each other a little bit.

The old man glided a hand up over his shirt, patted his breast pocket. He smiled. Something was there. Something good. He removed two tiny objects: a couple of gold-yellow sweets, wrapped in an oblong of transparent plastic, twisted at the ends. Before popping the things into their mouths, each did the same thing, as if it were part of a circus routine. They sniffed the sweet loudly, then, tossing the little lemon balls in between their lips, they smiled again.

From each there was a click against teeth as the tongue rolled it from one side of the mouth to the other. For a moment it formed a firm, still bulge in both cheeks, then each gave their sweet a hard, skilled crunch. Max wondered where they were off to.

The old man took a closer look at Max, sensing that the young man sitting opposite him was not a type. By no means an original, nothing startlingly unique; but not the mass-manufactured types that had so bored him in his last fifteen years of high-school teaching. He seemed to consult the younger version of himself upon the matter. There was an exchange of glances. Max wondered what their verdict was as he shut his eyes again.

At times during the journey, the older man would laugh a crazy laugh, which the younger had a higher version of. Every once in a while something in their exchange went chug and the old man would launch into his *ha-ha-ha* routine. Really hard, like it hurt. Kind of like the Joker in *Batman*, but unsuitable for family viewing. There was something just too weird about that old man, and his son.

As Max dozed, he was aware that his mind was juggling a jigsaw of thoughts about the subway map, and how the many colours of that map intertwined and how sad it was that so many commuters only knew the grey, the orange, the shit brown. There are so many other places to go, Max thought, besides those nine-to-five destinations. Other journeys you can take.

Next stop, Max thought. There at last. He was relieved the journey had come to an end.

'Pinstripes, overalls and uniforms,' Max spat. 'All variations of a straitjacket.'

So many people, all moving so fast to wherever. Coming from, going to. How, day in, day out, crammed together in the glaring, probing white light with their sports pages, magazines, petite story books and violent, erotic comics bound in thick paperback volumes, do they cope with all this? How do they feel when they return 'home' at the end of the day?

There are too many people on planet Earth. Something needs to happen. Some kind of momentary fault in technical defence. Bombs in New York, London, Paris, Tokyo – all at once. Hiroshima times ten. Actually, times a hundred. Or a virus. Not like AIDS. Too slow. Something fast, in the water or the ingredients of Dunkin Donuts. Something new and nasty that not even Osama Bin Laden had ever given thought to.

Too many people, Max thought. Too many stoopid, *demented* people.

The edge of panic at Furnace had quickly escalated from being a voiced concern by two members of the press office at eleven to a bubbling hysteria by noon. Management had not been aware how extensive the damage was.

'He's missed *how many* interviews?' the Head of Marketing enquired with a snarl, completely baffled that the press office were now admitting that all contact with Max had been lost since the gig on Thursday.

'Let's get this straight, we're talking Friday, the weekend, Monday, Tuesday . . . that's five days.'

'And he's never done this before, never missed a single interview or photo shoot. Right?'

Qwo-Li O'Driskill, Head of PR, nodded.

'Are we worried or are we worried?'

'On a scale of one to ten I think we're talking ten,' Qwo-Li croaked as he fingered his lengthy goatee.

'Not at the usual hotel?'

'No.'

'His parents' place?'

'Neighbours say they haven't seen him. We've checked.'

'Shit.'

'Listen, we can handle this two ways. One, contact the police and have him listed as missing, or . . .'

'I've already looked into that,' Qwo-Li piped up. 'The way the system works is that there are a number of categories of 'missing', and one of them is 'limited', which means that the details are circulated, but that's as far as it goes which, it has to be said, seems far from satisfactory.' Qwo-Li was about to stick his neck out. 'There was, after all, plenty of evidence to suggest that Max was unstable in recent months and that he may have posed a threat to himself.'

Everyone knew that Qwo-Li was right. The situation was suddenly abundantly clear.

'Shit, we should have been looking after him better,' shouted out Salwa Nassar, the tour manager. 'He doesn't even have a place of his own, does he?'

All the phones were ringing. The e-mails were flooding in. The fax machine was just about to run out of its second roll of paper that day.

'Okay,' said Alexia Exarchos of the management team. 'Qwo-Li, if we haven't heard from Max by tomorrow then issue a press appeal first thing. Anything could've happened, right? And hey, listen up. If he's okay and just decided to go AWOL for a few days, then we'll have to hype it a bit – make it rock 'n' roll. But I think we should be taking this seriously. Qwo-Li, check out the bars, restaurants, clubs and stuff that he goes to. Damon, phone all the usual hotels, car services. Erykah, check with the backing band. Maybe he's with someone.'

The mood was bleak. Max was always alone. There was no someone, never had been.

'Colleen, draft up a press appeal asap. That's it. Let's go!'

By five o'clock no one was any the wiser.

Exarchos was becoming rattled. He'd made a decision.

'I know I said we'd give it until tomorrow but I've just got a weird feeling on this. I think we should inform the police before end of play today, then the media. Hm?'

Heads reluctantly nodded.

Within the hour, Qwo-Li had reported Max as missing to the Metropolitan Police, who circulated his details to police stations nationwide. Simultaneously, Furnace hired the services of a private detective to try to track Max down.

Qwo-Li and his team stayed on until seven o'clock, fine-tuning the release that would hit the website and then every news desk the following morning.

ROCK STAR MAX IS REPORTED MISSING

Managment at Furnace Records and police are anxious to trace the rock star known as Max, aged 19 years, who has been missing since late on Monday 15 September 2003 when he was seen leaving the WKCI complex after a concert. Max's family, band members and friends are concerned for his safety and welfare and stress that no pressure would be put on him to return if he does not wish to. They stress that his privacy will be respected at all times. Police are asking anyone who has seen Max or knows of his whereabouts to call the number below, and ask for the crime desk or CID office. Should Max himself see this appeal, his family and friends are anxious for him to contact one of them or the police to let them know he is safe and well. They again stress that Max will not be urged to return or reveal his whereabouts if he does not wish to do so.

The appeal, which Qwo-Li had based on the police press appeal put together many years back when Richey Edwards of Manic Street Preachers had gone missing, then went on to list a visual description of Max: height, hair, build. The usual.

The barboy had skin still tanned from weeks on a beach all by himself. Ivory toenails, perfect fingernails: prepared for compliments. He was a handsome, sharply groomed, gym-trained young man who gave off just a little whiff of whore.

Atmosphere was one of those bars that Max had heard about, but never dared venture out to for fear of being recognised and – as a consequence – hassled. The joint went to town pretending to be laid back in a New Age kind of way. Lots of varnished wood, polished slate and lighting you would not notice. Key West meets Ikea. With very much a below-decks ambience, it was once a hip place to waste time. *Once*. The colour scheme, Max reckoned, was suited to a multi-ethnic reception class.

It was not yet seven, and the music was still on low. Without it, the only sound would have been the swallowing of Adam's apples and the creaking of necks as heads swivelled in synchrony, following the progress of anything trendoid.

There was a cluster of butterscotch-skinned Latino boys with lots of over-styled facial hair arranged balletically at the bar, waiting to be wined, dined and sixty-nined. To Max it appeared that they had come as some kind of victorious team, straight from the gym, keen to show what they were made of. What they were made of was dressed up in Diesel, Diesel, Diesel. Topic of conversation? Max quizzed himself. Oh, a fab bit of e-mail that had just come in on that clever little cellular that was now being passed around – nice toy. Or their latest T.4 cell count. Or Kylie. Place your bets, Max thought.

One kept turning to look over his shoulder at Max. He was sexy, and he knew it. Sexy plus steroid-knocker perfect. A tiny slackening of muscle here, a gob too much flesh there, would have utterly altered the balance. And the balance was, according to his personal trainer, just right. Just . . . just like something out of a skimpy underwear catalogue. A catalogue seemingly aimed at an entire new generation of new men, and their admirers. A catalogue with sculpted big-boy God-bods stretching and leaping and pretending to be sleeping – wearing little strips of something synthetic aimed at teasing/arousing.

His summer colour had just been topped up somewhere, he had that look. Maybe abroad. Probably not. There was something stung about his skin. And the more Max looked at it, the more he could hear the sizzle and pop. That youth, that body – laid out – surrounded by tubes of UV light going *vraa* and *kraa*.

Max imagined that the guy would have just a little chest hair, recently grown back after the summer pluck. It would be, Max thought, classic 'T' formation, with . . . yeah . . . just a little shaving here and there for emphasis along the abs. That guy has been everything but taxidermised, Max reckoned. Everything. Probably at an hourly rate. Faggot.

A little to the right of the guy's head, the bug light, the INSECT-O-CUTOR, zapped some little winged thing to death in a purple flash.

An anonymous sexual compulsive in search of a fresh face, a new body – some magical quality to feel complete – fixed his sad eyes on Max. In hopeful anticipation, that anonymous sexual compulsive moved to the table opposite, sat himself down. The state of anticipation he was trapped in was exhausting the poor soul. He had perfected that wanna-suck-you-right-this-minute look with years of practice – it was flashing across his forehead more garishly than the neon of Ginza.

As Madonna finished singing about the mystery of life, the man opposite Max, perhaps twice his age, removed his glasses gingerly, from one ear at a time, staring hard Max's way. Gently massaging the sore and reddened hollows at the side of his nose, he began to gobble up every detail. That crop, the zero body fat. Max looked away, began counting to ten.

Shit, Max thought, the sod's still staring at me. F-U-C-K *off*. He hoped that the man, who was now tapping a tired foot along to simple thudding computer pop courtesy of some dumb boy band, would soon shove off.

Distracted by the arrival of a gang of disco sodomites making a Big Entrance replete with tasteful tattoos, jolly piercings and jism-spattered combats – one of whom was marching around with the previous night's fuck like it was love – Max thought he would see what was happening on the upper level. Pushing past the prime, pumped, waxed, tanned, moisturised flesh, he felt distinctly light headed after the two neat whiskies he had downed.

Some guy in a new shirt was jigging about on the small dance-floor up there to some trippy, computer-generated dance soundscape, deluding himself that he was the sexiest person in the place, whereas he was just the drunkest person in the place and dancing in a really embarrassing way. There, Max thought, right now, right this minute: gross. The way his chin contorted into grotesque double folds, the consequence of a series of beery hip thrusts he was so intent on executing every fourth beat.

Max sat himself down at a table on which the wipe marks of a rag had just dried. It was with a slight annoyance that he realised he had seated himself in the restaurant/snack section of the set-up. He was a bit pissed about that – he had only wanted to have one last drink.

'Ready to order?' the waiter inevitably sing-songed, somewhat nasally.

Max took a quick glance at the laminated menu. Seemed like a toss-up between the smoked salmon and cream cheese bagel or the tender sliced ham and Gruyère in a toasted baguette. He went for the latter, with a side order of sweet yam fries.

'And to drink?'

Max's eyes zigzagged over the reverse side of the menu. He picked the first thing he saw.

'A glass of the Rioja, please.'

'Bottle only,' came the waiter's too-snappy response.

'A bottle, then,' Max said, very slowly.

The waiter's face seemed suddenly dejected, as if he were going to have to traipse all the way to some Valencian vineyard to pick the grapes, stamp them and all the rest of it.

'Jerk.'

A group, notably dressed in boots, beads and huge buckled belts, stood in that casual yet significant manner, bitching by the dance-floor. Showing off hard-gained masculinity while chewing sugar-free gum, they appeared to be waiting for something to happen. A revolution of some sort, perhaps. Or, more likely, the chance of a quick blowjob down in the toilets. Cash-corrupted, right-to-the-minute drug queens, squandering a few more glittering coins on a bottle of imported beer or a cappuccino that would take anything from a couple of minutes to an entire hour to get down. Waiting for a buzz to start or wear off. Waiting to roar and rage at the latest club in sweat-soaked tops or take a shower and sleep, recover from sensory overload.

'Hey, that's so *cool*.' That was what the girl on the next

table to Max kept saying *every* time a response was required to whatever her boyfriend had said. Out it would pop. That word. There she goes again, Max thought. Ouch.

Max gave the girl a somewhat lingering once-over. Mm, some new-to-the-metropolis kid, eighteen or nineteen, who has undoubtedly notched up an impeccable academic record in recent years. Judging by the club clobber she's decked out in she's an acutely televised young thing who allows herself to be dictated to every inch of the way, Max thought. The perfect consumer.

Double ouch, that word again, the 'C' word. *Cool*, such a convenient little soundbite.

'Like . . .' she starts, then thinks. Takes a while. 'Oh . . . whatever,' she says helplessly, stupidly, sexily.

Tonight, Max thought, or tomorrow, she'll be out at some dumb club. A club which'll be packed, packed like a death-trap fire-trap. Three to four hundred there. Club animals, tinted to all shades of bronze. Great-looking girls. More than a fair share of mad, bad, dangerous-to-know drug queens. Music way too loud, some DJ working a Nazi jackboot beat. All stomping in a uniform, pulsing undulation, performing all variations of aerobics – but nonchalantly. All in the same nothing mood, that 'cool' mood, hardly looking at one another but eyes everywhere – swivelling chunkily to the left and right in a tight, fashionable style they'd all picked up . . . somewhere. Maybe there. And while all the heads bobbed and jigged, while the heads veritably bounced with all the jogging on the spot – so itchy footed – dilated eyes would hunt. She'd think it was great. Heaven.

Max had been there, done that, just the once. Just the once everywhere. Quick international in-outs. At first that kind of club presence had been essential, useful in terms of establishing his profile. The clownishly intense party animals, however, were not Max's core audience. The stay-at-homes in the suburbs and provinces might have aspired to that lifestyle, but that desperately puffed-up mode was not Max's mode. Anything but.

When the sun goes down, Max thought, it's time to get the fuck outta here.

# 10

Standing opposite Max was a woman he had kind of grown up around – she was always there, somewhere. The supermarket, the cobbler's. She was the woman from next door. Very small, very thin, and for the last five years very deaf. Mrs B.

'Too much hairspray makes your hair look like a wig,' Max had shouted at her when he was aged seven. The woman had sniffed hard, pretending that she had not heard the remark. That was when she could hear, before the stroke had come along and gone *Boo!* to all things stable. Now she was a woman who had reached an age where ageing was a thing of the past.

Max knew it was inevitable that he would bump into someone either in the apartment building or somewhere close by soon enough. Most of the time he had been creeping around in the dark, just in case someone was watching the building. The phone had been going crazy. The record company had been phoning and phoning.

'Fuck 'em,' was what he had said each and every time he had heard Qwo-Li or Pshemko checking to see whether anyone was there. The tape was full of messages. 'Fuck 'em, fuck 'em, fuck 'em.'

The neighbour gave Max the once-over. Thought he looked better with that head of his shaved, less girly. About time, too.

'Jour-nal-ist,' she said in her distinctive style, 'askin' lotta question. Wo-man.'

Max nodded.

For a moment the old woman was absorbed in a half-smile dedicated elsewhere.

'Me say parents hol-i-day.'

Max nodded.

'Said you no here.'

Max smiled, touched by the old woman's efforts. It had taken a considerable number of years for her to be able to communicate verbally again after the paralysis of so much of her face.

'She *des-per-ate* to see you, Max,' the woman struggled to say. 'Hun-gry like a wolf.'

'They all are,' Max replied, taking in the fact that the old woman was now nearly bald, but for the wisp of long, thin, dirty hair which was pulled up into an oily bun that sat upon her head like a cinnamon roll.

'Hey, thanks,' Max said with a certain sadness, remembering the times when her hair was worn in all manner of shapes, flies caught in the trap of all that lacquer.

He gave her a wink which made the woman crank out her first laugh in a long while as she shuffled back to the confinement of her apartment with her little bit of shopping.

At around two, Max had managed to get himself motivated enough to go out. Hunger played a major part in that motivation. There was nothing to eat, not so much as a tin of peaches to be found. He had left the apartment with the intention of buying a big tub of ice cream, and some seed for the birdies. He fancied doing nothing but lazing in the park all afternoon and enjoying the sunny day. That was when he had bumped into his neighbour, Mrs B.

What he really wanted at that moment was a couple of lines

of that cocaine you see in films. Films about Colombians with private jets and bodyguards with steroid knockers and pony-tails.

The park was empty, except for crows. Crows were everywhere. As if signalling their comrades down the line of this intruder's approach, they let out short, sharp caws in Max's direction. They stood their ground, not even tempted to fly off as Max strode by. Close to, Max could see their sharp, weapon-like beaks and the vivid colouring of their claws.

Once past the unfriendly flock, Max had found a news-paper. Not something he wanted to read, something he wanted to lie on. The grass, Max thought, will still be wet after last night's thunderstorm.

It was just as well he had reached the spot. The short walk had tired him. He had to lie down quickly – everything was going dark inside him. The sky was suddenly pressing against his pores; maybe it was going to fall down on top of him. He had to close his eyes.

Laid out like that, on his back, he was like a boy on a screen. A projected, flat form. Not a person, but a character. A construction of shadow and light that cannot be touched. He looked fine, absolutely. Lucky. That big tub of ice cream beside him. That pack of bird seed.

The weight of the sky was hurting his head and at the same time that head of his was feeling so light. Was it filling with air, was it about to float up, up and away, or would it go BANG any second?

Something went glug in his left ear.

He felt he should sit up, get a taste of that ice cream before it turned into just a lot of melted goo. He could not move.

Lying on his back, Max watched the changing clouds. Northern clouds, massing up into crumbling snowmen, refracting the light. Always different. He felt upside down.

Felt that he should have been running across that sky, jumping into one of those clouds with his arms up, up, up above his head, knees bent, ready to execute a maximum-points landing.

Death passively awaited, Max thought, is a dishonour to life. That shabby, confused, agonised crisis was back again. Wham, just like that.

'When it finally comes,' a voice from behind Max said, 'it will probably be nastier than suicide, and certainly a great deal less convenient.'

Max jumped. More than startled, he was terrified.

There was almost a cigarette's-length column of ash on the Winston in between the old man's fingers.

'Didn't mean to scare you,' the old man said. 'I was just reading your mind.'

Max began to fuss with the carton of ice cream beside him, a strategy to avoid eye contact. A strategy to look 'normal'.

The look on the old man's face was momentarily awkward, then he was suddenly confident – it cracked his face alive. He could read the signs. That section of the park had long been his territory. He thought of it as his back garden. Home was a little tent in the bushes, a sturdy construction that was raised six inches off the ground and roofed with an enormous expanse of blue plastic sheeting.

The old man's eyes shone a minute twinkle. There was a strange healing power in those eyes. Half shy, half trusting.

'Nice day,' the old man said. 'This very minute is beautiful.'

Then he did what he always did when there was a troubled new recruit trying to sort his head out in the park. Some kid all fucked up and disoriented because of some trauma in the past, something looming in the future. The old man leaned towards Max and lightly punched his upper arm and smiled. It was a little bruiser of a punch, specific as a kiss.

'It's not worth it, whatever it is,' the old man said.

How can this old tramp know how I'm feeling? Max wondered. Am I that transparent?

'It's just . . . I feel as if I'm on the end of someone's fishing line and I'm just going to give up and get caught,' Max said.

The old man gave out a sniffy laugh.

'I'll be dead this time next year,' he said matter-of-factly, 'according to my doctor. Nothing withstands time, its capacity to macerate relationships. Any relationship, even the most true.'

Wrong guess, Max thought. I'm not all fucked in the head because I've fallen out with someone.

The old man briefly looked at his long fingers, fingers like tree roots. The cuticles showered with perfect, pale white quarter-moons.

'Whatever it is, it's not worth it, son,' he repeated. And with that, he did the inevitable. He kind of saluted and went on his way. He had his spring onions to water, some washing to collect off the branches of a giant tree.

Max felt hopeless. Stupid, guilty and hopeless. He ripped open the pack of bird seed and began throwing fistfuls of it at the sky. To his amazement birds began to gather, swoop down and feed. They had an instantly calming effect upon him.

He began to eat his ice cream. It tasted good.

There was a traffic jam all the way back to his parents' apartment. Dark rain. Max enjoyed that. Being in the cab with the noise on the roof. Warm.

'Next left,' he told the driver, whose geography of the city seemed limited.

As the cab pulled up, Max became aware of a number of

faces in the apartment building opposite his parents', all staring out. He froze for a second – he knew the signs. This kind of thing had happened before, and those faces weren't pressed against the cool glass of their windows checking to see whether there was a crack in the double glazing.

'Er, just a moment,' Max said to the driver.

There. Max had spotted the cameraman, with Oola Khan at his side. He slumped down in the back seat.

'Damn,' he said under his breath as he glimpsed the cameraman fussing with the legs of his tripod. Looks like they're doing a shot of the block while waiting for me, some nice establishing shots for their little feature.

The cab was close enough for Max to see that Oola seemed annoyed. As the cameraman changed from a portrait positioning of his camera to landscape format, Oola scanned the street.

They're waiting for me, Max thought. Maybe they've had a tip-off. Someone round here's got a big nose, I'm sure of it. I'm sure they get paid per sighting.

Max, his parents and the neighbourhood had grown used to the occasional flocking of fans or assembly of international journalists crouched at the entrance to his parents' apartment building behind a thicket of fluffy-headed microphones, waiting for the moment to pounce.

'Er, drive on,' Max said. 'Take me to the nearest McDonald's.'

An hour later there was no sign of Oola Khan or the cameraman. Max hopped out of the cab and ran into the building. The elevator was there, ready for him. His hands were shaking as key slid into lock.

He was in, had not seen anyone, felt okay.

He jumped when the phone rang, got the most tremendous burst of adrenalin. It was Qwo-Li from Furnace again. Max did not pick up.

'Right. Time to evacuate,' he said, making for the bathroom. He needed to piss and think.

A cockroach froze when Max flicked the light switch on. Maybe thought about something. Maybe made a decision. Maybe took in a deep breath. Maybe counted 1, 2, 3. Then off it sprayed towards a crack it called home behind the laundry basket. Max had not seen it; all he saw was his face staring back at him in the mirror, a face which seemed to be asking, Where next?

'Ten minutes,' he said to himself as he flushed the toilet.

He wanted to leave things right. His old room was as he had left it: perfectly empty. He stripped his parents' bed and put on fresh sheets. Those sheets were to go in the same direction as his father's clothes and the towels Max had used, into the laundry basket.

He loaded the dishwasher, did a bit of wiping down, put the trash by the door, then showered.

'Visa card?' he asked himself. There it was, right pocket. 'Cash?' Still plenty. Loads.

He looked at the note he had left by the kettle.

*Hope you had a good trip.*

*I'm fine – still alive.*

*Will call soon.*

*Max*

For a moment he tried to think very hard. He felt like a lost animal, trying to tune in for the route home. The idea of a hotel was oppressive. Clean white sheets, bleachy towels. The intrusion of room service.

He checked the address on the letter.

'Angela,' he said. 'Coming, ready or not.'

# Part Two

# 1

The sky was darkening, but it was still too early for the streetlamps to click on.

Sitting by the window, Minty knew it was almost time. It had been a weird day. The dog on the third floor had howled throughout the afternoon, then got a beating. The caged bird on the fifth, however, sounded cheerful enough. The little feathered birdie had a new toy. *Ding*, the bell went every few minutes. *Ding-ding*.

The cat shimmied towards the sofa, jumped up and settled herself down on the armrest. Signs of anxiety showed in rapid blinking and how the ears were, right that second, lowering to the sides. There, lip-licking: another sure sign of anxiety.

The sun was to the extreme far right of the window.

She'll soon be back.

The cat made an attempt to let out a little sound, one of the *oww*s which punctuated the day. No sound came.

'Here we are,' the cab-driver said, taking a glance in his rear-view mirror at the tall guy in the back.

'Thanks.'

Oh, this is ridiculous, Max thought. So silly. Should forget it.

He took a look around. There was a shop on the corner. What he saw were flowers, three red buckets of tall irises. It had been a long while since he had bought anyone flowers.

Ages. The last time had been typical of how he sent people flowers, via Interflora. Over the Internet. Once, when on tour in the Netherlands, he had stopped off to buy tulips – just to brighten his hotel room for the night. He wondered whether Angela would like irises.

Though his head was thinking, Don't, the fingers of his right hand were clutching a roll of notes.

Three bunches looked mean, six looked better.

He felt insane. Like some kind of stalker.

He had buzzed five times.

'No one home.'

He checked the address. Checked his watch.

Leaning against the frame of the door, Max felt hopeless. Lost. He was thinking knife to wrists. He was thinking bridge. He was thinking top of a building. He was thinking pills. He was thinking syringe full of smack. And it was beginning to rain.

I am such a fool. I am such a fucking fool.

The rain seemed intent on rat-a-tatting against his skull. The rain was doing a good job, getting what it wanted, and that rain was chilling Max. Those clouds were from the north. Those clouds were pissing on the last of summer.

'This time last week was . . .'

Max did not know what day it was.

'This time last week I was . . .'

Max could not recall which city, which venue, which TV network, which . . .

'This time next week I'm supposed to be . . .'

Lots had been scheduled for the following week. A block booking had been made by Furnace on a recording studio. A meeting with Seiko had been set up for a major advertising campaign which was being negotiated. RTL had been promised the opportunity to go looking at properties throughout the city with Max and a realtor for a forthcoming documentary about stars and their homes.

The rocking back and forth against the locked entry door was soothing at first. Then his forehead began to thump. Bang.

If you don't stop this you're gonna get a nasty bruise, an internal voice whined. But Max did not stop. Cradling that crudely wrapped bunch of irises, soaked to the skin, he turned the side of his face to the cold steel door. It cooled an eye which was boiling with tears.

He could not see the figure struggling along under a floral umbrella in his direction, bulging carrier bag at her side. What she could see was a hunched figure at the door, pressing the buzzer to *her* apartment.

Wearing delicate hoops of gold-plated silver and freshwater pearls through the lobes of her ears, she was dressed older than her years. Around her neck was a printed scarf based on decorative borders of first-century AD frescoes from Pompeii and Herculaneum. Classy, nice. Perhaps a little too conservative, though.

'Um, is it me you're buzzing for?' Angela asked as she navigated the first of the three steps up to the apartment building.

The figure did not move, something which made Angela begin to feel a little frightened. Oh no, she thought, taking in the shaved head. Oh no, some smackie trying to get into the building. Then she saw the heads of a massive bunch of irises.

'Hello?' she said, concern in her voice. Warmth.

Max swallowed. Over the last two years the letters had been numerous. Over the last two years the letters had been a line to another life. Unlike the other letters, they had always been the most welcome. Max was now gearing himself up for the disappointment. The fans were always fans. Just fans.

'Hey,' Angela asserted in a raised voice, 'can I help you? Is the buzzer system on the blink again?'

When Max turned he felt so tired. He needed that door for

support. His head felt so heavy and hot, then light and unsteady.

An enormously fat girl, that was what Max saw. The effects of at least three huge and ill-chosen meals a day were apparent. An enormously fat young woman, with an amazingly pretty face.

There was a moment in which it was appropriate, 'normal', for a person standing at the entrance to an apartment block to say something. Instead Max shivered. He felt the inhalation of a little breath followed by the inhalation of another little breath. He felt so inflated, but found he could not exhale. The flowers felt heavy.

Her eyes looked so kind.

'Angela,' Max said. Not as if it was a question, but the name of a destination.

'Oh,' Angela replied to this, not seeing Max but a person in need. 'You'd better come in.'

She was so excited that her ears popped.

It *is* him, isn't it? Angela asked herself, wondering what had happened to his beautiful hair. The fact that it was *him* was a detail. What she was dealing with was someone who looked pretty feverish, half starved and exhausted.

Out of her pocket came a distinctive keyring, a tiny penknife with a worn-smooth iridescent mother-of-pearl handle. Angela was surprised that she managed to put the key neatly into the lock. Straight in.

It was as if Max was rooted there, propped up against the wall.

Angela strode over to the elevator, pressed the call button and said, 'Can you manage?'

He obviously can't. God Almighty, what's going on here?

She placed her carrier bag inside the elevator, then strode up to Max.

'Here, rest against me.'

156

Angela placed Max's left arm on her shoulder, and put her right arm around his waist. As soon as she started walking, Max seemed to energise.

'Brought you some flowers,' he said.

She smiled, but ignored what seemed so irrelevant.

'Let's get you sorted, huh?'

He fell against the wall of the elevator, but remained upright, steadied by Angela.

*Weird*, Angela thought. What the . . .?

It was as if everything in her life had been nuked as the elevator rose up. The concept of Max entering her apartment any minute seemed impossible.

'Hope you're not allergic to cats,' was all Angela could think of to say.

Oh no, did I really say that? she scolded herself internally.

Max looked at Angela. His eyes seemed to focus for the first time. He let out a soft chuckle, a laugh at himself. Embarrassment.

'Well,' Angela said, about to open the door, 'beware of Tiger. She'll be hungry.'

Minty took one look at her mistress, then at the dripping figure beside her. The cat's eyes kind of went *Boiiing*. Instead of performing her usual acrobatics by the door, she retreated as far as possible from those towering humans. She felt safer by the window. Cautiously alert, the cat began to purr.

Max sat on a silver chair in the small white kitchen, gazing down at the cracked lino. Fake tiles, painted a cool green.

'Cats are weird,' Max said. 'They purr when they're happy, purr when they're frightened, even purr when they're dying.'

Then he sniffed. It was the kind of sniff that precedes the start of a bad cold.

'Right, I'll just get you some . . .'

Angela did not know where to start.

A towel. Mm. Would the offer of a hot bath be a bit forward? Definitely. Glass of wine to warm him up? I'll ask.

To the cat, this new addition to the household had the same smell as the veterinarian. Same kind of voice. Deep.

'Hey,' Max said to the cat, 'over here.'

Minty responded by rolling over on her back, stretching out her legs, yawning and exercising her claws.

'There,' Angela said to Max, taken aback that her cat was showing such friendliness to this stranger, 'towel.'

'Oh, thanks. But I'm fine.'

'No you're not, you're soaked through. Right, sorry, but I'm going to have to feed the cat or she'll get nasty.'

Max looked about as Angela rushed the usual home-time routine.

Next to an electric kettle that looked like a big toy stood a rice cooker, a fish steamer, a set of Le Creuset saucepans and a pine rack filled with assorted mustards: wholegrain mustard, tarragon mustard, thyme mustard, mustard that looked like bottled ant eggs, and the one that was obviously this young woman's favourite – green paste mustard with black bits in. That one was nearly all gone.

Max smiled Angela's way. She knew that look. He was going to be sick.

'Bathroom's that way.'

She read my mind, Max thought, as he skidded towards the bathroom.

'Oh, fabulous,' he groaned after he had spewed up, 'great first impression.'

He felt both surprised and thankful that Angela was allowing him the dignity of being alone at that moment. No fuss. He was just a guy spewing up.

He waited for a quiet double knock at the door, that usual 'You OK?' question. It did not come.

'I'll be out in a sec,' Max said. 'Emergency over.'

Must've been something I ate, he thought. He could feel himself regaining stability with each breath.

The bathroom was immaculate but for the damp. Red-and-blue plastic shower curtains, spotted with creeping dots of invading black. They went back in a whoosh. Grabbing the shower head, Max ran a stream of cold over the back of his neck and into his mouth.

From the plug hole rose the home-sweet-home smell of pine bleach. Where a germ settles, Max thought, it breeds.

He took a look at himself in the mirror. Breathed in, breathed out.

'Hey, sorry about that,' he said, all gentlemanly.

Angela smiled. She didn't have a clue what to say or do. The kettle was on, and she was halfway through unloading the shopping. The best thing to do, she thought, was to just carry on as normal.

'Er . . .' Max said, stretching out his hand. 'Hi.' He shrugged. 'I'm Max.'

Angela turned her head from side to side twice, then shook that hand.

'Angela.'

Max exhaled. Said, 'Whew!' Then laughed.

Her mother's nerves were in Angela's hands at that moment, wanting to rub down the sink, straighten the towels, tidy the shelves. Instead, she put her hands on her hips and said, 'How can I help you?' It was a simple enough kind of question. It seemed appropriate.

The last thing he wants to hear is 'I've got all your records, I'm your greatest fan' kind of thing.

'Well,' Max managed to begin. Then he pressed the palms of his hands against his eyes, which were beginning to fill with tears. 'I need . . .'

It wasn't Max the rock star Angela smiled at, it was a scarecrow of a human who seemed in a bit of a fix. It was a situation she felt she was having to deal with, a state. She had to fight the impulse to hug him.

Now here's something you hadn't planned on this evening, Angela thought as she watched Minty walk towards their visitor. With ears swivelled to the side, tail held high and bent over at the tip towards its back, she approached with a certain formality. Emitting a rough, loud, rasping purr, the cat stopped at Max's feet, then began head-butting his heels with long, sideways runs. Depositing its scent, the cat was marking this man, including him as part of her territory.

Max lowered his left hand and received an exploratory sniff in his direction. Max sniffed back. With eyes half closed, Minty gave Max an exploratory lick. That small pink tongue, covered with tiny backward-facing hooks, kind of tickled, kind of mini-hurt.

'Well,' Angela started, quite amazed at what she was seeing before her very eyes, 'I'm in the mood for a glass of wine. How about you?'

As she went to a kitchen drawer to hunt out a corkscrew, Minty headed off for a go at her scratch post. The cat's tail was upright, a sign of acceptance and goodwill.

'Made yourself a friend there,' Angela remarked.

She could not see Max standing, walking over towards the kitchen sink. He took a glass, filled it with cold water. Swallowed it down in just a couple of giant gulps.

'Something tells me you've got quite a story to tell,' Angela said quietly, in a voice close to a confidential whisper.

She was on the receiving end of one very tight grip. His knuckles, she could see, and feel, were turning white with the intensity of his grip. The tears that fell from Max's eyes to roll down the side of her neck felt too scary, too real.

Angela unhooked herself from Max's unexpected hug.

'Shit, Max, I don't know what's up, but I think you should go lie down for a while. Mm? Sofa or spare room, you choose,' she said, indicating the direction of the spare room. There had been just a hint of schoolteacher in her tone. It came out unintentionally but felt like what was needed.

'Take a nap. I'll make a bite to eat. If you want some you can have some. You know where the bathroom is. Tell me if you need anything. Um, phone's right here,' Angela said, indicating a standard portable model on its recharge stand by an old enamel bread bin marked 'BREAD'.

'Sure it's okay?'

'No problem,' Angela said matter-of-factly. 'Room-mate moved out just a short while back,' she fibbed.

It had been close to a year. None of the eight young women who had come to view the apartment in as many months had gone for it, based on what was in Angela's bedroom: all those posters. 'It's like an altar to Max,' one had said. 'Like some fucking shrine,' another had mocked at volume.

Max only felt weird for a moment as he stripped off. The logic running through his head rationalised that he had worked hard as an entertainer over recent years for fans such as Angela – a little reciprocation was not too much to ask for.

A single bed. Cotton sheets. Blank room. Safe.

Feeling like a criminal in her own home, Angela knew there was something she had to do. And quickly. The lock of her bedroom door seemed to turn with a gunshot click. It unnerved her. Made her jump, start to sweat.

'Got to take these down,' Angela whispered at the posters, which covered every inch of her bedroom walls. 'He'd think I was a right weirdo otherwise.'

The task was not as daunting as it had first appeared. The posters had been Blu-Tacked up, not taped or glued. After just ten minutes those posters were folded into a tight roll and stashed at the top of her wardrobe.

Angela had allowed just one area of pictures to remain. Above a small fireplace, post-Deco in design. There she kept a montage of visuals that held a certain magic for her. There was the A4 print and scatter of Jesus postcards, a few more postcards of the Virgin Mary; Kurt Cobain, Jim Morrison of The Doors, Jimi Hendrix, Bob Marley and an illustration of St Sebastian by Hasegawa.

'Right, that's that then.'

Taking a closer look at herself in the mirror, Angela tutted and made for a pair of tweezers on the second-to-bottom tier of the bathroom cabinet. She then plucked at two vomitous wisps of hair from the reddish-brown mole on her chin. A little lipstick made her feel better.

'Hey, Angela. Max is here. Taking a nap in the spare room.' She nodded, not believing a word her reflection was telling her. 'Yeah, right,' she said sarcastically.

It's obvious, Angela thought. He's going through a bad patch. Coming here, of all places, is a cry for help. But why here? Why *me*?

Then Angela smiled, feeling like the luckiest woman alive, which made a change. 'Better get some dinner on.'

# 2

Climbing over the edge of the mattress, down by Max's feet, a shiny-shelled monster cockroach with waving antennae tried to detect something edible in the room, which, in a roach's case, can be anything from television wires to coffee grounds to sweaty socks and banana skins. The creature was an erratic, darting runner, eager to fill its stomach asap. It was in a hurry – dawn was coming up.

Sunlight broke through the window, dappling Max's skin with warm splashes that moved.

Her kimono was softly printed with wild flowers, a garden of colour spreading the length of her body. One gigantic paint-by-numbers of an outfit.

'Max?'

'Yeah?'

'Breakfast.'

Angela left the tray down by the side of the bed.

Didn't eat any of his dinner, she noticed, picking up the other tray. Except the grapes. Then she noticed that the bottle of water was next to empty.

'What happened to the girl whose room this used to be?' Max asked.

'Got herself a boyfriend. Moved to New Zealand.'

Max nodded, wondering about that for a moment.

'How much was she paying a week? You know, rent.'

Angela was not there for a moment. The swift departure of the last room-mate still hurt.

'The rent? How much per week?' Max repeated.

'Why?' Angela began. 'Wanna take the room?'

She had only been joking, but looking a bit miserable as she had done so.

'If that'd be okay with you.'

Angela's forehead responded first. It crinkled. The body language: disbelief.

'You want to take the room?'

Then she laughed. It seemed like the funniest, most ridiculous idea. Just too impossible.

'Just for a few days. Like, say, a week.'

Angela shook her head in disbelief. Then she laughed herself across the room, making for the door.

'I'd better be off or I'll be late.'

She turned, looked at Max, who had propped himself up in bed as if posing for a photograph. Angela blinked. Her knees actually felt weak.

'I'll leave my work number by the kettle. Oh, and I'll sort out some keys for you.'

Angela left the room, going, 'Um . . .' to herself, trying to think of what else Max might need. This continued as she combed her hair over and over in the bathroom. Same direction, from crown down, stopping only when it felt right after numerous pats and presses and a curling behind both ears.

'The diet starts today,' she lied to the mirror. She knew 'diet' was not a big enough word for what she needed.

'Hey,' Max shouted out from his bed.

'Yeah, what?' Angela hollered back from the bathroom.

'Just, oh, you know . . .'

By the time Angela was standing in the frame of the door, looking towards him, Max had plucked up the courage to say the word.

'Thanks.'

◻

It's half past three, Max thought, and here I am tucked up in bed like a car crash victim. It feels wrong. Half past three and tucked up like a patient awaiting the next feed and wash.

He gave Minty a hug. The cat had been there beside him for hours. Purring, kneading, smelling so many regions of this human's body. Bliss.

'Come on,' Max said to the cat, 'time to get up.'

He spread the peanut butter thinly, taking no notice of the maker's instructions to lash it on. Neatly dissecting the bread into four squares, he began to eat. An observer might have suspected Max was curiously analysing as he savoured each bite, taking care not to miss a crumb. But there was no one there looking at him, only a cat named Minty.

Max patted the cat, ruffled the fur at its neck. The cat sniffed at Max's wrist. Waited for his next move.

'Hello,' Max said, fingering the cat's ears with a soft, very gentle kneading movement.

On TV two little boys were playing quietly and even tenderly with shiny, ultra-violent toys about to flood the market. Max had been flicking channels for close to five minutes. He had not found anything he had wanted to watch.

He began to read the titles of all the books, neatly shelved on three different levels by the window. There were so many about cats. *The Cat Owner's Question and Answer Book*, *House Cat: How to Keep Your Indoor Cat Sane and Sound* and a cartoon publication entitled *Games to Play with Your Pussy*, which evoked a dirty laugh. Besides these books were a stack of magazines bearing titles such as *Cats*, *Cat Fancy* and *Cat World*. Max looked elsewhere, and picked up a thick book about theatre design.

*Bunraku* is a thrilling combination of three elements: the narrator who voices all the roles, the *shamisen* player who accompanies the narration, and exquisitely robed puppets who enact the stories.

The unique art has a style and charm unlike that of any Western drama.

Max was surprised that he was not feeling totally shit. As he cuddled Minty close to him, he tried to work out why. His left eye squinted. Minty locked eyes with this strange young man, quizzically, and then began to purr.

Max lifted his right hand slowly, stroked the side of the cat's neck. The cat relaxed against his fingers, then asserted a little pressure against them. Max's fingers travelled up, gently rubbing the thin, crinkly ears. The cat's purring intensified. Max felt . . .

Max felt at *home*. That kind of feeling was rare. He had never felt that feeling in his parents' apartment. 'At home' had always been in music, or alone in a wood, up a tree as a boy. 'At home' was rare moments onstage when everything seemed so easy. When he could say 'Hi' to ten/fifteen/twenty thousand faces, to which he just got back this wall of sound as a reply – a sound that was international, a sound that could not be translated. A kind of 'Hi' which was kind of *rahhh*, or *ruarghh*. The cat was making that kind of sound now with its purring.

Max looked around. He wanted to stay. Needed to stay there, just for a day or two. That would be nice, he thought, just have some time out. Just do nothing for a change.

He looked at the telephone number Angela had left by the kettle. Thought about it. Decided. He would.

The cat leaped off Max's lap when he began to punch in Angela's work number. Minty lapped at the rare treat of a little milk, then began cracking away at some dried food.

As the telephone started to ring, Max became anxious. He did not know Angela's second name.

Before the voice blasted into his ear, Max could hear the rumble of corporate power in the background.

'Editorial,' that voice blurted, someone obviously in the middle of something. Slightly annoyed, busy-busy. A voice belonging to a body that had deadlines to meet. A voice that had no time for freelancers who were having difficulty e-mailing their copy, or for model agencies that wanted to send their girls out on 'go sees'. That voice was Angela's, and Max felt relieved that she had given him a direct line, rather than leaving him to navigate through a receptionist.

'Hi,' Max said. 'How's it going?'

The pupils of Angela's eyes sprang open, the roundness of her shoulders vanished. Facing her was one of a dozen pictures of Max. An entire glossy picture set full of sighs, smirks, rage and regrets, the tears and games of love and all his romantic melancholy, nonchalant cheek, his weaknesses and his ten million and ten emotions.

'Oh, hi,' Angela said, trying to sound cool. 'Everything okay?'

That was good, she thought, not too thrown by the call. Normal.

The effect of Max's voice on Angela, however, was so instant, so marked, that the other two members of the editorial staff present in that confined space known – almost ridiculously – as a 'department' turned to look at each other. She seemed transformed. They had noticed a difference since she had bounced in ten minutes late that morning with a secretive smile all over her face.

'Minty says hi, by the way.'

Angela breathed in sharply through her nose. It was an old trick she had learned long ago, something that was supposed to keep jagged breath and tears at bay. It was not working. She managed a little laugh, relieved that Max was taking the lead.

'Just wondered if you wanted any shopping doing. I'm feeling much, much better by the way.' He paused a second. 'Hey, thanks again.'

Angela did not know what to say. Max was not, however, leaving her a gap in which to say anything at that moment. He was aware that he was calling her at work and just got on with what he wanted to know. 'Shall I get some bits 'n' pieces in? Hm?'

'Oh,' Angela said, trying to sound casual. 'Okay, then.'

'Fish, chicken, ham . . . anything you don't eat?'

Angela managed to stop herself; a self-put-down would have been so easy.

'Oh, whatever,' she said. 'I'll leave it to you.'

'It's been a long while since I've made dinner. It'll probably be a bit Boy Scout.'

'See you six thirty, sevenish,' Angela replied, minimally.

'Okay,' Max chirped. 'See ya.'

Angela replaced the receiver with a movement that had plenty of glide to it. Two faces were pointed her way. One from the left, one from the right. Both were waiting, eyebrows raised. Heads tilted just so, ready for the tale she so obviously had to tell.

'Oh,' Angela said lightly, 'that was Max. He's round my place right now. Wanted to know what I fancy for dinner.'

How they laughed. Later, over a lunch-time drink, Angela's two colleagues reckoned it was not a man who had phoned but a relative or some old schoolfriend. Personal calls for Angela were extremely few and far between. A *man*? Calling for Angela? As if. Fat chance.

'I need a toothbrush. An' should get Angela somethin'. More flowers?'

Max put the set of spare keys in his pocket.

'Bye, puss,' he said to the cat before he gently pulled the door to.

Shopping, Max thought to himself. Weird.

Standing in front of a greengrocer's display, Max was confronted with over-choice. All the fare was laid out with a still-life artist's eye for colour and composition. The apples: red, yellow, green. Oranges from Spain, pears from England. Caulies beside cabbages and outsized broccoli, prominent. Eye catching. Spread out to show contrasts, contours, ascending order of sizes. Choicest to the fore. The grocer was wetting the floor; she was going to do one of her little sweeps with a nylon-headed broom of shocking pink.

Max had never done this kind of shopping before – there had always been gofers. He was surprised at how much a bag of apples weighed, the cost of asparagus and honeydew melons. He bought too much of everything and was laden before he had even reached the culture shock of the super-market.

Detergent, Max thought. Some of that, too. But here were so many to chose from. Where to start? He just wanted the one that washed whites the whitest.

That was all he could remember, an array of non-biological white powders. Then black.

'You fainted,' someone said as he came round.

The store manager was concerned. Women fainting, that was one thing. Men? Rare. It was something she found alarming when it happened.

ARE, followed by a YOU, very quickly followed by an OKAY. Question mark like a ting of glass –?

Work had become uninspiring and undemanding, but not financially unrewarding. Angela had moved from freelance work as a features writer for teenage publications to work on a food magazine out of convenience. Fashion and music were always changing, always moving. Fashions were adopted, then discarded. Knowledge gained, then outdated. Ideas created, only to be burned up faster and faster. Now she was twenty-four, the curvaceous rises and falls of the record sales charts no longer gripped Angela, with the exception of those relating to that rock star named Max. Food was food. Simple, easy. The samples were always welcome. The restaurant review opportunities rarely turned down.

The move from writing to working as a copy editor, a sub, was also more a matter of convenience. Angela did not want to compete in a specialised field of journalism in which her focus was the world of mass hypnotism with ever giddier pulsing cycles of nostalgia and buzz words.

The move to subbing had come as whole sides of Angela were shutting down. Taking life five times slower than the national average suited her. She got in, sat at her desk, had her breaks, left on the dot. Unless there was a film or restaurant review opportunity, she was always back home with Minty by 6.30. That evening, however, she would be home a little later than usual. As long as a month ago, it had been agreed that Angela would take part in a make-over shoot – one of six 'big' women who would get the magical before and after treatment.

The make-up artist knew what he was doing. Angela was relieved about that. She was hoping to transport some of the magical transformation from photographic studio to home.

Soft and light and warm and round and round went little dabs of cleanser, astringent and moisturiser. Gently around the eyes. Over and over. Circling. The lightest touches. Working on all those muscles around the eyebrows. Reshaping. Pulling up into the scalp. Patting, revealing a new definition to the features. Over and over. Pushing away surface fluid. Increasing pressure then reducing it suddenly to bring out that certain something from within. Making her feel good with all the patting. Angela knew one thing: I'm fat as a pig but I've got a pretty face. *That*, at least.

Angela's hair was arranged into short, sharp waves over her forehead. It looked as if a child had been busy squiggling with a pen.

The Polaroids looked good. Angela was told that she would probably make it to being main picture. It was the kind of boost she needed at that moment. She had been shaking like a leaf all day.

Chances are he'll have bolted, she had thought every half-hour since arriving at work. He'll have legged it. He can't . . . he just *can't* still be there. At my place? Oh, girl, get a grip. No way. Despite his call, no hope.

She had talked herself down, again and again. Max would not be there. There would be a note on the table, something would have cropped up. She would, she felt, have to accept that. What there had been had been nice. Lovely. But that was all there ever would be. Those few hours.

I should never have come into work today, Angela thought.

But she had. Had felt it had been the right thing to do. Natural. If the guy needed some kind of safe space for a while, her place was as good as any.

'The Virgin Mary,' Angela sing-songed. 'Some girls . . .' she continued, suppressing a giggle, '. . . get themselves the worst sort of reputations.'

Max did not get it. Again he looked at the postcard of the Virgin Mary. Then a smile cracked his face.

He was intrigued by the montage on Angela's bedroom wall. He was relieved that there were no pictures of him.

'What do your parents do for a living?' he asked, as the official tour of Angela's tiny apartment ended.

'My mother's dead. Happened ages ago. As for my father . . .'

Angela looked up at the ceiling, then down at her hands.

'He was an animal-feed distributor. He didn't want to be a dad, so he wasn't. Didn't hang around.'

Between her hands was that favourite souvenir from a long-ago week in LA: a coffee cup that changed colour according to the temperature of its contents.

'I'd like to get to know you better,' Max said to Angela.

She liked the blatancy, but it came as a bit of a surprise. She chose to kind of ignore the remark, not make a big deal of it.

Angela has an aura of seriousness which I like, Max thought. A sharp wit, funny without being over-jolly. But . . .

Underneath the bubbly exterior, Max could already sense the profundity of Angela's core. Beyond the cellulite there was a certain oppressive heaviness which she dragged around with her.

# 3

The him of long ago, enjoying a childhood of stuffed cabbage and *pierogi*. That was what Oola Khan's editor wanted her to dig up. Reminiscences of any sort. Max, the child, the boy. Those early years. What made him what he was.

Oola was getting nowhere. Max's parents were away on vacation, there were no old schoolfriends to chase up, not so much as a single sexual conquest to sniff out and bribe. Even his high-school secretary and premises manager declined an interview.

Her researcher had knocked on the door of every apartment in the block. No one was prepared to say a word. Not even the concierge. Oola Khan was at a loss. Her instinct was to go against the rather tired formula her editor had in mind, and focus on what interested her. A girl teen's world of wonder, Oola thought.

Over recent years, she had attended many a gig by some squeaky-fresh new boy band. Invariably the arrival of these pretty boy pop stars would be heralded by tiny, cheering voices pitched at much the same level as a junior school playground.

Oola began to type.

Every once in a while a band comes along and creates the full force of pop mania, making the teen nation sweat. Their focus is an audience of young girls who are at their most vulnerable and hormonal. Chosen more for their looks than anything else, boy bands are machine designed to get the money out of the hands of

173

parents into the hands of young girls, then out of the girls' hands and into the hands of the record companies. The music usually comes last.

Oola was not sure where she was going. Is this relevant? she asked herself.

These pop puppets pump and grind 24 hours a day, backflipping through dance routines into a million-plus hearts, practically brainwashing girls into being their daydream believers.

She began to list some classic managers. She had recently seen a television documentary about managers from the UK who had flooded the youth market over the decades.

Brian Epstein – The Beatles
Tam Paton – Bay City Rollers
Simon Napier-Bell – Wham!
Peter Rosengard – Curiosity Killed The Cat
Tom Watkins – Bros and East 17
Nigel Martin-Smith – Take That
Louis Walsh – Boyzone.

Oola shook her head, unsure. It all felt wrong. She knew that, ultimately, the music industry catered to a demand, a need. After reading through what she had written, she highlighted the lot, then pressed the delete button.

'I'll start again tomorrow.'

Angela was licking salt off her fingers when she spotted her department manager gazing her way. At least, she thought, at least I was looking at the screen. Looking at this shit copy I've got to do something with.

The department manager moved away.

Angela fancied another packet of the NEW! luxury nut assortment a major food chain was about to push on to the market. One packet was never quite enough, unless it was a family-sized packet. *Two* hit the spot just right.

Concentration was lacking. Dreamily and interminably, she bounced her knees together. Grinding round the interior of her skull was a loathsome tune heard on the radio that morning. A noise texture of fuzz guitars, whiny vocals and feedback. Flat, rhythmic, repetitious.

More than anything else, Angela felt stupid. Behind her placid, pretty face was an aching head with hysterics on cue but never released, a matter-of-fact feeling that she was about to implode, bursting blood, splashing everywhere.

The deputy editor came by. Jocasta. Someone who was never too far from a cup of strong black coffee.

'Hey,' Jocasta gushed, way too energised. 'New Thai restaurant opening up in town tonight. Here's the press release. You up for doing a review, Angie?'

Angela stiffened a little, all the way down her spine. That was the effect Jocasta had on her. Little Miss Perfect, Angela thought. Bet she even gets her nostrils waxed.

'Is it okay if I take a friend?' Angela asked.

Whoa. That was a new one. The look on Jocasta's face was puzzlement, slight dismay.

'Haven't found yourself a man at last, have you?' Jocasta teased.

'Might've,' came Angela's reply. 'And I'd like a nice quiet little table. For two. Sort it out, could ya?'

When Angela became assertive, she bordered on hostile.

Phone him, Angela thought. Tell him. You're going to take him out to dinner. Tonight.

As the bus lurched to avoid a large pothole, the passengers swayed as a body, they were packed in so tightly. Angela giggled but felt embarrassed about that. Getting the bus into town had been her idea. Travelling this way, Angela felt, lessened any pressure Max might have felt about dining out. Fatty and skinny, she thought. We must look a right pair.

'Now,' Angela said after they had been walking around in circles for a full ten minutes, 'this wouldn't have happened if we'd come by cab.' She was furious. Could not find the place.

'There,' Max said. 'Number nineteen, not ninety.'

'Right.' Angela sighed, sounding defeated and a little foolish at having read the details of the press release incorrectly. She was that nervous.

Max smiled. He was not annoyed. He had kind of enjoyed the walk, savouring the freedom that his new appearance gave him. He had not been recognised once. Not once.

He would not have been admitted, not dressed the way he was, so casually, had it not been for the fact that Angela was practically waving the press release right under the maître d's nose, as she insisted on a quiet table – *away* from the door.

'So,' Max began, once they had ordered, 'how was your day?'

Angela laughed at Max's tone. He had asked the question in that cloying 'So, how was your day, honey?' made-for-TV-film kind of manner.

'Oh, everything went wrong. The layouts for the next issue came in late from the art department, despite days of nagging. I had to do a load of headlines and stand firsts in, like, an hour.'

'What's a stand first?' Max asked.

'An intro. That bit which comes after the headline, you know.'

'Right,' Max said.

'Then there was all the picture captioning to do, but everything went to pit on the matter of George Clooney's age. I'd checked it and double-checked it but the editor said that the features writer wouldn't have made such a dumb mistake. Only wrote Clooney was thirty-nine which he ain't by a long shot.'

'Right.'

'Then I had to cut a load of copy on a travel feature because the picture they'd gone for took up so much space. There was something to run by the legal department about Michael Jackson. Boy, and that was just the morning.'

'Right.'

'After lunch the editor comes back from some do a bit worse for wear and throws out some fashion model's cooking tips feature at the last minute.'

'Uh-huh.'

'And when the color cromalin came in for the cover and opening pages I spotted that the photographer's credit had been missed out so I was in the shit.'

'Oh.'

'It's okay, as jobs go, but I'm always the last cog in the process, which can really piss me off. The lateness of copy is the worst. Some of these people who call themselves writers. Got a friggin' nerve if you ask me. Some of them don't even have a spellcheck on their rusty ol' computers. Can you *imagine?*'

Max began a soft, low chuckle.

'I think that waiter'd better hurry up with that bottle of wine.'

Angela's eyes shone bright. Max thought they looked pretty. The whites so clear, the pupils so enormous. And her teeth, the whiteness of a healthy kid's.

'There are perks every once in a while. Like, er, well, like this. And free books, the occasional cinema and concert ticket. Occasionally,' and Angela suddenly hooted, 'occasionally the typesetter will take the team out to lunch.'

Max raised an eyebrow. Angela was keeping something back.

'Oh, and PRs, of course, send stuff in all the time. Give-aways. CDs, hair and skin products – y'know. The features editor doesn't hog it all to herself, which is quite nice. The last one certainly did.'

'So,' Max said, teasingly, 'tell me more about the typesetter.'

Angela burst out laughing. 'No!' she practically screamed at the top of her voice. And then, 'Oh, okay, then. Well . . .' and she had to wipe her eyes because they were beginning to stream. 'He's obviously a bit of a fan of the woman with, how can I put this, the *fuller figure*?'

The waiter arrived with the wine.

'I think we might be needing a second bottle in a while,' Max said.

Angela gave him a wink, saying, 'Oh, that's what the typesetter always says.'

'And does it work?'

'Oh, every time.'

Max raised his glass.

'Cheers,' they said, together.

Mopping up the oil with a chunk of bread, Angela realised that Max was staring.

'Fat pig, aren't I?' she said, then downed the chunk of bread. 'Yum.'

She blushed as she chewed. Max just shrugged. He did not know what to say. The meal had been a veritable food orgy, but while Max had picked, Angela had gone through plate after plate with relish.

Food as a refuge? Max was thinking. It was just a starter thought, something which flared up, shone bright for a second, then fizzled.

'I fancy a brandy,' Max said.

'Hey, that's the spirit, ma boy,' Angela boomed in a dreadful attempt at a Texas drawl.

'Is there any other kind of work that you'd be interested in?' Max asked, serious for a moment. Angela was taken aback. She felt like a schoolgirl again. Max's tone was bordering on that of the charming man designated as careers adviser at the school she had attended.

'Well . . . I guess it's like this. I started reading *Look Here* at fifteen, and when I wrote to the editor asking for a spot of 'work experience', I was amazed that I got a reply giving me the green light. That led to me freelancing for a year, then I joined the magazine at sixteen as an assistant in Editorial. After a few months of that I was doing the pop page, book reviews an' stuff.'

Max nodded. On she went.

'The school I went to was a dump. All the people I work with at *Look Here* have this attitude that anything's possible in life. Where I come from it was always more a case of everything's impossible.'

'Fuck 'em,' Max said.

'Fuck who?' Angela asked.

'The whole fucking lot of them. The whole goddamned show.'

Then it registered. Max was pissed. Two bottles of wine, one very pissed man.

'Think we'd better get you in a cab.'

# 4

'Oh, sometimes – and this is one of them – I wake up and feel like a dog run over,' Angela groaned out loud. She heard Max laugh back at her through the thin wall that separated them.

'*Good morning!*' he shouted back too loudly, like some kind of speech therapist determined to conquer the gloom of a Monday morning staffroom. 'Hey, Ange, if you're feeling so shit jus' take the day off.'

'Mm?'

'Phone in. Say you're sick.'

She thought about it for a minute. Further persuasion was not what she needed.

'Y'know, I think that's what I'll do.'

Hearing the now familiar crack of a bone in Angela's left foot as she got her morning rituals started, Max rolled over. Just another five minutes of doing nothing, he thought. Bliss.

Minty was there beside Max. Disturbed from slumber, the cat began kneading with her toes. Once or twice she extended her nails while doing this, digging into Max's skin below the sheet. Max did his best not to yelp, knowing that such feline activity was a compliment.

When Max finally managed to get himself moving, Angela was cheerfully removing grit and ash that had blown in under a gap where the front door and lino parted. With a heavy plastic litter scoop she had already cleaned out Minty's little tray, something only just large enough for the cat to comfortably turn around in to bury its waste.

'Ooh, I hate dirt,' she sneered to the dustpan as she emptied

180

the contents of light and grey down on to the cat's stinking litter. That combination of wood chips, rolled newspaper and corn husks was nastily sweet.

'Pussy poo-poo,' she said with a shake of her head. 'Pussy *pong*. Yuk!'

Angela knotted the plastic bag and left it by the front door. Then she washed her hands.

'Now,' she prompted herself, 'sandwiches.' She thought for a minute. 'Any preference?' she asked Max.

Max shrugged.

'Oh, anything's fine by me.'

In an impulsive imitation of suicide, Angela took a small knife left out for the imminent chopping of cucumber and ham. With first a flourish, then a grimace, she drew the blade just an inch above her neck.

Max laughed, before heading off towards the shower.

No laughing matter, thought Angela. That small vegetable knife was just one of many knives she kept in a glass rack in a cupboard she had to stretch up to, a special place away from all the other cooking utensils. It was a somewhat fine collection of hand-honed zirconium ceramic kitchen knives. There was the fish/meat knife (length 156mm), the fruit/vegetable knife (length 130mm), the cook's knife (length 140mm), the general-purpose knife (length 110mm), the multi-purpose knife (length 105mm). Added to this collection was the shark knife set, packed in an aluminium briefcase. Cool stainless-steel handles with molybdenum vanadium steel blades. Very strong and very durable. These were kept in a cupboard which housed just this one collection, a cupboard that she had to bend to open. A cupboard beside another cupboard which was only opened occasionally, for special occasions of her very own. A cupboard which housed a 100mm filleting knife, a 120mm peeling knife, a 180mm flexible utility knife and a 200mm boning knife, all of which she kept in a durable Kevlar zipped wallet, plus a 220mm meat chopper and a five-piece carving set. These she had bought complete with a heavy-duty magnetic rack, but unlike the 260mm diamond sharpening steel, it was never used. Safer tucked away, out of sight.

'No picnic's complete without some chocolate,' Angela said. 'You wait here, I'll jus' be a sec.'

KitKats, Angela was thinking as she hurried along the train platform. A couple of KitKats and maybe some . . .

The moment came suddenly. The headlines were all the same, but different. Same message, different words. And the photos of Max, all recent. All looking wiry and strained, typical rock 'n' roll burn-out.

## MISSING CULT ROCK STAR SOUGHT

## FEARS FOR MISSING ROCK STAR

## RECORD COMPANY PLEA TO MISSING ROCK STAR

## MAX – SUICIDE FEAR

With all the speed of a sub, Angela scanned for the key words: eye-witness, bridge, disoriented.

## IS MAX – THE WILD REBEL OF ROCK – ALIVE OR DEAD?

The last of these headlines ended with the melodramatic, italicised cliffhanger, 'Friends fear his demons told him to leap off that bridge, and the dark waters closed over him.'

'The usual ill-informed rock clichés,' Angela muttered through gritted teeth.

Most of the papers were following the bridge-jump theory, based on the account of a fan who had asked – and got – an autograph, accompanied by the shocking phrase in capitals, 'DIE HAPPY', something which a graphologist had both verified as Max's handwriting and as being 'of a disoriented nature'.

The bridge was hyped up in many of the tabloid reports as a 'notorious suicide spot'. No body had been found, but Max had already been placed in the lineage of such famous excess-all-areas fuck-ups as Hendrix, Morrison and Cobain.

Even supposedly decent, moral papers were not above squeezing some juicy sensationalism from this rumoured tragedy, running a Max-related story on the cover of their entertainment guide supplement, dramatically asking, 'CAN ROCK LYRICS KILL?'

'Here we go,' Angela sing-songed chirpily when she got back to Max. 'Lots of lovely chocolate.'

As the train pulled in, she was anxious to spot an empty carriage.

'There's one,' she said, pointing. 'It'll be nice and quiet.'

We'll have to run, Max thought. Wonder if she's up to it.

Angela was keen to enter the carriage first, just in case there were any discarded newspapers left on seats. Much to her relief there was not a single paper in the carriage. The train was devoid of all the usual rubbish, being fresh on to the tracks.

Angela could already feel time ticking away. Max would have to return to his other life pretty soon. All she wanted was one full day. Just that day. She knew he would have to go soon enough. She knew he was going to have to leave her.

In three or four days, she thought. Just three or four days, at the most.

'It's a bit of a trek,' Angela said as they left the train station after what had been a smooth forty-minute journey. And it was. A trek through still-dewy meadows, the last of a chilly fen mist.

'Used to come here years ago every Sunday, with my mother.'

'Uh-huh?'

On they went, past occasional PRIVATE FISHING notices. Just as Max was beginning to think this long walk to what Angela described as a 'special, special spot' a bit of a pain, he caught a glimpse of scampering moorhens, cattle down to drink at a peaty bay. Sparkling and transparent water, so many lilies.

'Almost there,' Angela reassured him. 'Not long now.'

The sound of buzzing bees visiting buttercups and fox-gloves.

They had been walking for close to an hour.

'Here we are.'

The spot was film-set perfect. A sunny knoll beside a circular lake.

'Oh,' Angela said, sounding a little disappointed as she looked at the lake, 'it's covered with duckweed.'

Indeed it was, but that did not stop Max stripping down to his boxers and wading in. Sinking through the opaque green cloak of that duckweed lawn, he began breaststroking like a fly trapped in soup. It was just a dip. He emerged a minute later resembling the Incredible Hulk.

'Oh!' Angela laughed out loud. 'I've gotta get a picture of this.'

Max did not feel exploited – Angela was not acting like a fan. It was a natural impulse, and he enjoyed the three shots she took of him. It was one of those funny/bizarre moments for which a camera was called.

Soon the sunlight dried the duckweed upon his skin and off it fell. Like confetti.

'Okay?' Angela asked.

'Feel crisper than cornflakes,' came Max's smiling reply. 'Y'know,' he started, 'I would've liked to've been a carpenter, to have worked with my hands. A carpenter, or gardener. Growing things. Making it green where it's grey.'

He inhaled, held that breath, exhaled slowly. Right that second, Max would have preferred to have been by the sea. A sea choppy and flecked. Swallowing a taste of ocean spray.

'Just nipping off to spend a penny,' Angela said, a little shyly.

Max hardly registered any kind of response to this. Off Angela went, choosing a spot beyond a clump of bushes where the imminent *schweeesh* of her pissing would not be heard.

'The tide is in,' Max imagined out loud to a space some-where between the branches above his head and a wasp intent on settling on his face, 'and I can feel my feet sinking in the wetter sand at the edge of the tide. And now, now I'm lying on the softer, dry sand. Warm from the sun. And now a big wave is rolling towards me. Here it comes.'

That's what we'll have to do next time, Max thought, go to the seaside.

'Damn, fucking wasps everywhere,' Angela said, returning slightly out of breath. 'Oh, shit. And here's another one.'

She made crazed swimming movements in the air with her hands.

'Leave it alone and it'll be off soon enough.'

Angela looked at Max as though she were a girl who had

been told off by an uncle or a new teacher. She hated wasps. And bees. Anything with a sting.

Ten minutes of silence came to an abrupt end when she had grown bored with gazing at the view.

'Tell me about the syndrome you have,' she started up out of nowhere. 'I mean, I've read a bit about you having it, but . . .'

'Kleinfelter's,' Max said with a sigh. 'Kleinfelter's syndrome.'

He did not look too keen to talk for a moment.

'Well, it's a chromosome disorder. Instead of having the normal complement of forty-six chromosomes – 46XY – I was born with an extra X chromosome, so my make-up is 47XXY.'

'Right,' Angela said. She knew that much. She felt she had activated some kind of weary monologue in Max that had long taken a certain path and he was already some way along it. 'Symptoms begin in puberty, right?'

'Correct. Whilst all the other boys at school were beginning to . . . er . . . well . . . Basically my testicles were unable to respond to the chemical changes occurring in the hypothalamus and pituitary gland.'

'And that's why you grew so tall, huh?'

'Yeah. Without testosterone to signal an end to the adolescent growth spurt, I was suddenly this basketball-player height at fifteen. But, well, the muscles remain unstimulated and undeveloped – so basketball was out.'

'Am I right in thinking that there are varying levels of your condition?'

Max looked uncomfortable.

'Oh,' Angela suddenly rushed to continue, 'hey, sorry. Demanding too much information. That's me. Comes with the job.' She laughed nervously.

Max's discomfort evaporated. With the exception of a brief radio slot in New York a few months back, he had never discussed the matter except with the doctors, his parents and his head of year at school. It was a big deal that he had never treated as one.

'Guys with the milder form have low sexual desire but enjoy brief intervals of potency. Many are infertile, often impotent. *C'est la vie.*'

Angela did not take it any farther. Max, she felt, did not look uncomfortable. It was as if something had been dealt with.

'Guess what,' she said as she began to remove her sandals. 'Blisters. Ow-ow *ouch*!'

Five minutes later Angela was cooling those sore feet down as she assembled massive fern leaves beside sea holly, strawberry clover, glasswort, prickly saltwort, woolly burdock, welted thistle and – for colour – some alpine forget-me-nots.

'Aren't you hot with that top on?' Max asked, glancing at Angela's armoury of clothes. It was the sleeves he was looking at. She could at least roll up her sleeves. She's gotta be sweltering.

'No day for wearing silk-feel viscose, I'll give you that,' Angela said as she struggled to stand. 'I'm just going to go for a little walk,' she added. 'Back in five.'

Max nodded, but felt something was up. He watched Angela stride off, into a darker part of the wood. The walk seemed intentional, very direct.

He wondered whether he had said something to upset Angela. He felt he had.

'Oh, hormones.' He exhaled as he lay back to get some more sun on his face. 'Women.'

And then he was sleeping.

Her feet did not feel grounded. The words she had been

speaking had felt like lines. All interaction with Max felt distant. She knew what she had to do.

The tears running down Angela's face were hot, they felt acidic. The familiar surge of mounting anxiety, racing thoughts and rapidly fluctuating emotions had hit her like a tidal wave. She knew what she needed, that familiar sting on her arms. It had been thirteen days since she had last gone at herself.

First she found a blackberry bush which had some pretty nasty thorns on it. Then she found a rusty nail and a broken bottle. She opted for the thorns. Safest, not too much spillage.

Pulling up her left sleeve, that old desire was there: to symbolically, and permanently, vandalise the body her mother had brought into the world. Cutting had long been a life-saving, pain-sparing survival strategy that few knew about.

'Fat pig,' Angela said as she suddenly, impulsively, ran the sharpest edge of a thorn over her skin. 'Wish you'd never been born,' she whispered, repeating a line her mother had all too often thrown her way as she scratched up those babies.

She had long been the caretaker of her wounds, soothing those self-inflicted injuries, watching them heal, only to scratch up those scabs again and again. Her arm was like a giant, very complex bar code. Years of self-injury getting some air, some fresh red. Those criss-cross cuts, all those burns which had so long provided a perverse sense of self-esteem, an identity and a structure for a life so bereft of meaningful human connections. Those scars were her stories, history written on her skin.

'No no no,' Angela said under her breath as she felt the yes yes yes of pain.

Above her, a treetop swinging. Voices in the wind singing.

You're ugly. You're fat. Four words that she had dotted along her left arm, aged fifteen, with the point of a compass. In a maths lesson. No one had seen. No one had ever taken too much notice of the fat girl who sat at the back. The constant chewer.

When she saw the blood well up the relief set in. She had opened her safety valve, was letting off steam. With a wound Angela knew where the pain was coming from. It came from a specific place. The other pain she felt did not come from a place she could pinpoint. That place moved about, crept into strange regions. It haunted her. Always.

Her left arm, scratched like a patchwork quilt, was bleeding now. With Max only a short distance away it felt wrong. After a few deep breaths the feeling changed, she was at a remove. The fleshy part of her which was now beginning to run red in the usual way was just exterior, shell.

I'm weak, she thought. All my life I've felt weak compared to others. If they want to crush me they can. But I can do things that other people can't. This.

She wanted to go on and on. She wanted to go deep. All she was doing was scratching, getting a ration of what she needed: a top-up. There wasn't much blood. Not this time. Had she been alone, at home, there would have been the comfort of her shark knife set, so coolly unpacked from that smooth aluminium briefcase. Had she been at home it would have been the 100mm filleting knife, a 200mm boning knife she would have laid out beside her, perhaps the Stanley knife.

The glinting glass of the broken bottle had been tempting. The nail, too.

Barbed wire, Angela thought for the first time, that would be good. Reels and reels of it around my waist.

'Three or four days,' Angela half whispered into the air around her. 'Then, *la fin de la visite*.'

# 5

When Max first awakened he was, he realised, not alone. Angela was bending over him. She was breathing in through her nose, out through her mouth. A distinctive sound.

'Max?' She whispered the single syllable teasingly. 'You awake?'

The night had been moist, heavy with heat and a throbbing whirr of insects only briefly shut up by a heavy shower just before dawn.

Max rolled over and said, 'No, I'm fast asleep,' then rolled back to the position he had been in.

'Rock Star Needs Beauty Sleep,' Angela said, in the tone of a tabloid headline, to which Max responded with a firm, 'Mm, he does.'

He slept through the sounds of coffee being slurped, toast being crunched, the toilet being flushed nine times. Over the last few days Max had come to think that Angela was some kind of cistern addict – every time she went into the bathroom she felt the need to flush.

What eventually woke Max was silence. Angela had gone off to work. There was a glass of freshly squeezed orange juice beside the bed.

He had been dreaming. It was one of those dreams he often had which brought the start of a song, sometimes entire lines of lyrics.

Stumbling out into the kitchen, Max searched around for a pen and paper. Already the dream was fading. Faded.

He rushed back into bed and shut his eyes.

'The little boy walked into the park, eating an apple. Wearing blue jeans, bright orange and green Reeboks and a white T-shirt, he was feeling sad. He had lost his doggy. He had lost his ball. Only had one parent. Didn't feel loved at all. Wanted a cuddle. Walked towards the bushes. Needed to cry for five minutes.'

From this he wrote down a few key words:

> Boy in the park, eating an apple.
> Wearing blue, orange, green, white – he was feeling sad.
> Lost his doggy? Lost his ball?
> Didn't feel loved at all.
> Wanted a cuddle. Needed to cry.
> Wanted a cuddle. Needed to cry.

Max looked at what he had written. Thought about it. Said, 'Crap.' Scratched out a few words. Then a few more. Most significantly, the boy became a girl.

> Girl in the park, girl in the dark.
> Wanting a cuddle. Needing to cry.
> Wanting a cuddle. Wanting to die.

'Angela,' Max whispered.

He was silent for a moment, and very still.

'"Girl in the Dark,"' Max said aloud, with certainty. He knew that feeling: song title.

> Girl in the park.
> Girl in the dark.
> Needing a cuddle.
> Angela.
>
> Girl in the park.
> Girl in the dark.
> Wanting to die.
> Become an angel

'No,' Max said.

He thought for a second.

'Start again.'

Sipping a cup of flavourless coffee, Max thought they all looked the same. All wanted the same things. Camden Town, Portobello, St Mark's Place, Haight Ashbury, Harajuku, Osaka's 'American Village' . . . all the same. It's all about shopping, Max felt.

Watching all the toing and froing of tightly dotted heads on necks on shoulders on bodies carrying bags with names on, Max felt older than his years. And not particularly human. Perhaps more like an alligator watching an unwary batch of baby ducklings. The dedicated followers of fashion, Max thought, doing the same things every weekend – like lab rats – hoping they'll find fun.

If all your cells completely replace themselves every seven years, Max thought . . . and the thought fizzled. Right there.

He enjoyed the combinations of the street market in that fashionable but rough part of town. The teenaged girls with babies, two black punks with the white-blond hair of a perfect plastic dolly. People in brown and grey, all the gradations of blue denim. Whatever the brand, blues. Children's shoes. The cheap outfit accessorised with something too grand. Nerves. Giggles. Candyfloss. Bad teeth. Each irreducibly him/herself. Each different. All sheep.

They are so *mediated*, Max thought, shocked at the realisation. Every move, gesture and expression, absorbed as if by osmosis from ads, soaps, pop videos and stand-read magazines. God, look at them. All so desperate to be some tiny part of a passing culture dreamed up by stylists and advertisers and . . . record companies. Each wants to be 'now' – and, Max thought, 'now' is a hysterically short time. Clones, every one of them. They probably think they're all being so individual, but indie means group. Group consciousness. Look at them, with their shop-bought goodies. Parts of a franchise or two, right down to what goes through their heads as they wank.

This, Max thought, is what it must be like to be a detective. Sitting. Watching. Waiting for the right moment. Other than that, he thought nothing for a moment. Nothing. Immobile. Alone. Not once getting a second glance, not even when, at 16.02, he laughed out loud for five seconds as if at a good joke.

There was a girl in the market who never ceased to amaze Max with her changes in hairstyle. She had gone from pink to red to mauve to ash-blonde to auburn and once – just briefly – green. From beehive to cornrows, plaits to haphazard bun, cutesy pigtails (of course), blue Mohican and dreadlocks with extensions, naturally. That day she had a hat on. Max was amazed. It was one of those very tall, English policeman's hats. A real one. This girl, whose skimping on fruit and veg and compensatory chocs was written all over her zits, was not alone. Her friend was an almost identical girl, but wearing some ancient deerstalker hat she had picked up in some Berlin flea market and had dry-cleaned for ten times the price. She was, naturally, heavily pierced with all manner of up-to-the-minute body bric-a-brac pushed through her. Beside that girl, a whippety kind of dog that would rather have stayed at home where life would have been quieter.

As she drew her friend close with a tug on her pigtails to whisper tender atrocities beyond a castellation of ear studs, they were suddenly embracing like footballers. Perhaps she had finally got some fella she'd had her eye on, finally got him licking and nibbling her sexy teenage details. Got herself sat down on more than a courting finger.

A third girl with a poodle trotted up. The pink-bowed mutt took a long, uninvited sniff of the whippety creature's behind in that louche canine etiquette. The whippety creature did not want to be sniffed at and planted her pussy firmly down on the sidewalk.

Whatever the wind thought it was doing, Max did not know, but dust in his eyes was pissing him off. He had to get out of there.

There was panic at Furnace Records. The fan who had spotted Max on the bridge and got that startling 'DIE HAPPY' message and autograph was now being questioned by the police. An estimated time when the two had met having been ascertained, footage of a CCTV video was being examined.

The footage came from a camera that was 150 feet up in the air, fixed to one of the highest points of the bridge, designed to record traffic flow and nothing else. The police and world media were hard pushed, even with sophisticated video enhancement techniques, to tell whether any particular vehicle was a lorry, bus or car.

'I can say categorically that the idea that you could identify somebody from such a grainy VHS is arrant nonsense,' the chief investigating officer had said earlier that day to gathered media. 'The camera was so far away that any figure would be totally unidentifiable.'

Although there was an image of a figure on the murky film, then two, there was nothing conclusive in this line of investigation. Soon after the second and smaller of the two figures had moved on, what little clarity had attached to the first figure had disappeared in the glare of headlights during a spot of congestion which killed all vision.

'So, what's the official line today?' Qwo-Li asked. 'He's not dead, he's not alive, he's just missing?' he added, sarcastically.

It sounded good, it sounded great. It sounded . . . *cool*. It was today's statement.

Max made a tentative start, dotting over the vanishing lines, determined to master an art for which he had absolutely no spontaneous inclinations. His left hand smelled of the eraser he held tightly for when the right hand deleted, adjusted and smudged the sketch he was doing.

He scanned the apartment building opposite. By looking, and looking again, he was seeing. All those windows. Some with venetians turned to a precise angle, some with curtains tightly shut. Seeing. All those lives beyond. In there. That building. How many people?

Minty made a headlong dash from one end of the apartment to the other, for no apparent reason. The animal positively flung herself along and then, just as suddenly, came to rest as though nothing strange had happened.

Cats shouldn't be kept in, Max thought. Poor thing's been deprived. Has no opportunity to express its inborn urges to hunt and flee from danger. The cat had been in a listless, frustrated mood all morning. Max had noticed that the animal had shown no interest when he had opened three different tins of pre-killed food for it. Maybe it's sick, he thought. *Something's* wrong.

Max put down the pencil and eraser; that part of the process had been completed.

'Now for some colour.'

The paintbox Angela had bought herself three years before opened slowly. The metal felt cold. An enamelled palette unfolded, revealing a double tier of rounded, labelled colours with convex top surfaces like silk or satin cushions. Each pretty dollop of colour – scarlet, carmine, umber, ochre, chrome, viridian, cobalt, indigo, ultramarine and forest – among others – had been set into clinical white frames which would soon be spoiled. Angela had never used the paint set. Not once. She had lost interest in the idea of painting as a hobby soon after the expensive purchase.

It had been a long while since Max had held a paintbrush, and he was nervous about looking silly to himself. At school he had always been pretty good at drawing, had enjoyed charcoal and chalk, found working with Indian ink and wash exciting, but felt too challenged by paint. The variety of strokes, the whole range of tones, unnerved him.

'You don't get stray hairs with a pencil, don't get a run with chalk,' he said to nobody.

Sitting by the window, Max noticed a change in the days. A chill(ish) jet hit him for a second. His eyes scanned red roofs, blue roofs, cubes and oblongs of grey. Intolerable geometry.

Someone in the building had their TV on far too loudly. Occasionally there were laughs. Max moved from his position to switch on Angela's TV set to see what was so amusing. The remote control switched from NTV to TBS to NHK. Flash: a laughing chat-show audience. Flash: a seagull gliding over Sydney Harbour. Flash: some pop star jumping through a hoop of fire, like a lion. Girls going crazy. In between words he does sexy things with the microphone, puts it between his legs, touches his chest as if he's got massive mammaries. Really turning the thirteen-year-olds on. Flash: highlights of the previous year's horse racing from Fukushima and Royal Ascot came and went in seconds. Just as he tuned in to what he could hear from two floors below – commercials on TV Asahi – whoever it was turned off. He'd missed the big joke. Before him some dumb cartoon of teenage boys and girls bowling skulls at thighbones set up as skittles jumped out in too many Day-Glo colours for his liking. He hit the OFF switch, furious that he had bothered.

'Imagine you're in a cinema,' a voice in his head said, 'sitting there. Alone. The film begins. The opening shot is of . . .' And then there was a pause. Max was schizophrenic all of a sudden; lines from the last stage act were running uncontrollably. '. . . and the opening shot . . .' Must've been that drink he'd had. 'And the opening shot is of a boy walking – walking across a featureless landscape. A landscape like a grey stage. There's a hint of rain in the breeze, a breeze which flops the boy's perfect fringe. Photography: grainy black and white which turns to colour as the boy's progress gains in interest. Aged nine, maybe ten, the boy wears nothing but a pair of white, skin-tight, thin cotton Fruit of the Loom pants. He looks up at the sky then crouches down, knees touching chin, bottom skimming the air an inch above the sand. He carries an umbrella which looks black until the colour comes up as it does – yes, now. It's a shiny red umbrella – an item more suited to a little girl. Cheap. Cheap plastic. Bright red. Heavy rain begins to fall. The boy makes eye contact with the camera, then looks beyond the lens into the mind of the viewer.'

Shortly after this, Max heard the steady sound of rain, first approaching from some distance, then passing directly overhead, splashing down hard on ledges, dusty panes of glass.

The first brush strokes were strong, confident, unerring – no hesitancy in expression.

'Small Black Flowers that Grow in the Sky,' Max said aloud as the brush punched the canvas with globs of blue-black.

# 6

She wore an outfit that was antique, to say the least. Someone, somewhere, had wasted a life creating this object of white-on-white, eyelet-embroidered linen.

'Like it?'

Max nodded, smiled. He did. Angela could tell that he actually approved of what she was wearing. Found it interesting, at least.

'We going, then?' Angela asked.

Max smiled, nodded.

'Ready when you are,' he said. But something had felt a bit odd.

As the door had closed behind them, something had felt just not quite right. As they had waited for the elevator, something had jarred. As they had travelled down from floor to floor, something . . . That feeling of not having turned the bath water off, or having left the gas on, a window open.

Back in Angela's apartment, Minty was fascinated. That little birdy on the window ledge wanted to venture inside. It could see so many crumbs to swallow down. All it had to do was hop from there, to there, then swoop over to there and . . .

The cat was no longer a thing of stillness, of hard (but fluffy) edges and clear (but fluffy) outlines, but a whizz of grey, claws and canines, in the air. On the bird. Down on to that warm little thing. But the window was shut, sealed tightly. The cat's tail deflated, lowered fully, curled in between its legs. Off it went towards its bowl of water. The cat had been drinking much more water than was usual. Angela had noticed this, but had not made the connection.

Although Angela knew all there was to know about fleas, lice, ticks and mites, she had not thought through why the cat's litter tray was much damper than usual. Being a member of AACA, ACA, ACFA, ACF, CCA, CFA, CFF, FIFE and TICA, Angela knew all there was to know about tapeworms, whipworms, roundworms, hookworms, lungworms, kidneyworms and heartworms. Knew all the ins and outs of internal protozoans and toxoplasma. But, like the cat, Angela was not herself.

When she was a kitten, any sneeze or discharge from Minty's eyes or nose had not gone uncared for. Any sudden bald patches or splotches of dry skin had been blasted by expensive medication quickly. Minty's little ears had always been clean and pink inside. For too long the cat had been all she'd had.

Within a minute of Angela and Max having driven off in that rented car, Minty was defecating outside her litter box, then pissing in the bathtub.

Rain was coming down hard on the metal roof like nails being hammered through.

Angela's knuckles whitened on the steering wheel and she bit her bottom lip, then dared a glance towards Max, sitting beside her in the passenger seat. They both burst out laughing.

'Great day we picked,' Angela said.

'It might brighten, weather forecast was okay,' came Max's reply.

'I have as much faith in weather forecasters as I do in astrologists. Zero.'

Hanging from the rear-view mirror was a violently green, tree-shaped air-freshener. Beech nut was fighting against the brand-new matt plastic upholstery.

As neighbourhoods turned into other neighbourhoods, the dark clouds were left behind. Max could not remember the name of the place they were headed. Some seaside resort that had a weird name which sounded like the squelch-squelch water makes in wet boots.

'So, how come you don't drive a car in the city?' he asked.

'Can't be bothered, basically,' Angela replied. 'Y'know, all that maintenance. Looking after the cat complicates my life enough. I'd rather just get a cab, anyway. Easier.'

Then Max detected a shift in mood. One thing he had noticed at the apartment was that the phone never rang. Friends? She doesn't seem to have any, he thought. It's just her and the cat. And, I suppose, me.

The skin at the sides of Angela's eyes began to lightly bunch as she smiled. She had scented the water, the sea.

'Almost there now,' she said. 'Won't be long.'

There was a complicit gurgle at the back of her throat. She was having fun, repeating words her mother used to excite her with. Being a naughty girl, by again phoning in sick to spend the day with Max, she was enjoying herself, having a naughty bit of fun. It felt like playing hookey, something she had become quite an expert at between the ages of fourteen and sixteen.

They stopped off just the once, for a few minutes, to purchase just-from-the-baker's-oven rolls, takeout coffees and some fresh fish.

They look so pretty, laid out like that, Angela thought. Boxed according to size. The herring had suffered silver-grey deaths in the nets earlier that day, hauled aboard, drowning in the air. Glittering gills squashed by the weight of others on top of them. Within an hour they would be lunch.

When she switched off the engine she heard it, the slow sweeping of the waves which were churning glittering gravel as if it were a massive win of pachinko balls. The glad lifting feeling of arrival was heightened by the fact that they were so generously alone. The day was now warm. Not yet hot, though. Not yet.

Max was suddenly as animated as a puppy, straining on the leash. Off he ran, carrying an old wicker picnic basket under one arm, a large tartan blanket under the other.

Their stage was a luminous sandy green bay, backed by stacked dunes that stretched. Dunes like a wall that went on and on, sand too bright to look at. The location had the expectant air of an amphitheatre, a sense of elaborate theatricality to it, heightened by the view of two graveyards at either end of the stretch of coastline.

Max could imagine that in the months of July and August there would be more than the occasional sun-worshipper to be seen popping up from the dunes, as if carrying out some kind of essential surveillance duty, then back down to a read of their paperback or tabloid, or a listen on their mini-headphones to the cricket, a little Puccini or something at a relentless 184 bpm.

The insect hum of a really hot, slow day was approaching its height. Max's eyes tightened as he spotted a bumblebee bobbing towards him. It landed on his elbow, froze, kind of curtseyed and then flew off.

The sun was audibly frying seaweed that hung from odd rocks here and there. Pop, it went. Pop, pop.

Max attempted to unbutton his shirt quick as could be, but each button seemed an obstacle. They were too new, stiff. The soft leather of his belt snapped back easily. The new jeans collapsed down around his ankles in a soft shackle. He stepped out of them, their smell smudging the air. Kicking off his Reeboks, he was left standing wearing nothing but a pair of baggy Gap shorts, decorated with a pattern of little black boxes on white.

Angela pretended to divert her eyes as Max walked towards the shoreline. She gave the picnic blanket a couple of good shakes, then laid it down flat. A corner was flapping in the light breeze. Four rocks soon landed down on each of the corners of the blanket, securing it in place.

And there he was, hesitating at the water's edge with crossed arms clutching each shoulder as he tested the chill water with his toes. He seemed so still for a moment. Max wanted to be in the silent folds of all that silky water, hovering there, fluttering his feet, the fingertips of his outstretched arms only lighly anchoring him, maintaining a frozen hover.

Angela's eyes followed the arc of the front line of Max's upper leg, pausing on the balanced, adequate fullness at the back. The way the opposing curves slendered into the knee. It was a fixed and reckless stare of a view that would soon be shielded by the waves. She could not take her eyes off any movement, any moment, snapping every opportunity with a memory that would later replay them, freezing and enlarging certain moments, working the zoom of her memory.

Angela watched Max march in, ducking himself down once at waist level for five seconds of total immersion. Then he eased himself along, breaststroking so slowly, so quietly. Eyes at water level.

Angela's mind was dissolving, absorbing, dissolving as she walked along the only sandy stretch there was on the beach. The sea was out, and each step whitened the sand like pressed skin. After just one minute of walking she realised that behind her, on the beach, was an almost straight line of deep foot-prints.

Reflected in the wettest sand were nature's bagpipes, the incessant gulls that were stalking the air above. Threatening, but doing nothing. What they could hear were millions of tiny worms in their mudholes, wriggling down.

Angela would have liked to have stripped off and entered

the water too, but the water would sting. It would hurt wounds that had not healed. She had to keep her body covered.

'Oh, Jesus, fuckin' Jesus, it's freezin'!' Max shouted, now standing in the shallows like a truncated statue. 'Oh, well. Here goes.'

Submerging himself backward in the sharpness of what seemed like raw water was a mad moment of masochism. It was, at first, scaldingly cold, and Max could not believe he was doing what he was doing. He began a doomed ritual in which swimming could easily turn into drowning, forcing himself to perform a frantic twenty seconds of rocketing front crawl against the thick of the shuddering waves that shone like lasers. Practically swimming out of his skin into pure spirit, he arose from the single-breathed exertion slippery as a dolphin, shiny as silicone-sprayed rubber. Panting, he was, Panting.

For a few supersaturated moments, Max could see, feel, hear and smell everything. He was breathing deeply, stertorously, as if he could gulp into his lungs the precious components of that moment. His body appeared to be well pleased with itself, high from the cold.

The light breeze was chilling his shoulders, so back in he went. He entered with a dive that went kind of wrong, something just a step away from a belly-flop which splashed up water like diamonds. Glittering. Strings of them. Attached, one to another.

Hoping Angela had not seen or heard that crap dive, Max surrendered his body to the temperature again. Flexing as he did so, he was floating face down in the clear salt water, feeling quite comfortable after just a few kicks. Once again he was soon acclimatised, lulled by the water.

The world of Furnace Records seemed a long way away. The likes of Qwo-Li, his parents, the prospect of the next few weeks laying down tracks for an album he only had a few songs ready for.

I don't want to think about any of that right now. It's so good to be away from all that. The likes of Oola Khan picking my brains.

As he sank deeper into the unconscious world of the sea, there was only his breathing, and Angela. The two of them, in what seemed like a huge field on a windy day. The two of them, together, navigating themselves through their young lives which, like the sea, had so many sudden dips and seductive channels, often carrying a surprise ambush of icy cold.

A soft jostling swell with a dancing rhythm. Max had already forgotten his fear of coming up with material for the new album. Another soft jostling swell, the water forever changing tempo.

'A great place to drown yourself!' was Max's shrieked verdict, before clearing his sinuses of more snot than he would have thought imaginable. Up from his throat too, and out of his lungs, came stringy catarrh.

Seems as if my body is intent on a bit of spring cleaning, he thought.

Each breath seemed so much easier than usual. Straight through the nose, directly into the lungs. Then out. He felt shiny and new.

To amuse Angela, Max attempted to execute the classic Tarzan yodel. Well, Angela thought to herself, that would have had Johnny Weissmuller in stitches.

With his arms behind his head, the rhythm of his breath changing, slowing and deepening, Max was enjoying himself in the shallows of the gravelly shoreline as waves thumped the cliffs just a hundred metres away with great thuds that ricocheted with the incoming snowy waves. Waves that fondled and groped and sucked him into the undertow every few seconds, changing his position with abrasive yanks that dragged him under, only to be rescued with the impacting shove of another.

Waves that buffet, swirl and creamily shampoo, that was what Max was dancing in. Waves that clasp, circle and spray fireworks in your face, shooting in your mouth, eyes being forced to clench tight against the threat of sting. Waves heaving with rage, swollen. Waves delivering thuds that head-butted, leaving him dazed. Waves, wrecking the seat of his baggy boxers, making it hot with friction, achieving a small rip, a scratch that would bleed unseen. Though Max felt hot in all that steely cold, he was close to ecstatic hypothermia.

The moment served as a generous clemency, a beneficence. Max was feeling refreshed and felt grateful to Angela for taking the day off work to drive him to a spot where she used to holiday with her mother many years ago.

'This is fan-tas-tic!' he shouted in Angela's direction.

She turned. Even at fifty, sixty yards away, he could see that she had a pretty but sad face.

'Come on in and I'll give you a kiss!' was what Angela's mother used to holler at her daughter. 'Come on in and I'll treat you to a chocolate milk shake.' That was the tease which always got Angela running in for one minute's worth of salty wet.

It was a spot that Angela's mother would only ever bring someone to under an oath of secrecy. It was a section of coastline just that bit too far from snack bars, toilets and car parks. The fact that it was between two cemeteries was, Angela had always thought, the main factor deterring the frolics of holidaymakers. Locals, Angela knew, thought it was a little disrespectful for lazy sunbathers to be looking on, munching their sandwiches, as a loved one got lowered six feet down.

Max emerged from the choppy waves stunned and galvanised. Teeth all a-chatter.

'Here,' Angela said, handing him a two-litre bottle of water which was surprisingly warm. 'It's tap water. Rinse yourself down with it or your skin will be all salty 'n' dry 'n' 'orrible.'

Max smiled.

'You think of everything,' he said as the water ran over his face, down his neck, back, chest and further.

'I love it, Angela,' he said as he began to dry himself.

Angela almost did not hear. Her focus was upon his chattering teeth, all those goose bumps. His little nipples, both so sexily popped-up.

Angela had collected some driftwood which she had arranged and was ready to set alight.

'My mother taught me this little trick,' she said as she sprinkled a small can of something first over then into the centre of the collected wood. 'Lighter fuel.'

She struck a match, dropped it, and within seconds the wood was wearing blue flames.

'Robinson Crusoe, eat your heart out,' she said, taking a glance at Max, shivering beside her. 'Hey, Man Friday, feeling peckish?'

Max was wearing a towel wrapped loosely around his waist as he first sat, then lay there on his side, enjoying the warmth of the sun on his body. He took in a long look at all the colours the sky was playing with, then exhaled. Closed his eyes. He imagined the aerial view, the map cul-de-sac they were in.

Beyond the smells of sea and seaweed, all that limp bladderwrack on the rocks, Max was detecting the change in temperature, the air cooling fast, bringing with it some stubborn fragrance which was clearly autumnal. Some kind of mix of chrysanthemums, marigolds and burned pine needles.

Angela began unwrapping a shop-bought apple pie. She

sniffed. 'Mmm.' The smell was marvellous, as if it were baking all over again.

Max was surprised to feel himself beginning to slip off to sleep. He went with the feeling, allowed it. Flat on his back, arms at his sides, head tilted just a little in Angela's direction, he was dead to the world in minutes.

The waves broke on the shore. Again and again. A mosaic of shatterings, never quite the same twice. Breaking again now. Foam bubbling. Nothing, nothing to them. The crisp little waves expired and expired so unremittingly and tirelessly on the sand. There, breaking again, a little harder this time. The going-nowhere of the waves, like heaps of melting, whispering glass. Softening and shifting thoughts.

Sitting on the ridge of the dunes was a family eating sandwiches. Upright and dignified. A family that went down in steps of size: a man, a woman, a girl, a boy. They seemed intent on watching the tall man collecting wood, the fat woman up to her knees in the water.

No sound but the waves. Large grey waves, rolling towards Angela. One after another. Large grey waves, rolling towards her hypnotically. Some bigger than others. Some which looked as if they intended to rush the young woman, dragging her back into the cold sea. Down and under. Sharp, focused, precisely detailed grey waves. Ready for her.

Max was not looking where he was going and slipped on the remnants of a broken surfboard covered with weed. Carrying three fair-sized logs, he had fallen badly. At first he thought he might have broken a rib. He knew he would bruise up soon enough. Lying in a crater of loose sand, however, he felt strangely relaxed. Uncaring.

Aged nine and maybe ten, the two children who had been eating sandwiches nearby ran to his rescue.

'You okay?' the little girl asked.

'Not too bad,' Max answered.

The little girl studied Max's face a moment too long. Max knew the look, one of recognition. She knew the face, not the hairstyle.

'You . . .' she began, then changed course. 'You sure you're not hurt?'

'I'll live,' Max said. 'Thanks.'

As the girl and boy moved off, Angela approached, doing her best to run. She was red in the face, breathless. Sweating.

'I slipped,' Max said.

'Looked like you were having a heart attack from where I was.'

Max said nothing. If anyone was going to keel over from a heart condition it was Angela, and she knew it.

A huge wave roared up. It was a sudden onslaught. A roaring as if the sea had teeth. Frilly white lace splashed up over the caterpillar softness of Angela's feet.

She looks different, Max thought. Alert.

'The fresh air's doing you good,' he said.

'Mm,' Angela replied, stretching her arms up above her as if posing for a picture. 'Haven't felt this alive in ages.'

Max sneaked a sidelong glance. This was still Angela; she had not made that transition to fan. She was still herself.

'Have you ever had sex by the sea?' she asked.

Max burst out laughing.

'You what?' he answered, feeling a little awkward.

'I never could. All that sand. And haystacks, doesn't seem very sexy to me. I'd be all itchy an' sneezing my head off.'

She wants to talk about sex, Max thought. Just talk about it. His theory was that talking about sex was perhaps Angela's way of flirting.

Maybe she's on GO, Max thought. Maybe the internal mechanisms are already gently sliding from one gear to another. Maybe she wants to hear what I'm into, what turns me on. That kind of thing. Would she be disappointed by my total *lack* of experience?

When they got back to the blanket and fire, Max lay down. He was snoozing again in minutes.

Pretty as a picture, Angela thought, and she could not resist snapping that picture with her trusty Nikon. Neither the metallic click nor the auto-wind woke him.

She framed the pictures carefully. A profile, focus on his eyelashes, narrow depth of field. Head and shoulders. Cut to waist. A three-quarters, a daring aerial view. Then another. There were just ten exposures left on the roll.

Just ten to go, Angela thought.

'Hey, sleepy-head. Time to eat.'

Max woke. Smiled.

'I was dreaming. Was I asleep long?'

'Nah. Few minutes. Thought the pong of these roasting fish would have woken you up.'

Max was amazed. Angela had cooked the mackerel in a little picnic frying pan upon the fire.

They ate in silence. The combination of olive oil and freshly squeezed lemon upon the fish tasted, and felt, so good.

'What were you dreaming about? But, hey, please, no kinky shit. Mm?'

Max laughed, then turned his head to one side and gazed towards the horizon, as if that would jolt his memory. He said nothing and remained perfectly still for long seconds.

'"I have eyes in the back of my head," my mother was forever saying,' Max began, in the style of a children's party entertainer. 'Aged five I was treated to some art exercise of painting my parents at school. Well, my picture showed two tortoise-like aliens with eyes popping all over their hard-shelled bodies, pincer-like hands. The teacher took me aside for a chat about it. She was only, oh, y'know, one of those art therapy nuts.'

Angela laughed. She knew *exactly* what Max meant.

'Well, when my mother came to collect me at the end of the school day, she was shown the picture.' Max clapped his hands at the memory. 'It was unpinned and folded very carefully, and my mother said, "We'll see if we can improve on this over the weekend." I thought she was joking, but no. She was mortified.'

Angela laughed hard, then began ten seconds of uncomfortable coughing. Something she had just swallowed had come up, then gone down the wrong way.

'That evening, all day Saturday and all day Sunday, I painted over black-and-white xeroxes of my parents' wedding photo. You know, the 'best of' one.'

'Yeah, actually I think I read about this in *Spin* or something.'

Max kind of jumped. Angela wished she had kept quiet. Oh, fab, big mouth strikes again, Angela thought. Look at him, he's recoiling by the second.

Max shrugged, obviously uncomfortable at the unexpected mention of media.

'Yeah, ho-hum. My personal history ceased being personal long ago.'

He said that in a snappy kind of way which hurt. Then, to right that mini-wrong, he added, 'The past few days have been, you know . . . It's been *cool* just, you know . . .'

'Hanging out,' Angela said.

'Yeah.'

'Oh,' Angela said, making herself busy by wrapping the

plates in a carrier bag as an avoidance tactic, 'you just needed some time out. Bit of a rest.'

Max smiled.

She's sweet, he thought. She's . . .

They'll be wondering where you are. That was attack thought number one. Recording studio, new album. That was attack thought number two.

'Right,' Angela said, stretching towards the apple pie which was warming in the sun. 'Pud, then we'd better be moving back home. Looks like rain again.'

The two of them sat in silence, watching a far-off figure take all his clothes off and walk out into the water. When the lone swimmer was at a depth just past his knees, he dived in – surfacing a considerable distance from the point of entry. He then began to do backstroke against the waves. Effectively, he swam on the spot. And while he swam he sunbathed with his eyes shut.

Max wondered whether the swimmer thought he was going out a fair distance, or if he was just happy going nowhere.

Another damp patch on the carpet. Minty had not wetted in the living room for a long while. Angela cleaned with a vinegar-and-water solution, then applied a commercial odour neutraliser to the spot.

It hadn't been so long since the cat had suffered pyometra (pus in the uterus), ascites (fluid in the abdominal cavity), anaemia, otitis (ear infection), nephritis (kidney inflammation) and chronic constipation. Angela was worried. It was one thing after another with Minty.

She began another home examination. There was some further eye discoloration. The veterinarian had said it was likely that Minty would be at risk of cataracts and other afflictions in this region. And the cat's hearing, Angela thought – not what it was.

The cat's teats were beginning to sag, her nipples becoming enlarged and wrinkled. Being an unspayed female, particularly one who had never been mated, Minty was at risk of developing cysts, tumours and cancer of the mammary glands.

The cat's teeth had not been cleaned in a long while. Angela felt bad about that.

She had told Max everything about the cat, from purchase to litter-box lessons and the need for the occasional pedicure. She knew the cat was unwell – there were slight traces of blood in her stool, crying for no apparent reason, loss of hair, sleeping more than usual, eating less or actually refusing food, even loss of interest in her favourite toys. Even catnip was not having the usual desired effect.

From three to five, Angela had cradled the cat by the window. At times like this, she remembered Minty's sister cat. They had arrived together. All had been well the first week. Then Angela had returned home to a very frightened Minty, and one very dead Scoot. Scoot – silly name for a cat, Angela had always thought, but it had seemed so appropriate. The cat was always scooting about. Not after it had chewed through the electrical wires of the television, though.

Angela looked down at the several heavy-duty plastic strips of the kind designed to conceal cords that travel across the floors in office cubicles. To be doubly sure of no repetition of this tragedy, Angela had smeared Tabasco sauce over the casing, just to be certain that no harm came to Minty.

From five to seven, one-third of a bottle of Jack Daniel's Old No. 7 brand Tennessee sour-mash whiskey had been downed by a slightly wobbly Max and one very cheery Angela. The litre of whiskey, 43 per cent alcohol by volume, distilled and bottled by the Jack Daniel Distillery, Lynchburg, Tennessee, USA, had cast quite a spell on them both. Maybe it was the pure cave spring water and a little something in the unique mellowing process perfected by Mr Jack Daniel, the man himself, in 1866 that did it, hitting their respective metabolisms very nicely. The flavour brought about through the slow, time-honoured methods insisted upon by the founder certainly made the trawling through Angela's photographic collection distinctly pleasing.

'I'd never planned on becoming a collector. It began, as obsessions do, quite by chance,' she said, refreshing first Max's glass, then her own. 'Cheers.'

'You've got quite a collection,' Max said, casting his eyes over five fully packed shoeboxes of old postcards. 'When and *how* did it all start?'

'Well, back in September of '98 I literally stumbled over a shoebox at a flea market. There it was, beside a battered mannequin festooned with costume jewellery and a box of delaminating jigsaw puzzles: an old shoebox for size-nine brogues. Sticking out from under a table it was, thick red rubber band holding in the contents.'

'Right,' Max said, taking a sip of his drink, enjoying listening to Angela as he looked at the real-photo postcards.

'Nobody seemed to be in charge of the stall. I looked around, almost guiltily, as if about to read someone else's mail, but there was no one. Well, *b-doing b-dang* went that rubber band as I removed it to discover a precious collection of daguerreotypes, ambrotypes, tintypes, *cartes de visite*, cabinets and real-photo postcards. Some of the visuals were in raggedy envelopes, the majority were rubber-banded tight in categories that soon became apparent.'

Max was mesmerised by the visuals, which he handled

carefully, holding them by the very edges as if they were delicate transparencies.

'Faces stared up at me from rumpled albumen paper prints and slivers of metal. Faces almost pleading for me to take them home. Expressions that touched my heart.'

Angela seemed so alive at that moment, so pleased to be sharing something that she valued with someone else. Her every sentence carried pent-up detail.

'The majority of the images were frozen in time long before the invention of the automobile, telephone, radio or aeroplane. With just one blink of an eye the single compelling possibility of ownership was pumping adrenalin fast, believe me.'

Max could imagine the scene. All around, voices bargaining, calling out prices and weights. The caramelised aroma of home-made berry pies mingling with the damp of old coats.

'Eventually a man appeared inch by inch from the rear of an old van, bottom first. "Twenty each," he shouted my way. I pretended to appear uninterested as I shuffled through a pack that was nothing but men in couples. Soldiers, sailors, university students and 'theatrical types'. Some of these men resembled each other as brothers might, many didn't. For the most part their ages didn't seem different enough to suggest a father–son relationship.'

'Uh-huh.'

'I looked through another pack – women dressed 'butch'. Some decked out in men's suits, some in army uniforms. "How much for the lot?" I asked, trying to sound more curious than interested. "Fiver," the guy piped up. Well, as the bustling crowd tested the plumpness of tomatoes, and scrutinised free-range eggs, I rejoiced that he wasn't asking the earth. "Give ya three," I said. Not so much as a second elapsed. "Sold!" the stall-holder said.'

Angela had described the scene well. Too well, Max

thought. He had the suspicion that she had either told this story time after time or, more likely, had written a piece about collecting old photographs for that magazine she worked for.

'Most of the subjects were documented in the form of "real" black-and-white picture postcards. Brothers, sisters, best mates, lovers . . . whatever the relationships or my interpretation of them, someone somewhere had spent a lot of time – and maybe money – putting together this abandoned collection. And suddenly they were mine.'

Max turned his attention to the picture of a young man and woman, figure-eighting on their skates. A frozen-over lake. Austria, perhaps, or Switzerland. Sometimes, on the back of the images, there was a telling communication, hastily written and provocatively. Sometimes an interesting postmark, a collectable stamp. More often blank, nothing. The one of the two skaters simply had a date: Sunday, 14 February 1904.

'Images taken by travelling tintypists frequently became inserted into a ring or cuff links,' Angela went on, as she opened a little box that contained some jewellery.

'Once these items were gifts,' Max said, moved by the faded photos of a pale youth from long ago, 'tokens of affection.'

Angela sighed. No one had ever shown any genuine interest in her collection before, a collection few had seen.

'Costs quite a bit collecting this stuff. I go to all the fairs,' she enthused. 'All the dealers know me.'

She thought of those dealers as friends; they thought of her quite differently.

In that apartment building, just as in so many apartment buildings throughout the city, the bedtime rituals of locking doors, checking taps, straightening towels, setting clocks, kissing photographs goodnight and darkening rooms was in progress.

Shoes, polished to parade standard, were ready to be worn in many of these apartments. Breakfast cereals and vitamin pills ready to be swallowed. But first – sleep. Or a bit of rumpy-pumpy, then sleep.

Down below was brimming with cheerful, resonant and inept exclamations ending in a volley of goodnights. Peace and quiet exploded regularly with the racket. Two-door thumps of car doors as couples prepared for the one-door slam of their home. The person waiting for a cab, the person last to leave, was extravagantly sick. Max could hear the *wroarrrgh-wroarrrgh*, then the *splaaat-splaat*.

Whilst Angela was already snoring, Max was more than wide awake. Unable to sleep, he started to count sheep. Not your average white sheep, but red and yellow and pink and polka-dotted sheep. Some with stripes. The occasional one with a sequinned crash helmet for variety. But the colourful combinations and occasional accessories were too much to keep up with; in the end they became boring, regimented white sheep. Despite that, Max could not sleep for one reason: there it lay, like a whale stranded and dying on a deserted shore. It was not going to let him get a wink of sleep. Gradual, pulsing jerks, pumped with warmth, stiffened the object. It became enormous, somehow detached from the now stubbly mooring.

It waited, quivering stupidly. That nineteen-year-old body, just three months from its twentieth birthday, was what this well above nationally average-sized penis was straining to detach itself from.

Penis, swaying. Not obeying the requests to settle down and relax. Penis, persisting obstinately in swollen silence. All feelings, intelligence, drained into that erectile tissue. So pumped up, so red headed, so animatedly erect, it looked like a falsie, like something which had been on a charger then plugged into his groin. Two very red veins like car traffic in a night-scene photo lined that penis. Ready, it yelped. Come on. Hanging upside down, it would not have looked out of place in the window of a delicatessen.

The tip of his dick bounced beneath his fingers: hot, damp and rubbery – like a dog's toy bone. It seemed to radiate like a hunk of plutonium, or the bleeding heart in Catholic pics of Jesus Christ. It kind of hurt, kind of got on his nerves.

The wrinkled puckerings of his scrotum heaved, smoothed out. Max weighed his balls lightly with one hand, non-committally.

My prick's like a pet dachshund living in my underpants, Max thought. Sometimes, at least-expected moments, that dick of mine takes it into its mind that it wants to go walkies. And it won't stop yapping until I do something about it. Frustrated by the demands of his penis, he rolled over, scratched himself in irritation.

The apartment building opposite was a jigsaw of lights. Max looked at the patterns formed. Maybe, he thought, maybe a little orgasm will help get me off to sleep. Yeah, he thought. Yeah, he would. He had convinced himself. Already he was under starter's orders.

The sheet beneath him puckered as he squeezed. Bending it, bruising it, he smiled. Felt nice. That thing – whew – felt *good*.

Nah, I won't. To hell with it, he thought. Rolling over to the other side of the bed, Max felt instantly cooler. For a moment he thought he might drift off, any second.

'Oh, go on, then, if you must,' he whined, resignedly seizing the base of that part of his anatomy, tugging the thing back and forth a few times, enjoying the warmth of it in his right hand but looking furious, desperate and frantic.

Rattling those testicles into confusion . . . contracting the muscles of his abdomen close to doubling up . . . rolling a little like an epileptic . . . remembering the cheap flash of a sapphire ear stud on a New York City cop . . . remembering Oola Khan's orange-squash blouse . . . jerking away swiftly and sweating.

He jerked himself off silently, but for occasional breaths and the friction of spit. His heart, pounding with racing blood, felt more worrying than F-U-N. His left eyelid began to flutter violently. The fleeting, contemptible moment was on its way.

In his throat he felt an ache he got when on the top of high-rise buildings. His stomach briefly hollowed. The ache spread from his throat down over his thighs as he hit the pre-climax shudders.

The bedroom looked on with polished indifference.

# 7

Angela could hear Max moving about in what had become his room. Only a thin wall separated them. She listened intently. She could hear him humming as his jeans slid on and up. She wondered what he looked like. How he conducted himself when alone. Just beyond that wall, Angela thought.

She stood, approaching the wall with opening arms. It was as if she were about to give that large, cool, flat expanse a hug. At the last second she turned her head to one side, positioning her right ear against the fragile partition to listen all the better. Max was still humming, not a tune she recognised. Then he went quiet, but he was still there.

In there, somewhere. Just beyond this construction of wood and plasterboard, Angela. Just a few feet away, girl.

The tip of the index finger of Angela's right hand *itched*. It lowered to a point that, on the other side, would be somewhere around the small, cluttered bookshelf.

Angela jumped when Max opened his bedroom door. Though her door was locked, out of habit, she moved away from the wall and got busy fluffing up her pillows.

Then the click of the bathroom door, the turning of the lock in there. Angela walked directly over to the far wall, again with outstretched arms. First placing the palms of her hands against the flat surface, then the side of her face, then her body, she relaxed into that surface. Max was beyond that wall.

That was his pissing she could hear. That was him flushing. That was him running water into the sink. That was him

219

splashing his face. That was him, now being quiet a moment. What was he doing?

Again the tip of the index finger of Angela's right hand itched. It lowered to a point that, on the other side, would be somewhere around the small, cluttered shelf of neatly lined seashells, that unhealthy air-plant which was dusty with talcum powder.

Now the tub is filling. He usually has a shower, Angela thought.

What would he look like laid out in the tub? That was the question which tormented her. Max, in there, alone. Naked.

'Hey, Angela,' Max called out, unnerving her, making her feel that he could see through that thin partition between them. 'Fancy going for a swim?'

Angela opened her bedroom door, stood outside the bathroom in knickers and baggy T-shirt.

'Nah,' she said, 'I'm going to stay in this morning, do a bit of tidying up. You go, though.'

Half an hour later Max was ready to leave.

'I'll buy a pair of shorts or something on the way, I guess.'

'There's a little shop that sells swim stuff by the ticket desk. Well, there used to be. Ages since I've been.'

Max thought it diplomatic to say nothing.

She wanted to hug him, but did not dare touch.

'If only . . .' she started.

The words were left hanging. It could well have been the beginning of a silly sentimental verse with no rhyme or reason or rhythm, heavy on regret.

'If only what?' Max asked, maybe a little too abruptly.

'Oh, nothing.'

It ended there, with the scent of camellia oil lightly applied to her hair and eyebrows just one hour before.

Ears lowered to the sides, panting, Minty was anxious.

Naked, sitting cross-legged on the kitchen floor, Angela surrounded herself with her tools, tools which all too frequently induced euphoric agony. When that fine collection of hand-honed zirconium ceramic kitchen knives came out of the cupboard, Minty always scampered under the sofa. It was the crying the woman made which she did not like, not the blood. All that blood.

'There, now,' Angela said as she slowly lowered the fish/meat knife, the fruit/vegetable knife, the cook's knife, the general-purpose knife, the multi-purpose knife.

'There, now,' she whispered to herself as she opened the aluminum briefcase, before slowly laying down the molybdenum vanadium steel blades which had scarred her arms, her legs, her breasts, the expanse of her stomach.

Her face was reflected in the largest of these knives. The other knives also reflected parts of her body, at a variety of angles. What she could see was a jigsaw of horrible anatomy. A grotesquely obese odalisque, staring. Absorbed yet detached.

'There there, now,' she said in the voice of a mother comforting her distraught child as she quietly unzipped the black Kevlar zipped wallet before neatly positioning the filleting knife, the peeling knife, the all-too-familiar boning knife.

Lastly, in its usual place, went the diamond sharpening steel. Everything would be sharpened. Made ready.

Angela was not feeling the usual fall of calm. She knew time was limited. Max would soon be back. The last thing she wanted was for him to find her there, like that, with her favourites out.

'And what if I cut too deep?'

Excessive bandaging would take time. The discomfort might arouse suspicion.

The carpet cutter in the top drawer, she thought. That fearful Stanley knife. She longed for just five minutes with that. Just pins and needles for now, she decided, controlling the urge. Just a piece of glass. One small piece of glass, at most. It was the Stanley knife she wanted. She'd need more than shit paracetamol to lessen the pain that she could inflict upon herself with that thing.

Her fingers were not ready. The air was still swirling in the apartment from when Max had swung the door shut, from when Angela had thrown off her clothes and whipped out the knives.

Eyes closed, she knew she had to tidy all this away. Knew she was on the wrong track. Knew what she wanted to do.

'He's been gone fifteen minutes. Loadsa time.'

The spare room smelled of him. She had got to know his smell. From his bath towel, his sheets, the clothes he threw across the back of a chair so casually.

She knew what she was about to do was wrong, but she still wanted to do it. There was no need to rush. Max had said he would be gone a while.

Standing on a little stool, Angela removed the books from the shelf, careful to keep them in the exact order they had been in. Holding the drill firmly to the lightly pencilled 'X', Angela began to squeeze the bright orange power button. The drill jumped to life, shaking about like a massive trapped bug. The vibrations set the loose flesh of her drilling arm jumping. Her chins began to wobble, her brow to quickly sweat. Eyes set, there on the 'X', she was determined.

Drilling from Max's side of the wall, there was less chance of getting things wrong.

'There. Through.'

Running around to her room, Angela raised herself up on tiptoe for a peep. The hole was small. For a moment she considered the possibility of changing the bit for one slightly larger, the next size up.

'No, too risky.'

That'll do, she thought. That'll have to do.

Angela wiped the shelf free of dust, base-board too. Then she repositioned the books. Her vantage point on the other side of the wall would be via two books on cats.

She hoovered carefully, then sprayed some air-freshener about to cover up the stink of plaster dust that floated through the air.

She was less confident about doing likewise in the bathroom. The room was a quarter the size of the bedroom. The chances of seeing a hole in the wall far greater. It was something that occupied her mind as she munched through a packet of biscuits.

'Sod it, I will,' she whispered to the wallpaper.

Drilling from within the bathroom, Angela pointed the bit at the dark centre of a flower in the wallpaper: a daisy. The drilling was easier this time round, faster. The paper around the edge of the achieved hole, however, had frayed untidily a little around the edges. She tidied this up with a few dabs of a felt-tip pen.

To divert eyes away from the hole, Angela decorated the other end of the shelf with a jug of dried flowers that she had kept in the corner of her bedroom since before Christmas.

'Mm.'

From the other side of the wall, the view of the toilet, bath and full-length mirror was good. She felt like a burglar planning a break-in.

Outside the room, by the front door, Minty was mewing like a kitten. The message? 'Let me out!'

Max bought himself a cheap spiral notebook on the way to the local pool. This, he thought, is a bad sign. Looks like I'm not going to check out for a while yet.

'MY BADLY SCRIBBLED NOTES' is what he wrote on the cover of the pad. Huge capitals, in a diagonal.

'No remembering,' is what he wrote on the opening page. 'No more remembering of times past. No more remembering of the old you. All the yous. They are all past. All gone. Good as dead. REMEMBER: NO MORE REMEMBERING.

Max felt self-conscious as he paid the admission charge. He was hugely relieved that the swimming pool changing room was quiet, only two old men down at one end, one of whom was having difficulty getting his key into locker number 176.

The white moulded silicone Speedo swimming cap and the smoked pearlescent-blue goggles gave Max an anonymity he felt was necessary. The goggles were of a soft resin frame variety, with a tough black tubular strap which fitted around his head comfortably. It had been a long while since he had been to a public pool. Years. He felt like an actor as he walked towards the edge, preparing himself to dive.

With his soles flattened against the rough surface of the block, Max repositioned the smoked lenses so that the nose-bridge adjuster did not pinch. Having already hyperventilated to expand his lungs, he gripped the very edge with his toes.

He looked at the water. The glints and shatters of sunlight and fluorescent stabbed through his eyes. He was ready.

The dozen or so people in the pool were aware of the unusually tall, slim young man. Not one of the Saturday regulars. Some were more curious than others. Two women, a teenaged girl. One very obviously gay man.

There was something so charged about the way Max flung himself from the side of the pool. It was the dive of someone who was looking forward to the feel of the water, the sensual refreshment of a rapid entry. The dive made the surface shatter into a million wavy panes.

Max thought the water would have been cooler. He shrugged and floated to the surface. Already too warm and not yet ten. He would would have preferred the water ice cold, like a mountain stream. A temperature that tightens every pore. A temperature than makes you sleep well.

He got out of the water to dive again, then swam six lengths of easy crawl. The giant white soles of his feet fluttered with the one-two, one-two of someone who had been trained long hours in his early teens. Added to this was the precise curvature of his hands, scooping the water, scooping it past.

He sat by the poolside a while, watching kids take their turns on the diving boards. They were having fun.

I want to think in nice sentences. Easy-to-read sentences. Smooth sentences, Max thought. Sentences for my mind to glide over. No hard, broken-up bits 'n' pieces. Not fragmented. Smooth. Nice smooth sentences.

Looking at him was a woman whose eyes had heavy bags. Her chins had heavy bags. Her body appeared rather like a collection of purses of flesh, untidily heaped into that potato sack of a swimming costume. From armpit to ankle, wobbly flesh. Just like Angela, Max thought. Poor Angela. All that extra baggage.

That queer guy was looking at him, too. Checking him out.

Max said 'Hi' to the guy as he walked past, which seemed to really freak the guy out. Off he swam to the shallow end, then made for the showers. Then he thought again. Maybe I just got recognised, even with this cap and goggles on.

The cat was wearing a relaxed but alert facial expression. Face tightened, eyes sharply focused, pupils constricting, Minty stretched her right paw out in front of her. Hey, the body language seemed to be whispering, you okay? Five minutes earlier the cat had brought a toy mouse to Angela, in an attempt to initiate a game. No response.

She is suffering. She's longing for that refuge in herself. The utmost pain, nature's lukewarm pleasure.

'Now is the time, but there's no time. He'll soon be back.'

Everything is tidy. Done. Completed. She has checked, over and over. Just to keep herself busy she has chopped up an apple, a peach, two large carrots, half a punnet of strawberries and a handful of parsley. Juiced the lot. Made a jug of juice, she has. Enjoyed watching the colours mix, change.

She is waiting. Suffering while she is waiting. Not used to existing in the shadow of someone else.

A little balm might help me, she thinks, as she applies a dab to the Taiyang point (left and right of side of head). And a little dab here to the Yaoyan point (left and right of upper buttocks). And here, at the Shenyu point (left and right on either side of the spine in the small of her sweaty back). And here, the place she felt she needed it most, at the Fengehi point (at both sides of the back of the neck).

The heat started up within a minute.

'Ah, that feels good.'

Right that moment she wanted to punish that body. The body she despised. Her body. What she wanted was the sight of her own blood, over the floor. So much blood it would appear that someone had torn apart a huge bouquet of red chrysanthemums, leaving the petals to dry in the sun. That deep dark red. That colour would remind Angela that she was real, alive. All that colour would have a calming, reassuring effect, creating a welcoming reduction in her heart rate. She'd have to wait before she could have a cutting binge.

Angela knew that time would come soon enough, knew she would soon be alone again. There would be plenty of time to indulge in what she felt was the beautiful dignity of her chosen form of self-abuse.

'I hurt myself to get pain out,' she whispered over to Minty, whose head was turned a little to one side, as if interested. 'That's why.'

The cat looked back at her. What it wanted to emit was a strange, throaty, yowling noise – a *mhrhrnaaaoua*, then a *mhrhrhrnnaaahooouuu* quickly followed by a *mhhngaahou*. It stayed silent. Did not move.

Try and look normal, Angela thought to herself. Make yourself busy. Do something. Take that juicer apart. Wash it.

Just as a final section of the juicer was being rinsed, then placed the draining board, Max gave the front door a couple of kicks. This startled Angela.

Max was laden – he had bought something and seemed joyous about his purchase. His face was flushed from running.

'Hey,' he said, breathless, 'look what I've got. Some fella was having a yard sale down the road.'

Angela looked at the packaging while drying her hands on a small towel.

'A synthesiser?' she asked, unsure.

'Uh-huh,' Max replied, laying the keyboards out on the kitchen table.

'Hey, plug this in, will ya?' he half asked, half directed. Angela complied.

All numbers and symbols on the buttons of the VOICE/STYLE group had faded away with wear long ago. Max took the greatest of care when plugging the cords into the rear panel jacks. The internal speaker system was fine, no problems there.

The old Yamaha synth, a PSR 300, looked so black against

the fresh whiteness of the plastic kitchen table. Though the internal circuitry featured a maximum polyphony of twenty-eight notes which could be played simultaneously, with extra notes when the automatic accompaniment, split or dual voice features were used, Max hit one note at a time like a kid, still mesmerised by the touch response facility after all these years. The way the volume of the sound could be controlled to a certain degree by how hard he played the keys had always been something of a comfort to him.

'I had this exact same model when I was about eleven,' he said, delighted by his bargain buy.

When Max pressed the SUSTAIN button, the indicator lit up welcomingly. He selected a fretless bass sound, then improvised on the lower end of the keyboard. Sounds decayed gradually as his fingers lifted from the keys. The familiar hum and slur made the corners of his mouth curl upward in the slightest hint of a smile.

A spatter of rain hit the window. Max looked out. Down below a woman was running for a bus, a handbag held atop her head. Her free hand was holding her skirt away from her body so that it would not cling. The bus made a rare exception, pulling up fifteen yards or so from the stop, and Max smiled and shivered at the driver's kindness.

By the time the woman was looking through her bag for loose change or a bus pass, Max was searching through his favourite sounds for something suited to his mood: synth piano, synth strings, cello. FANTASY 1 AND 2 were particular favourites. The rhythms he then sifted through were NEW JACK SWING and EURO BEAT. Hideous names, he thought. He set the tempo at 170 beats per minute.

Playing minor, seventh and minor seventh chords in the SINGLE FINGER mode, Max forgot about himself for a while, lost in the easy manipulations.

Angela just sat there, on the sofa with Minty, watching.

White, Max thought. White.

'Tell me some things that are white,' Max called over to Angela as he played random chords.

'Er, seagulls, storks, cockatoos.'

'Mm, go on.'

'Lilies of the valley.'

'And?'

'Carnations. The petals of a daisy.'

'Uh-huh, keep going.'

'A mother's milk, flag of surrender. The whites of my eyes but not a sheep's.'

They both laughed at that.

'Go on,' Max said, as he changed from one sound treatment to another.

'Teeth. Bones. President Bush's house.'

'More.'

'White rot and maggots.'

Max turned to face Angela, gently pressing the power button as he did so.

OFF.

■

# 8

'MAX FAN TELLS OF ASTONISHING VISIT,' ran the tabloid headline. Oola Khan was stunned by the news.

Head-shaved and barefooted, rock legend Max has surfaced after being missing presumed dead over recent days. An eighteen-year-old fashion student named . . .

Izzy's well-built, conscientiously exercised body was squeezed into an outfit that the tabloid's news desk and fashion editor thought would make for a sexy cover: a little black dress. A *very* little black dress.

Talking exclusively to our reporter, sexy Max fan Izzy Constantinou said, 'It was like a dream come true. As soon as I opened the door and made eye contact with Max I got this tremendous tingling feeling. My heart started beating very fast. I almost went hysterical. I wanted to throw myself at him and cover him with kisses, but I didn't. It's my one regret. I'm sure Max would be a very passionate lover.'

Oola groaned inwardly at the usual formula. 'Typical. Yuk.'
    Izzy had sold her story through a celebrity PR who had gained a reputation for negotiating hefty sums for sensational revelations. The way Izzy looked at it was simple – the money would get her through her three-year fashion course, pay the rent, and could work as publicity in her favour in the fickle world of fashion. That photograph she had snapped of Max sitting at the kitchen table had come in handy. It may have been a simple 35mm 400ASA disposable Fuji camera snap,

but the negative had been scanned at a high resolution and digitally enhanced. Splashed across pages two and three of that day's edition, it was a picture that was already being syndicated for considerable amounts of money on a global basis. The picture had been cropped for the cover, just showing Max's shaved head, with an insert of his bare feet.

Splashed across pages three and four was another shot of Izzy. Again dressed rather sexily by a member of the tabloid's staff, Izzy had been photographed sitting at a kitchen table, holding the cup that Max had drunk from.

'I've kept everything that he touched or handled,' sexy Izzy admitted with a smile. 'This coffee cup and saucer. This spoon. This yoghurt pot.'

There was an insert shot of Izzy sprawled across her double bed, gazing longingly towards the camera through a mirror by the bed. Focus was more on Izzy's behind than on the framed pictures of Max by her bed.

'It's his voice, it just makes me go kind of funny inside,' Izzy told our reporter. Izzy is such a Max fan that when she makes fries she cuts the potatoes so that they make 'M', 'A' and 'X' shapes. 'I hope he's okay. He looked very stressed out when he came to visit me. I hope our time together helped him. I'm sure I'm not the only fan who loves him with all their heart.'

'Oh, please,' Oola sighed at the tabloid drivel.

Another insert shot had Izzy leaning towards the camera showing plenty of Photoshopped cleavage. Behind her, on the shelves of a vintage glass display cabinet, sat dolls with composition heads and limbs, pretty little things with smiling mouths and deep dimples. In her hand she was nursing the pride of her collection, that unbelievably rare 1965 developmental Barbie prototype of which she was so proud.

'We talked for hours and hours,' attractive Izzy told our reporter at her comfortable apartment. 'He told me all about what it was like being discovered, the thrill of success, the strain of touring. Maybe he just needed someone to talk to. I'm glad he picked me. The fact that he did still gives me goose pimples.'

Both the PR to whom Izzy was now contracted and the tabloid journalist who had interviewed the girl had embroidered what little of a story there was into something that the likes of MTV, CNN, NHK and the BBC would highlight in news broadcasts later that day.

Izzy, a young fashion designer who hopes to establish her name in the world of fashion, is currently a student at . . .

The paper had set up a telephone line which Max fans could call, recording their Max fantasies for a forthcoming feature. Oola sneered at the small print – the charge per minute was exorbitant, both peak rate and off peak. But it gave her an idea. She picked up her cellular phone and punched in the number of her radio producer. What had been planned for that night's show would have to be postponed.

'Hi, Wai, Oola. Hey, listen. I've got an idea.'

'And tonight on Capital Radio's 'Open Heart Surgery' slot we have Oola Khan, who *very recently* interviewed Max on the last night of his sell-out forty-two-date tour before his mysterious disappearance. Good evening, Oola.'

'Hi, Robbie,' Oola replied, lips just an inch from the microphone. She favoured a close-mic approach; it gave her quiet voice a distinctive, intimate feel.

'Many of you will have read that Max has been sighted, shaven headed and barefooted, on two occasions in recent days. Tonight's show is dedicated to the life, spirit and fans of Max, hoping he's doing okay out there, maybe getting some time to chill – something we all need to do from time to time. That's what Capital's "Open Heart Surgery" is all about,' the DJ gushed. 'We'll start the show with a treat for the fans out there with a repeat of a live session recording of Max's third single made in July of last year. Here's an acoustic version of "Come. Hear Us Rage".'

As the track faded, the DJ pointed to the fan who had some opening lines written down in front of her. 'Max is the first thing I think of when I open my eyes in the morning,' the fan began. 'I feel that I cannot get on with my life right now or make any kind of decisions because he has gone missing.'

'Carla, tell us what most appeals to you about Max,' Oola said encouragingly.

'Oh, just *everything*,' the seventeen-year-old began.

There was a difficult moment. The girl had gone blank.

'Ever find yourself *fantasising* about him?' the DJ interjected. His style was too harsh, too direct. Bad start, Oola thought. Damn. The fan, however, had been expecting such a question. The DJ's sensational approach had not thrown her.

'When I fantasise about him it always begins with me imagining that I am washing his hair. Combing through the conditioner, that kind of thing. Running my fingers through the length of it. Just him and me, just the two of us, his head in my lap. His eyes . . .'

'Yes?' the radio DJ prompted, just a little too eagerly.

'His eyes just looking up at me, waiting for me to lower my head to kiss his eyelids.'

The girl's bottom lip was quivering. What the DJ was hoping for was a little breathing difficulty, erratic breath hitting the microphone before the start of tears. Unless listeners had logged on to the website, seeing what the webcam was picking up at that moment, they would not be able to see the tears running down the fan's face.

'I've been so worried about Max. When I saw the paper today I felt so relieved, but I feel something was wrong and . . . I'm . . . I'm so *worried*.'

Right on cue the girl put her face into her hands and started to sob.

'Time to take a break,' the DJ gushed. 'Back in a minute with Oola Khan of the *Observer* for more in this one-hour special on Max.'

As an advert began for the launch of a new slimming aid, the second Max fan was ushered into the studio. There was plenty of time for the sixteen-year-old to get seated, calm herself in the new surroundings and take a sip of water to sort out her mouth, which was cotton-wool dry all of a sudden. Two more adverts ran, then – after a slight technical hitch which created five seconds of complete silence – the DJ played the first minute of 'Deep Love Scar'. This fan, like all the others, had been contacted by Oola via the fan club. There had been no time to do what she thought of as 'quality testing'; the criteria for the selection process had been absolutely basic: can you make it to the radio station by eight tonight? Twelve of the fifteen contacted had.

'And we're back, live in the studio with Oola Khan, me, Robbie Dario and Mandy.'

The DJ pressed the PLAY button and the four-second signature jingle of the show burst and faded.

'Mandy, tell us . . .' Oola began, leaning ever so slightly towards the denim-clad girl nursing a Max doll. 'Tell us what Max means to you.'

For a moment the girl bit her bottom lip, staring up towards the ceiling. The DJ shot Oola a glance which communicated a thought: feed her a starting-off point.

'How does it feel, for example, when you are alone at home,

in your room, looking at your posters of him. I'm presuming you have posters of him, right?'

'Oh, yes,' the girl blurted, '*loads*. Every inch of my bedroom is covered with pics of Max. My form teacher wrote on my school report that I think about him too much and should be getting on with my school work in class, not looking at pictures of him that I've taped to my files and pencil case. I buy anything with a picture of Max in it. I check the website each and every day when I get home from school just in case there's a new limited poster on offer for my collection – it can all get very expensive. [Laughs.] Well, when I look at posters of Max I look beyond the printed picture. I fix my eye on the picture, but look beyond. It's just something to fix my mind on. I don't really look at his face or what he's wearing, it's into his eyes I look. They're great posters an' everything, but they're not the real thing, just like the music's not the real thing. That's what upsets me. That I can't touch him. When I masturbate, I imagine he's in my room. Just stood there.'

While the DJ was gulping inwardly at the sexual explicitness of what had just been said, he looked beyond the glass panel into the control room to register the reaction to this on the producer's face. Oola smiled at the girl, nodded. That nod said go on. Keep going, it's okay to talk about these things.

'I feel Max is kind of like a safe place that is always there for me to retreat to.'

'Right,' Oola said. She knew exactly what the girl meant. Exactly.

'When I listen to his records I feel very close to him, as if he's my friend – someone I've known for years. When I'm fed up or upset about something I just plug in, y'know, and he seems to sort me out.'

Oola nodded encouragingly.

'I've got one poster in which he's wearing a baggy white shirt which is buttoned up all wrong. He's sitting on a bed with his legs wide apart, surrounded by three girls. It's a real turn-on. He's got this look in his eyes which says "Come on now". I often imagine kissing the top parts of his shoulders, then undoing his trousers as he lies back on the bed with his arms behind his head. [Giggles.] I love the way he smiles and laughs in interviews, that's how he is in my fantasies. [Giggles again.] I've got another poster in which he is completely topless except for a black scarf around his neck, something very sheer. If I look at this poster long enough, Max is kind of beamed through the air into my room. One second he's there, leaning against the wall. "I'm here!" he says, then he's gone. Next second he's by the door. "Over here!" he says, then he's by my wardrobe. And he's, like, wearing nothing but this scarf and his black leather trousers, the top button of which is always undone. That goes on for quite a bit and eventually . . .'

She stopped herself. An instinctive moment of self-censorship.

'Yes?' Oola whispered.

'And eventually' the girl sniffed, unsure, then decided to take the gamble and admit it. 'And eventually I come.'

She had said it proudly. Her chin was up, her look straight ahead into the eyes of Oola.

'Once I tore up all my posters of him. It was like killing him, and I can understand that guy who killed John Lennon twelve or thirteen years ago. My sister couldn't believe it, all of a sudden I was screaming, "I don't love him, I fuckin' hate him. I hate him for what he's doing to me, he's ruining my life. He just wants my money." [Laughs nervously.] Love and hate can be so close. [Laughs again, semi-hysterically.] I'm just one of many, many fans. I find that annoying. Sometimes I'll eat a whole cake in exasperation, I get that wound up. It's sort of like frustration or anger. Just wanting attention, maybe, but from *him*. You see – and I'm not the only fan who feels this, I *know* – I want to explore Max, really find the [inaudible] person beyond the hype. The real person. That shy and very sensitive being, be with him for a while to understand *that man*. The more successful he has become the more inaccessible and brilliant and famous and wonderful he has become, too. And me? I'm just plain old spotty me. Each night I listen to his music. I lie on the floor with the speakers right next to my ears, wanting to have him inside me.'

Then the girl burst into tears.

'Oh, I feel so ashamed for saying all that. It sounds wrong, sleazy. And what I feel for Max is beyond lust. If anything has [inaudible] to Max I don't know what I'd do. I really don't.'

The DJ flicked a thumbs-up sign at the girl, which she interpreted as a sign that they were off the air. Time for another jingle, time for another track by Max. Oldest trick in the book. Out came all that emotion, held in since the first rumours that Max was missing, presumed dead. Broadcast, over the airwaves, her sobs, her wailing.

'God, please help me!' she said. 'Oh, what are we going to do?'

Oola leaned forward, hugged the girl. From behind the glass partition the producer gave a signal to the DJ to spin the moment out.

After much sniffing, Mandy seemed to right herself.

'Do you ever dream of Max?' Oola asked.

'Oh, do I? I dream and double-dream,' came the curious reply. 'He's my very own personal Jesus. One dream I've had a few times is that I go to a record store signing and as he passes back the signed book or whatever there's a note with a time and place written on it. Some hotel. I go there, right, and knock on the door of Room 505 or whatever and the door swings open and it's him. Max. Standing there. White satin shirt, black leather trousers and his purple suede boots. And he opens his arms for me to walk into them. That's when I wake up. I usually start crying because I have to leave that lovely feeling and just be me at home in my lousy bed all alone again.'

The girl put her arms around herself, squeezed her knees together. Began to rock back and forth very gently.

'Touch plays a really big part in my fantasies about Max. I lie for hours and hours imagining his lovely, long fingers caressing me. In my fantasies it all happens so romantically. It's about love, not sex, and everything's in slow motion. Sometimes we are on a bed, surrounded by candles, and sometimes we're on the side of a grassy hill, under the stars.'

Not a word from Oola or the DJ. The producer had given the signal for another track to be played. That meant Mandy out, next one in. On came a live version of 'Hidden Bruises'.

'And I bet that surprised a few of you out there. Recorded at what we all hope was not Max's last gig, "Hidden Bruises" with backing vocals by Marnie Actil.'

Oola was looking distinctly uncomfortable. Oprah was not quite her style. This conveyor-belt approach to the fans was proving distasteful, but she knew it was the direction her career had to go in to achieve the kind of success she wanted. She swallowed her professional integrity and proceeded as planned.

'Thanks to Mandy for being so honest and direct with her account of what Max means to her. Once again, I would like to share my hope with all you Max fans out there that he is safe and well.'

Oola took a look at her clipboard. Fan number three, a nineteen-year-old girl who said she wanted to be identified as 'Beth', though that was not her real name.

'Beth, *goood* evening,' the DJ chirped in an attempt to lighten the tone, swing things along to keep the advertisers happy.

'Hi,' she said, a monosyllable in a slow, deep monotone.

'Well,' the DJ began to rant, 'sightings of Max have been

flooding into the radio station all day. Members of the public have claimed to've seen him all over the city looking distinctly fragile. Max, if you're listening out there, why not phone in to put all our minds at rest or, even better, pop by the studio. You know where we're at.'

Oola rolled her eyes. She could not wait for the present contract with the radio station to reach its full term. This guy, she thought, was such a jerk.

As Oola was about to ask the question she had ready, the fan named Beth jumped the gun.

'Y'know, this last week has been just horrible,' she began. 'Max means so much to me. I've been really frightened, frightened of my own emotions, of what I've been feeling. When I first *discovered* Max I thought, oh, lucky little mousy old me, someone really worth following at last. Someone with substance, *heart*.'

Oola had a feeling that this one was going to take over the show, talk her heart out. Behind the panel the producer and engineer were both gazing intently towards this Beth character. The DJ had raised an eyebrow. The tone of the young woman's monologue was magnetic. Irresistible radio.

'I am quite confident that Max will turn up in a week or so. I reckon he's just burned out after the tour and's taking time off. Some of the gutter press have suggested that his going missing might be a publicity stunt, but I don't think so. I feel that he is alive and I feel that he *will* go on and be better for whatever he is going through right now.'

Oola looked at the black nail varnish, the silver rings on every finger, the combination of black leather, purple suede and white satin.

'How does Max inspire you, Beth?'

'Oh, in so many ways. I've become so much more aware of the beauty of nature since Max came into my life. Sunrises, sunsets, the chill in the autumn air, the nostalgia of the sea.

Being in contact with Max through his music has most definitely changed me for the better. When I look back on my life before Max, well . . . it was so mundane. I feel more confident now, more my own person.'

Oola thought she sounded anything but. Brainwashed, more like.

'Have you ever written to him?' Oola asked.

'I haven't, no,' came the instant reply. 'Sometimes, when I have unmanageable emotions, I'm tempted to put pen to paper but I don't. I never push my emotions on to other people. You hear of fans who have sent forty-two-foot letters to the fan club and stuff like that, and I just think how *pathetic.*'

'How many times have you seen Max perform live?'

'Eleven times. I've tried to see him more than that but tickets jus' go so fast. Often I have to travel to see him. It can all get expensive, what with trains and hotels an' all.'

'Tell us about the best time at a gig.'

'Oh, undoubtedly when I was in the third row, over to the right of the stage by the piano in January last year. It was freezing cold outside, baking in – like the heating had been turned up too high by accident. Just as the backing band came on to take their positions, I felt like I wanted to scream and scream and scream. I was very tense. I'm so envious of the girl who plays the harp, the three who make up the violin section, the four backing singers. When Max came onstage I clapped so much my hands were swollen afterwards and I had no voice for days.'

Oola nodded, then shot a glance towards the producer beyond the glass partition. Something was worrying her, something she could not pinpoint.

'After Max had finished singing a ballad at the piano, he shielded his eyes from the lights as he looked out into the crowd and . . . he looked at me. Right into my eyes, for like three or four seconds. Our eyes just locked. When I smiled he

240

seemed to chuckle, but nicely – not taking the piss, like. It took me a month before I could play one of his CDs or look at one of his DVDs without tears rolling down my cheeks.'

Beth suddenly sat up. Something in the interviewee had changed. She seemed to grow in stature. The atmosphere in the cramped studio altered suddenly. It was a power-cut transition which filled Oola with fear. The studio became grave and quiet. Though up on the sixtieth floor, high above the city, it felt like a padded cell, underground.

The fan's face had paled, become glazed. Then she smiled and did something that the listeners could not see or hear. There was a clatter of bracelets as her left arm was unveiled of an embroidered tulip sleeve, revealing a forearm that made Oola gasp.

'I should say, at this point,' the DJ interjected rapidly, 'that Beth has just shown both Oola and myself . . .'

Oola raised a hand to stop the DJ.

'Beth,' Oola said in as controlled a voice as she could muster, 'I can see your forearm, but the listeners can't. Could you please describe the tattoo on your forearm for the listeners?'

Beth inhaled quietly, exhaled theatrically.

'Well, it's a six-by-three-inch, four-coloured tattoo of Max as he appears on the cover of the second album, *This Very Moment*. It took three sittings to complete, each sitting taking three hours. It'll be there until the day I die, and so will this one.'

Beth ripped the blouse she was wearing, from neckline to waist, with one motion. There, across her stomach, was an enormous tattoo of Max's face.

'Beth,' the DJ burst in, shielding his eyes from all that exposed flesh, 'thanks for coming by and talking to us.' He moved on swiftly. 'Now time for a few words from Max himself, a repeat of some questions I put to him during his tour earlier this month.'

As Beth was escorted not just out of the studio but out of the building by two security guards, following an instinctive concern the producer felt he had to act on, the next fan entered the studio.

'You okay, Roberto?' Oola asked.

'Getting there. It was what was written across her tits that freaked me.'

Oola nodded.

'What was that all about?'

'Fourth single,' Oola answered authoritatively. 'Title.'

'The devil's a gentleman' is not something I'd want tattooed in red and yellow capitals across my boobies, Oola thought to herself. Wonder how many times that one has been sectioned.

A tall young man in his early twenties entered the studio, sat himself down. Very much a Max lookalike, from newly shaved head to purple suede boots, he picked up on the weird vibe that had been generated in the studio.

'You're *Blue*, right?' the DJ asked. His manner was just a little too clinical. A little dismissive, Oola thought.

'Correct,' the Max devotee replied rather briskly.

Oola checked the wall clock, then her clipboard. When the taped interview with Max came to an end the DJ gushed about how the lines had been jammed all day by well-wishers; he then read out a list of names of fans, promising to dedicate the next song to them all. On came a rare demo version of 'Up To The Edge', Max's chart-topping second single.

'Oh, *wow*,' Blue said under his breath to Oola. 'I just hope my girlfriend is taping this right.'

Recorded in a subway tunnel on the east side of the city, the footsteps of commuters seemed to act as an an accompaniment to the song.

'Did you know he was making this up as it was being recorded?' Blue said to Oola. 'He was improvising. All the first songs were made up that way, complete improvisations. He

242

used to do that at all the early gigs, there'd always be a spot towards the end of the show where he would get out a notebook, put it on a stand, backing band offstage for a while, and he'd just go for it.'

Oola nodded. She was tired. Wanted this to finish. Go home. Bed.

'Next up we have Blue,' the DJ said. 'How's it going, Blue?' he asked, bright and breezy.

'Pretty fuckin' shit, obviously. Asshole.'

Oola struggled to keep the smirk in. He had made his point. Max was missing and chirpy small talk was inappropriate.

'Max obviously means a lot to you,' the DJ said a little sheepishly, though becoming aloof as he recovered from the rebuke.

'Soon as I wake up there he is. The first thing I think of is either my girlfriend, then Max . . . or Max, then my girlfriend. He's just the best. Best in terms of lyrical content, best in terms of being a solo performer, best in terms of being a . . . *spiritual* influence, I guess. There are so many different kinds of love. There's the love I have for my girlfriend, Yelena. There's the love I have for my parents. There's the love I have for my friends. Then there's the love I have for Max, which feels like the biggest love affair ever. What I feel for Max is what I feel love should be. I don't expect to ever meet him, I don't want anything from him, I just want him to be there for me, doing what he does. I want him to be happy.'

'Right,' Oola said, nodding. Encouraging him to go deeper.

'I hope he's okay. I feel that he isn't gone. I don't get a dead feeling in the air. I feel that he's here. Y'know, *alive*. Just floating right now, do you know what I mean? That's what I hope, that he's in limbo and will be back soon.'

Six foot two, and beginning to cry. The DJ did not move a muscle. Oola, too, stayed absolutely still. The engineer turned the volume of Blue's microphone up so that his sniffing and breathing difficulties were being picked up clearly. All those little exhalations through his nostrils, all those occasional wipes of his face with dry hands. The webcam was getting it all, on zoom.

'Y'know,' Blue said, struggling to control his voice, 'it's such a great feeling being at his gigs. Complete strangers catch hold of your hands. You're all united, united as one. He creates so much magic, and the warmth that runs between us is like an electric shock. Jus' wonderful.'

Then he broke down again, fully, and the fluctuations of tone in his voice brought tears to Oola's eyes. There were sounds like iron being dragged against iron.

'To think that one man can do that to so many people,' Blue continued. 'Am*aaa*zing.'

He sniffed. Inhaled. Was suddenly back in control.

'I can be a bit of a neurotic when he comes on TV, just like I was a minute ago when you played that demo of "Up To The Edge". I'm always worried that it hasn't taped properly, that I haven't got it. Y'know?'

Oola nodded.

'Yeah, I know that feeling. I think we've all been there,' she said with the warmth of recognition in her voice.

# 9

An imaginary finger began stroking his shoulder blades. That imaginary finger then travelled up his neck, to circle the outer edges of his ear. Max, on the other side of the wall. Sleeping. Unaware. Watched.

The enormous weariness compounded of gratitude, melancholy and frustration that suffused Angela's face pressed through that little hole into Max's side of the bedroom wall. Such was the young woman's intensity of feeling, it was surprising a little snaking smoke did not rise up from her vantage point.

Max's sheet had shifted in sleep. His long, pale, totally passive form was laid out for her, and she gulped down the view. How she wanted to push down that flimsy physical barrier between them and swoop down to kiss and kiss that waist of his, licking along each rib. Those fragile bones, displayed in a neat tracery under that thin skin. His. *Him.*

Angela put her left nostril to the carefully drilled hole, inhaled. She wanted to suck in the undiluted odour of him as it rose from the nape of his neck, his hair, from that gap just under each shoulder blade, the wrinkle inside his elbows. It was rising now, that odour. Off him. Like a gentle breeze. But nothing. Only plaster dust, a hint of yellowing paperbacks.

Angela began to sob. Only by changing her spread fingers into cold, tight fists did she manage to gain control over her breathing, concealing the outpouring.

Unaware that she was outlining the wall with the sweat off her body, she took another look. Her warm lips wanted to skim over the twin flowers of his bare feet, tasting salty toes. All she could taste were her tears.

You should stop, stop right now, Angela told herself. Go and rustle up some breakfast. She had the routines of the day to activate. Routines with their respective, unvarying courses – measured and ritualistic. The first of these would be to flick the television on. Get the news. See what the weatherman had to say for himself.

Normally Angela did not pay much attention to the stuffy old bore who did a three-minute review of what the papers were full of, but that morning she was hanging on his every word. Three papers were running headline stories on some radio show featuring Max fans. One had an EXCLUSIVE!. Some weirdo named Beth had . . .

Angela was so unnerved that she found the news report hard to follow. She felt her body temperature first lower then rise steeply as the gradual loss of ownership sank in. Some *fan* had sold a story about Max. 'THE MAX I KNOW,' the headline ran.

Angela dressed quickly, ran all the way to the newsagent's.

Through the tiny cracks of pretend-asleep eyes, dim fingers of light hit his retina. The field of vision was small. He could smell her, and then the stink of the newspapers she was holding. Max wondered what Angela was up to. He struggled to keep his breathing sleepy.

Now he could hear her, that jagged breath as her lips joined and separated quickly. Attempting to breathe the deep, re-laxed breath of sleep was too much of a challenge. Inhalation and exhalation ceased. He froze.

'You awake?' Angela asked two freckles and a mole.

She wanted the delicate bloom and loveliness of him to stay

with her for ever. But he would go. Soon. She knew it. She felt powerless.

'You'd better see this.'

Max rolled over, propped himself up. Headlines were not such big news to him. It was not the first time there had been a cover story about him. As he glanced towards Angela, a stubbly eyebrow raised sceptically, he wondered how much this latest whoever had been paid for some cobbled-together EXCLUSIVE! story.

Max took in enough information within just a minute. Radio show. Oola Khan. Fans.

With a smile towards Angela, he said, 'Today I think I'm going to . . . go swimming.'

Angela was amazed.

'Then maybe go to the park, feed the ducks.'

Angela was at a total loss for words.

Max sniffed as he looked towards the window.

'Looks like it's gonna be a nice day.'

Angela stood.

'Back at the usual time?' Max asked.

'Yeah.'

'I'll fix some dinner.'

Angela smiled and backed out of the room pretty fast. The tears were starting up again. She felt that dinner was probably going to be a last supper. The front door closed quietly behind her.

When Max left the apartment, close to an hour later, Minty stood by the door, sniffing the world beyond through the letterbox. First the tail was swishing with anger, then it drooped, indicating despondency, resignation.

That dive was a moment. Instantly he was loving the water, the *feel* of the water.

Diving into the perfect smoothness of an empty pool to swim a whole length alone, Max thrilled to the sight of his pale hands showing in sharp focus through the clear water before him, feeling next to zero resistance. The fast rising of all those tiny bubbles breaking around his legs tingled. Some of those polished bubbles seemed to be sticking there, glued to him, buoying him up.

Still no one – the pool was his. It was like being a kid again, first customer of the day through the turnstile. There'll be others soon enough, Max thought.

He swam a length, fast. Then the turn. Sudden, as if he had just remembered that he had forgotten something and needed to return to fetch it. It was 1 – flip – 2 – flip – 3 – the astonishing whites of the soles of his feet turning on that slippery tiled wall no problem. Back and forth, one end to the other. 4 – 5 – flips, converts, and gone all in one yet again, breathing to the right every four strokes.

Here we go, he thought. There, an elderly couple, following their doctor's good advice. There, a teenaged girl, all alone.

Just for a micro-slice second, Max thought the girl was watching him as his head emerged from the aquamarine blur of breaststroke. A millisecond. Long enough to greedily, guiltily, sneak a peek. Was she? Had Max been recognised, even with the disguise of the Speedo swimming cap and reflective goggles?

The intimacy of the girl's gaze was long and detailed.

Max swam for another ten minutes. Crawl mainly. He felt safer face down, concentrating on his streamlining, shoulder touch and bilateral breathing drills.

When he emerged from the water the young girl was still watching.

She knows, Max thought. I've been sussed.

The lights were green all the way, something which seemed to displease the cab-driver.

Max had not visited the capital's main park for many years. He had forgotten what a tourist attraction it was.

Feeling like a pervert, looking worse, he made for the lake. He sat for a while on a bench by the water, watching a few grebes enjoy the stale white bread he had brought with him. Crows in the branches above, he counted nine, were making a lot of noise with their incessant cawing.

Time moved slowly.

Two women passed by with a little boy who looked as though a terminal disease was winning against the immune system behind his skin. They sat down by the water's edge and took a few snaps of the child feeding the ducks. Just as they were about to leave, the little boy ran up to Max and whispered, 'I'm not well, y'know.'

He felt like an invisible man under the branches of that huge, solid old tree. That section of the parkland felt more like a heath. Wild.

It had been a long while since Max had climbed a tree. The desire to climb had not been resisted. The impulse to get naked was subjected to only a few seconds' delay. At first Max thought he would just remove his T-shirt, but when he felt the sun and air against his skin, off came everything – even the protection of his Reeboks.

Storing his clothes in the safety of an old bird's nest, up he climbed.

'No one about. Not a soul.'

It felt good up there, in a spot where he could lean back against the main trunk of the tree, arms supported by branches, legs splayed.

When he felt the need to piss twenty minutes later, he did so schoolboy style. Down, spraying the leaves, swerving his penis in slow figures of eight to see the glittering drops.

He felt so free. So liberated. And, finally, in control.

He would, he decided, have to be the one who steered his future, not pig management, not pig record company, not pig PR. None of that lot.

More than anything, Max felt it was time for him to get himself a base. A home. Something of his own. Money, after all, was no problem. He could have what he wanted, where he wanted. Anything.

The cat's mouth was open, tongue protruding slightly over bottom teeth in the suckling position, her throat occasionally making a gentle swallowing action. Legs twitching, face occasionally twisted with fear, the cat was dreaming: dreaming of being a kitten.

Max followed the cooking instructions carefully. Buying the ingredients had been the worst part of preparing the meal. So much to hunt out, so much to sort. The gnocchi pasta, the making of the tomato-and-garlic sauce, sprinkled with pine nuts which he had roasted himself.

'Shit, I've made enough salad for six.'

Enough salad for six, enough Dutch fries for more. But he knew Angela would go for those potato chips, smothered with cheese and spring onions as they were. She liked that kind of combination. Hot and creamy.

'Nearly time,' Max said aloud as he glanced towards the kitchen wall clock.

Up he went to the roof of the building one more time. Everything was nearly ready up there. The picnic blanket was out, scatter cushions, bottle of chilled white wine, candles for later. There was still plenty of heat in the last of the sun.

The heat was rising up off the concrete of the street and roof, the grey metal of the building's air ventilation system.

'Oh,' Angela said, genuinely touched when Max led her up to the roof. 'I've lived here ages and have never thought of coming up here once. It's lovely.'

She did not say thanks. Thanks would have been too much. There was already a finality in the air, the feeling of closing curtains.

To Angela, the view was a blur: shape without form, shade without colour. She felt paralysed as she lowered herself on to a cushion.

Minty joined them up there, delighted by so many new places to explore.

'Yum,' Angela said, eyes wide, as she got a first taste of the avocado starter. Max's home-made vinaigrette dressing was a scorcher, sharp with ginger and black pepper. The flavour seemed just right to her. That hint of sweet red peppers and tarragon.

'Let me get your camera,' Max said. 'I'll take a pic of you 'n' the cat.'

Angela usually felt self-conscious in front of a camera, but she knew he was going. Knew he was leaving her. Time was up. Her concern was that she would not be able to hold back the tears as that big black eye of the camera focused upon her.

'Hey,' she said, and Max knew what was coming, 'let me take a couple of you instead.'

Sensing her discomfort, Max succumbed.

'Over there,' he said, pointing towards the grey of the ventilation system.

All he was wearing was the outsized Bermuda shorts he had bought for swimming.

'You've caught the sun,' Angela said as she sorted out a

depth of field appropriate to the fast-failing lighting conditions. 'Look really well.'

'What a difference a few days makes.'

*Click.*

Angela took a step closer. *Clickclickclick.*

The point of focus kept changing. The curve of Max's shoulders, his mouth. Ultimately, it was those eyes which Angela chose to zoom in on.

And again. *Clickclickclick.*

'Look away. Now look back at me.'

And he did. As instructed. Straight into camera. Perfect. A stunning facial expression. Then something to do with the mouth, a moment which was pure magic. The way he was stretching forward, leaning towards Angela.

*Clickclickclick.*

'That's it,' Angela said, as a little red light atop the camera began to flash. 'Film's come to an end.'

*Our* little film has come to an end, Angela thought.

'It'll be interesting to see how these turn out,' she said casually.

Something felt wrong as Angela pressed the rewind button on the camera. Was Max resenting the fact that she had taken these photographs? The photographs of him by the duckweed-covered lake, the photographs by the sea, too?

'Hey,' she said, handing the roll of film to Max, 'souvenir.'

There, again. The finality. Recognised.

Max wanted to nod just a little. Or smile. He did neither as he pocketed the roll of film.

In this last of meeting places they avoided too much speech.

Max's smile was the sweetest moment of unexpected appreciation.

A second's clumsiness, then Max moved forward. Breathing in through parted lips, he held that breath, then exhaled just the tiniest little bit as he moved towards Angela to give the lightest fingertip touch to the side of her face. Then he moved closer. Held her.

A goodbye hug.

Part Three

# Part Three

# 1

The staff at Furnace Records made Max feel special as a piece of junk mail, the kind where your name is filled in by a computer on a pre-printed letter. From reception to press office, it was as if a memo had circulated, instructing all to be just a bit off with Max, if not a little frosty. Only Pshemko in the fan club showed any warmth.

'Hey,' he had said on seeing Max's cropped head, now perhaps the length of a number three, 'Hitler would have approved.'

Only Pshemko had given Max a smile and a prolonged hug in which he had noted a new mould of muscles that had formed under Max's soft boy skin, anything but the usual clingflim-on-bone feel. It was an embrace from which Pshemko withdrew a little shaky, the whites of his eyes clear through the tears which had suddenly welled up.

Max smiled. Said, 'Now, let me take a look at *you*.'

Pshemko's outfit of the day was a candy-striped suit with a colour scheme perhaps based on sweeties made in chemical factories and Henley Regatta. On Pshemko the effect was part dandy, part schoolboy. Not unattractive – just loud. A full-on, head-to-toe clash.

Max had always been fond of Pshemko. He had already decided that this young black guy was to be the vital member of his new team. There would be him, Max hoped, and – if she agreed to it – Angela. Max had done a lot of thinking on his recent walks, in that pool, up that tree.

Angela – she's too smart to be a sub at some dumb

magazine. Way too smart. Once I've sorted everything out this end, I'll call her, ask her whether she'd be interested. She'd be good for me, good to have around.

'Live through this?' Angela asked the contents of the glass knife rack beside her. 'Can you?'

That fine collection of hand-honed zirconium ceramic kitchen knives stayed silent, did not answer. Their only communication back to her was a shiny jigsaw of fragmented reflections. There was the fish/meat knife (length 156mm), the fruit/vegetable knife (length 130mm), the cook's knife (length 140mm), the general-purpose knife (length 110mm), the multi-purpose knife (length 105mm).

Beside her, the shark knife set, already out of the aluminium briefcase and ready. Cool stainless-steel handles with molybdenum vanadium steel blades, ready. Very strong and very durable, ready. To her right, that durable Kevlar zipped wallet, unopened as yet. Close by. Ready.

Max had been sweet, Max had been a dream. Now Max had gone. The number of his cellphone, that was all she had, just that point of contact. He had said that he would call, but that it would be in a few days at least. Getting back into gear, he had said, would take a while. But he had promised, said he would call.

'Yeah, right.'

Angela looked at the telephone. She should have been calling the office. Work. To phone in sick. But she felt that she would not be able to talk. Her throat felt so tight. Her head – *bleached*. She had cried that much. Cried for hours.

He had left at noon after one last night in separate beds. She had watched him sleeping from dawn until ten, when he had rolled over – turning his back on her until she had woken him with freshly squeezed apple juice.

'Alcohol,' she announced to Minty, 'that's what I'm gonna have to go shopping for. Lots of lovely alcohol.'

Her mind was replaying those final hours, over and over. She had no control of the flashbacks. Within minutes of getting up, Max had gone to the bathroom. Angela had seen it all, taking it all in like someone in a fairground tent.

Max, Angela thought, lying there. Just lying there, looking up at the ceiling. With his arms stretched out behind his head, the gulley of his left armpit had been the focal point. Then the line of his neck, from where jawline connected to collar bone. His little nipples: flat and boyishly pink. The outer tips of his shoulders, rosy with sunburn.

Though her fingers had done a certain amount of roaming, all she had felt was doors slowly closing.

He won't come back. Even though he took the spare set of keys with him, that's that. The end. Finito.

Some grit had blown into Angela's eyes as she got off the bus. She had spent the last five minutes rubbing them as she'd walked and, as a result, they were heavily bloodshot.

The slow simmer of anger was building to a bubbling-hot rage. Internally, Angela began to chronically excrete higher levels of catecholamines – the chemicals epinephrine, norepinephrine and dopamine. This triggered hyperarousal. A familiar chain reaction.

'Alcohol,' Angela said as the glass filled. 'See, I went out and got some.'

The drinking started as soon as Angela had fed the cat. She uncorked two bottles of Côte du Rhône which she left in chambré on the kitchen table. She then peeled off her clothes, showered, brushed her teeth, applied a dab of Chanel No. 19 to her temples, and then filled a blue Moroccan goblet to the brim.

'Cheers,' she said to her cat, who was watching her coolly.

Angela took a swig, swallowed loudly. Quite a gulp.

Minty vanished, under the sofa. She knew the old routine.

Angela emptied the contents of two carrier bags out on to the table. She looked with satisfaction at the chaotic spread which would soon fill her: all her favourite things. How would she start? Brie on Pringles?

No, not yet. She wanted to get some kind of lighting concept going. Dotting the kitchen, bathroom and her bedroom with candles took a while. It was a little cool in the flat, so she turned all four rings on the gas hob up high. A neat little blaze. It was then that she started on the Brie and Pringles, the olives and hummus, the Bounty bars and cup cakes, the . . .

The ochre glow given off by the dozen candles lighting the kitchen did not soothe sufficiently. This combination of alcohol, food and lighting and . . . Angela realised she had forgotten the fourth ingredient, music. She had not sorted out the music concept. The idea of a Max CD was out of the question. She hunted out some vintage dub, old scratched vinyl by King Tubby.

By eight, Angela was pissed off that she was still sober. Although she was well into the second bottle of wine, that floaty feeling was not there. She still felt too real, too Angela.

Sitting cross-legged on the floor, she held the reluctant cat close to her as she continued to chew through her extensive comfort shopping.

'Go on, then,' Angela spat at Minty, 'fuck off, then.'

The cat had wriggled around in her arms too long. Had scratched.

Lips stained red, breasts dotted with crumbs, splatters of chocolate and a few dribbles of her own making, Angela began to cry.

Picking up a candle, she wondered whether what she was about to do would hurt. Perhaps as much as a soup spoon's worth of hot red wax had accumulated atop the candle. She held it close to her face, then turned it sideways. She let out an involuntary gasp. The hot red wax which had splashed across her throat travelled down to the base of her neck then slowed up as it hardened.

It had not hurt, not half enough.

This time Angela picked up two candles. Again she held them close to her face. This time she lowered the candles slowly towards her nipples. Applying the wax slowly to the focal point of each of her flabby, saggy breasts, Angela knew that she would soon be milking each candle in the apartment for the hot wax they could supply her with.

Where might it hurt most? Angela thought. She soon found out. Answer? Inside leg, close to cunt. Almost in there.

More teasing than the hot wax, however, was the idea of that flame. The small, flickering flame of each candle had the potential to make her forget about herself for a while. A burn here, and here, she thought, would soon have the endorphins coursing through her.

Angela put a teaspoon over the flame of a candle. When the handle became warm she knew the thing was ready. She turned the spoon over, saw the blackened underside. Wondered how much that would hurt if she put it on her tongue.

She decided against using the hot teaspoon upon herself. 'Uh-uh.'

Reasoning that a teaspoon was way too small an object, that a greater pain was what she merited, Angela stumbled towards the kitchen drawer and pulled out a soup ladle. It took a while to heat, but the pain that lowered ladle inflicted upon the target of her navel was instant. She knew she would blister, knew the area would be marked – a new fixture among the existing collection.

Now that she had the one wound, the one pain, she knew that the way of lessening the intensity of that focus was through diversion. Her forearms itched for attention. Old wounds pleaded to be reopened, reinvestigated. Her flesh needed air. Her hot blood needed release. Angela needed the reassurance of the sight of her own blood. That would calm her and, eventually, make her come.

She sniffed. Poured herself another full goblet of wine. Downed it. Then she shook her head at the candles she had been using. In terms of foreplay they were passable, but only that. She needed pins, now. She needed long needles to scratch with.

'No hurry,' Angela said to the third bottle of red wine which she cracked open. 'Plenty of time.'

She hacked off the rough skin of a pineapple, cut out the bad bits, then chewed with delight.

Crawling across the kitchen floor, she was intent on scuffing her knees. She wished it were rough concrete that she was grazing her knees raw upon. She wished she were being beaten, not by a man but by many women. For being a fool. For being such a bloody, fat fool. She felt she deserved a good whipping, a branding.

At times, and this was one of them, when she was on the border of what she was about to start, about to do, she felt she should flee the apartment. Run to a phone box, call one of those helplines. She had done it once. Frightening herself with a boning knife one time, a boning knife which she had stared at too long, a potentially lethal instrument held above her heart with both hands, she had managed to drop the thing, throw on a raincoat, grab her purse, her keys and stumble out into the night.

Hadn't done her much good. The person on the other end of the helpline had not been able to make out so much as a name. All that sobbing, all that difficulty with breathing. The one slurred, staccato sentence that she had managed was 'Fat bitch, fat fuckin' bitch'. The person at the other end of the line, new as a volunteer and someone in need of improving their listening skills, had slammed the phone down on Angela. Too much at 2 a.m. in a small room all alone.

That was a year back. The memory faded from Angela's mind.

'Time to start on the vodka,' she said to the fridge.

It took Angela a while to get herself moving, but once she had started the routine of making a nice strong double, she looked remarkably in control of herself. That felt good. Then she fell over, not only dropping her drink but shattering the glass.

'Shit!' she screamed. *'Shitshitshit!'*

Glass, one of her favourites. As a seventeen-year-old, Angela had started with pins, quickly graduating to needles, nails, screws, razor blades, glass, knives and – top of the class – a carpet cutter she still treasured. One large shard glittered so invitingly. Long and elegant, it was still attached to the stem of the glass. The shard possessed a delicacy. Press too hard into the skin, that shard seemed to whisper, and I will snap. You have to go lightly with me. Be gentle with me and I will be gentle with you.

Angela got to her hands and knees and shuffled across to the shard. She picked it up with one hand, then held it close to her face for a good look at the point of the thing.

Her breathing calmed her. Became steady. Deep.

'I want to cut my life into pieces,' she said. The words were the opening line to a song. She was sure of that. Just could not remember *which* song, *which* band. It was a line that had been swamped into her head by the tide of the unhealthy mental filth rising up from the charts, she knew that much. American kids, she could recall, raging. Pierced and tattooed. Screaming themselves hoarse, spreading the negative word.

High levels of dopamine, adrenalin and norepinephrine were driving Angela to do it: cut. Skin that had once felt the warmth and softness of a cuddly blanket felt numb. Skin that had felt the discomfort of a wet diaper, the pain of a fever, nothing. Skin that had never felt the exploring hands of a lover – blank. The sight of blood flowing from that soft exterior would prove there was life inside.

'This'll do nicely,' Angela said. 'Time to cut the skin, draw some blood.'

Methodically, tracing her skeleton, mapping the pain she felt inside, Angela began to cut. The pain she felt was mute, her only cry a bright red scream. The unkindest cut, she thought, was Max's departure. She felt cut off, cut out of the picture.

After three neat, shallow cuts, the entire world wore a 'CLOSED' sign.

'Good girl, bad girl,' she whispered to herself as the endorphin response began to flood her with the body's natural opiates, providing a form of analgesia. She had got to know a lot about the raising of enkephalin levels from self-help books which held so many handy hints in the tales of self-destruction.

The worry circuits of Angela's brain which had been hot and buzzing began to cool and calm as the equivalent to an injection of eight milligrams of morphine hit her. The critical neurotransmitter that influences mood and aggression, serotonin, was now at a decreased level.

She could feel herself floating to the top of the room and disappearing into the wallpaper. Soon the sense of peace and euphoria would recede, Angela knew that, and all she would feel would be shame and regret.

Taking a look at herself in the bathroom mirror, at what she had come to term her 'time suit', Angela found some comfort in her appearance: her outside was beginning to match her inside. The sight and sensation of her flowing blood were not, however, having the usual effect.

'Not at all.'

There was the old temptation to lop off her breasts, invade her vagina. Acts which she always thought of as 'painting the town red'. She looked deeply into her eyes. These eyes told her nothing about who she was, what she was. Only what she was going to do, eventually. Soon.

She raised both hands, so that the warm flesh of her palms met the cold reflection of glass.

Angela knelt at the entrance to her bedroom, resting her head against the frame of the door. It felt like a stage direction. [Angela enters room, kneels.]

Kneeling there, clock ticking down internally, she surveyed the room.

Lines which Angela could not get out of her head were circling her brain. Piano. The swirling came to her at the strangest moments. The gentle tinkling of a piano, over and over. Single notes in slow succession. Simple patterns, stuck. Repeating with a sustained clarity, a hypnotic buoyancy. A persistence.

It had been a long while since she had gone through her record collection. All the vital elements of her life were in a suitcase she kept under her bed. Music. Music she had hunted out by herself. Recordings she had somehow managed to hear about and had sought, found, purchased at – sometimes – considerable expense.

'Laurie Anderson, Elgar, Brian Eno, Felt.' She said the names quietly to herself, perhaps the way a school teacher might, remembering the names of pupils past.

'Philip Glass, Josquin, Billy MacKenzie.'

The tears began, as she knew they would, as Angela looked at the cover of *Beyond the Sun*, MacKenzie's last album before he took his life in a cold garden shed. She held the CD to her forehead, cooling her brow.

'And Wim Mertens,' Angela said with finality. She had found the CD she had been looking for, something entitled *Stratégie de la Rupture*. There it was, track two. 'Wia.'

'Three minutes, thirty-one seconds.'

She pressed POWER, then PLAY. And on it came, track two. Angela began to bawl as soon as the music started, and continued to cry long after she had pressed the STOP button. Thirty-four seconds, that had been enough. All she could take. Her last listen.

The CD mirrored her face too cruelly as she returned it to the transparent plastic casing.

All Angela had was her music, she realised that now. Nothing but music, music, music. She had been a consumer for years, got through so many shopping lists for 'product' at HMV, Virgin, Tower Records. All those stores. Shiny black vinyl, smear-free CDs. Her collection. Destined for the bin.

That morning she had wondered whether a bin was the right place for that collection. She was tempted to box it up neatly, leaving it in the elevator at different times of the day, or out on walls, the seat of an empty train carriage. A park bench, perhaps, she had thought. Lots of park benches. Kind of like spreading my ashes.

'Wim Mertens,' Angela said, wishing he were there with her now. Surely, she thought, someone who could produce such music would be capable of giving her the hug she needed right at that moment.

Inhaling deeply, steadying herself, Angela was intent on continuing what she had started. She wanted to play another track.

Laid out in front of her was everything Mertens had ever recorded – she had the lot. Warm fingertips touched the edges of cool black vinyl, CDs reflected (none too prettily) her upside-down reflection. A decision had been made. She would have just the one track: 'Maximizing the Audience' from the album of the same name.

'Eleven minutes, forty-three seconds,' Angela said, perhaps in the same way a junkie might measure the amount of morphine about to be imbibed.

As soon as the paired voices of Ine van den Bergh and Valerie Koolemans-Beijnen started up, Angela began to fizzle and melt. When the soprano saxophone began, her eyes felt as if they were bleeding. These were hot tears. The hottest.

She gazed up, vision blurred. Her eyes met his, Max's crudely mass-reproduced eyes.

Her favourite poster of Max had been shot by Sabdy Zaitchik. In Holland, perhaps, France or Germany. Max, with his arms wrapped around himself, self-comforting, wearing nothing but his black leather trousers. All that long hair of his, blowing. Before it was all cut. Off.

Max, in a field of poppies. All that red behind him, out and out and out of focus. All those gradations of red. Red gone increasingly grainy. Splatters of red, red, red.

That poster was something Angela particularly enjoyed after a few initial cuts, that almost lifesize poster of Max. A little perspiration on his forehead had run, matting his eyebrows. Eyelashes, too, stuck together, perhaps with tears. Max, in those black leather trousers, based on the design of classic Levi's. Beltless, cheap brassy zipper appearing exposed, forced out by his no doubt delicious genitalia. Cheap brassy zipper, glinting like a precious metal. It was a zip that led eyes in. There were dark shadows there. What would that entrance smell of? Fresh cake? Raspberries? A hint of popcorn? Angela wondered about that for a while. The perfume of Max's body.

Max, there in front of her, long-haired Max, just staring, staring out. Staring out above Angela's head for ever, the way he had stared out above the photographer's head momentarily as instructed.

Long hours Angela had gazed at that picture, that mass-produced image.

A shutter of hardness dropped down the length of the young woman's face. The flash of realisation was so swift, so overwhelming. It was like being jerked into consciousness from a week of deep sleep. The absolute certainty was too much. He had gone and that was it. Over.

Angela kicked her record player, ending the music with a *wrrruuup*.

That felt good, that outburst. That release of anger.

Angela sat on her bed and shook the frame with her heaving cries. Every detail of the world within that cramped room was the same. It should not have been. Pictures should have been crooked, curtains torn and flapping in the wind. But everything was the same.

Measuring out ingredients with speedy confidence, preparing with dexterity, cleaning up carefully as she went along, Angela began to make a cake. Tentacles of dough hung from her fingers.

I can't bake a cake with so many tears in it, she thought. Then she felt the need. Oh yes I can. She added more chopped nuts, more sultanas.

The mix got dumped into a tray, shoved into the pre-heated oven. There was another bottle to get through before that dessert would be ready.

Angela was sat there, by the window, on the sofa, snoring. Like a bean-bag sculpture with a loud mouth.

A spot above her lip was ready to burst.
She didn't hear the phone ringing. And ringing.
Her loss.

# 2

Slow morning rain.

At first there was no one about. Angela liked the bench, thought of it as hers. A quiet spot, surrounded by the tallest of fir trees. She liked that, too. Always got the sun so nicely at that time of day. At night, lovers would sit on the bench, hidden from streetlights as it was.

Being just that bit tucked away, Angela felt quite comfortable about letting her absolute misery get some air – it was totally unzipped for all to see.

She needed the family-sized bottle of Coca-Cola. Needed the fizz and glug of it. Needed that internal tingle. Also much needed was the crunch of those Pringles. One was never enough. Three at a time was just right. Three gave a good crunch, plenty to chew on.

'Damn.'

Once in a while it happened, company. Behind her, in the bushes, there was a rustling. Flasher, rapist or dosser? Angela wondered.

A man emerged from the bushes. Not realising that a young woman was sitting there, watching, the man shook out two old blankets with much muttering to himself. No costume cupboard, no wardrobe manager, could have dreamed up the rags the man was wearing.

He was not alone. Now emerging from the bushes was a

similarly dressed man with no teeth. He was speaking in a dialect which, to Angela's ear, not only sounded of far away but also of long ago.

Angela stopped breathing, just for a moment. No inhalation/exhalation at all. She did not want to be seen. A triple Pringle sandwich in her mouth softened with jets of warm saliva. She dared not chew. Dared not move a muscle.

Perhaps they will disappear if I close my eyes. Or maybe I will become invisible. Or maybe they will think I'm deep in meditation. Or praying. I certainly wish to God they'd fuck off.

They did. Two old men, in search of a bite to eat – only that – moved away.

When Angela opened her eyes again all she saw was their backs. Old coats, even in the sweltering heat of the day, tied around their waists with long strips of bright orange nylon string. Blankets over shoulders, bursting carrier bags at their sides.

Angela took another glug of her Coca-Cola. Stared straight ahead, beyond the fence of the school playing fields. This time she felt momentarily comforted by what she saw. A teacher, leading a class of girls out for a lesson.

'Fifteen, sixteen, seventeen . . .' Angela half whispered under her breath, counting heads. Class of twenty-eight, or thirty. She was not sure.

'Right, line up!' the teacher barked – a sturdy professional who had the air of someone who had spent half her life working alongside students with reduced hearing.

They all looked so happy, so light and carefree, wearing the whites of a new school term. Angela had always loathed PE. Being the fatty of the class had always been made so patently obvious during those dreaded twice-weekly sessions. To Angela, PE lessons had only helped build a certain amount of mental strength, not physical. The changing rooms were dreaded. The showers? Torture. The humiliation. Teachers were the worst. Was cruelty a part of each school's induction training?

Between the ages of fifteen and seventeen, Angela had attempted the dizzy rapture of starving. She'd failed. After just three days she would binge, gorging herself on everything she had been denying herself times three. She had wanted to be all powerful, stopping the menstrual cycle, reversing the bodily changes of uninvited puberty, denying the process of what she had always thought of as 'motherfucking nature'. The purity and lightness of the anorexic were not for her. As a bulimic, she had attempted to fill that void inside her, soothing herself with food and more food.

Fifteen to seventeen: a cycle of starving and stuffing before the repertoire of self-injury made itself known to her. Fifteen to seventeen: years when a room with a good lock on it was a number-one priority, a room with a sink in it being a plus. Fifteen to seventeen: misery.

'Stretch! Go on, right up. Tiptoes. Over. Hold. Back. Keep breathing. Upupup. Keep the trunk stretched *upward*, no leaning forward. Come on, Quintes. Stretch! Radermacher, don't rush it. Tiptoes. Arms down and re-lax. Well, that was useless.'

The teacher's tone was that of a (totally lesbian) sergeant-major. Echoing off the concrete walls, the voice came from all angles as if by the wonders of Dolby Surround. All more or less the same size, all quite alone on the white lines of the sports pitch, thirty or so teenaged girls in neat rows stopped their clumsy efforts.

Thirty sets of eyes faced forward. Those who had seemed to be fast asleep in a geography lesson just fifteen minutes ago had wakened with leisurely chat with friends while removing jacket, white shirt and all manner of shoes, skirts, socks and silently ticking wristwatches. Each face was intellectually very alive, each had a perpetual listening quality. All looked emotionally blank.

'Right, watch me.'

Smoothly, evenly, again and again in lovely slow motion, the somewhat fierce teacher showed the class how to do the required exercise. How strong, how taut. She dominated the scene. All thirty girls watched the elegance of muscle, cutting through air. It was a stretch, a plain stretch.

'No bouncing at this point. And here . . . push as far as you're comfortable with.'

Unlike Angela's own former school PE teacher, just a few years back, a sadist who felt exercises were only effective when students were on the verge of collapse, this teacher didn't seem to want to hurt: inflicting pain was not her aim. What she wanted to see in her students was sturdy, physical development. Not an inch to pinch.

'Take it gently. Right, let's try it again.'

Eyebrows bunched, waiting for the orders to commence, some of the girls were shivering in anticipation. Every muscle, every sinew, tense. Ready, in rows, on white lines.

'And stretch! Right up. Tiptoes. Over. What did I say about bouncing? Hold. Keep breathing. Back. Upupup. Come on, DiCampo. Stretch! Tiptoes. Very nice, Gitta. Arms down and re-lax. Mm, better.'

Angela was mesmerised. If only I could start again, be that young.

The index finger of her right hand entered her mouth. She gave the finger a light bite, then a harder one which comforted. As a toothing child, Angela had bitten her hands to manage pain. In the following three minutes, her teeth became aggressive attackers.

'Right, four volunteers.'

Thirty arms that could snap like brittle ice shot up. A

chubby girl, not unlike Angela at that age, raised her head, black hair falling across her clear olive face.

This was the same sports pitch on which Angela had once endured the most tortuous PE lessons. The section nearest the fence, however, had been a playground for the juniors. Once there had been a roundabout close to where Angela was sitting, something she had gleefully jumped upon many a time. She shivered a pale green coating of goose bumps at the memory.

Little Angela, a girl who was forever skinning her knees when out riding her bike. Little Angela, a girl forever wearing plasters. Little Angela, who confounded both peers and professionals alike with that odd childhood habit of hers – running backward, fast as anything, to bang herself against a brick wall. So many symptoms had gone unrecognised. Little Angela, the girl who was forever inserting her tiny fingers inside the razor-sharp mouth of a soda can, cutting herself.

Somewhere, back at the apartment, in a suitcase under her bed, was a Hi-8 of her as a child in that playground, screaming. Screaming her head off in delight as she dizzied herself going round and round anticlockwise fast. Days when she often returned home with a headache or nosebleed.

Her mother had been good to her. All those games they had played together in the shade of great trees. All that quality time, even when her time was running out. Even when she was on the way out, chemotherapied sideways, she had removed grit so carefully from between the toes of her little girl after an hour in the sandpit, saying that she was to remember one thing – 'Mommie will always love you.'

Angela was many worlds away from the wonderful world of her first years, when she was a trusting little girl in a nightdress softly printed with kittens playing with balls of wool. The little girl who never knew her father. The little girl who had a day out at the zoo while her mother got buried. Everybody had thought it best. 'You wouldn't have understood your mother's death at that young age,' Angela's aunt had explained with a nagging frequency over the years.

For too long there had been no one to keep her under their wing. No one to guide her through the final years of school, the first years of employment, setting up a home. No one to help out with a little pocket money. Dinner. A night out, something special. A surprise. With the exception of Max turning up on her doorstep, completely out of the blue, there had been very few surprises over the years. She had no gun to protect her, no squad to back her up, no training for the constant combat of her life.

She wanted to be the centre of someone's deep attentiveness. Attention hot as a spotlight, as if she had been picked for something. Encouragement with some kind of unidentifiable excitement behind it.

Halcyon and Prozac had not worked wonders for Angela. Just had not worked.

Oblique reminders of the past swam into Angela's head to tease and torment her: the anarchy of memory. Gently, she began to tear small clumps of hair away from the nape of her neck.

From nearby, a crow let out a sharp caw.

Dissociating into the personality of a five-year-old child, Angela began reliving the things that were once done to her by someone who was supposed to be a carer. Her eyes closed, the reel-to-reel began to play, a film in her head in which she was the screaming star. A film in which she was 'Angel', a vile paedophile's 'Baby'. She had liked being called 'Baby'. All value was lost when she became too rounded. Briefly she had been 'Fatso'. Then 'Porky'.

Not all abusers are men, Angela thought. Not all abusers are men, Angela knew.

With arms folded in front of her, Angela stayed there a long while, on that bench, reciting Japanese syllabary aloud, rolling them off perfectly: 'Ra, ri, ru, re, ro; sa, shi, su, se, so . . .'

# 3

She's not answering, Max thought, as he put his phone down after the twentieth ring. I'll try her at work again later.

He had already tried calling Angela at the office three times, each time getting only her voicemail.

Why isn't she getting back to me?

Despite all the things he had to do, the media whirlwind he was now sucked into because of his 'return', he was concerned about Angela. He knew she'd be missing him.

The reunion would be sweeter for the first of the few tracks he was soon to record, he felt. Later that day he was expected to start the recording of the new album. He had taken the helm with management by insisting that he was only ready to do a few demos, that the time in the studio had to be seen as a time to develop ideas – not lay things down for ever.

She'll enjoy being the first to hear something, even in such a raw state. She'll listen, really listen. Tell me what she thinks.

'I've been rethinking the relationship I have with my fans,' Max said to Oola Khan as the photographer's three assistants were busy taking light readings, setting up reflector boards and arranging and rearranging a backdrop of soft black velvet. 'I feel a certain responsibility that I didn't feel before. Lyrically, I think I need to be kind of careful about what I put out.' He left it at that.

Oola preferred this new Max. Gone was the long hair, the

emaciation. In was that soft, fuzzy crop, making him appear like an Olympic swimmer. He looked so well, had a good colour on him. Seemed to have gained a little weight, toned. That vivacious sclerosis of the spirit had also been spring-cleaned away. He's attractive, Oola thought, and he's attracting me.

'Emil?' the photographer called out to the make-up artist. 'Ready to get started?'

The make-up artist extinguished his cigarette, put down his cellphone, took a few gulps of black coffee.

'What are we going to do about your eyebrows? Do you want me to pencil in a bit, or leave 'em?'

Max took a look at his reflection.

'Leave 'em,' he said.

Max had always liked Emil around on photo-shoots. He was so relaxed, though some interpreted this as a complete lack of interest.

Tiny brushes of mascara lengthened and thickened Max's eyelashes.

'No need for foundation or anything,' Emil discreetly whispered to Max. 'Maybe we'll add just a little gloss to your lips an' leave it at that, mm?'

He smiled at Max, nothing too invasive. Eye contact from Emil was rare.

When he had finished preparing Max for the cover-shot session, Emil made for the kitchen area of the photographic studio to shed a discreet tear. He had always been very quiet about the fact that he was a Max fan. Had all his records, videos. The lot. *Adored* him.

Pshemko strode in, wearing mashed-up Nikes, a pair of old Levi's on which the waist and rear pockets had been hacked off, and a shirt of the girliest pink which, ironically, only enhanced his masculinity. The look of the day seemed to take reference from fifties Italy and *Miami Vice*.

'Everything okay?'

'Mm,' came Max's reply.

Pshemko could tell that Max wanted an update.

'I've been calling that number every fifteen minutes. The voicemail's still on, no answer with the home number.'

Oola Khan was intrigued as Max checked his cellphone. Four messages. Nothing from Angela, though.

'Ready to do a Polaroid?' the photographer asked.

'Sure.'

It was time for Max to get dressed. On went a judo-style top which sported a traditional white shirt collar. Pshemko's choice.

The cellphone was put down on the armrest of the sofa. As if the thing had a mind of its own, it slipped. From armrest to cushion edge to internal base. Max's cellphone was lodged in among some long-lost loose change and dust-balls the size of golf balls.

What with one thing and another, Max forgot two things at the photo-shoot. His sunglasses, and his cellphone. The sunglasses had been found, the cellphone had not.

'I'm sure I left it by the sofa,' he said over and over to Pshemko. 'Get them to check again.'

Pshemko had a sneaking suspicion that perhaps the journalist Oola Khan had pinched it. Those pigs, he thought, capable of anything. Every dirty trick in the book.

# 4

He gave me his number, Angela thought, and I'm gonna call it. Just say hi. Be cool.

Minty curled her tail around her owner's leg. The last three days had been weird. The litter tray had not been changed once. All routine was out.

Angela decided against leaving a message.

Her hands and feet felt paralysed. She could hardly catch her breath. She managed to rock herself for a while. That soothed her, sorted her out. Got her ready.

Rather like a painter imagining the splash of the first few brush strokes, Angela cut through the air again and again before lowering the Stanley knife – held in her right hand – down on to the back of her left forearm. The essential foreplay before penetration.

Burning left better scars than cutting. *Impressive.* Boiling water, too. Pretty much exactly that time last year, Angela had burned the inside of her right thigh with an iron. Forty-eight times. Consecutively. Set, almost laughably, at MAX.

The thick, hollow metal handle had popped out that replaceable, retractable short blade so automatically. Ready. Always so ready, willing and able.

Arms. It was her mother's arms Angela thought of as she methodically made the first incision. Arms that did not adequately hold Baby A, arms that did not keep the child safe.

Angela's self-portrait painting as a child at school had always shown her without arms: helpless, and unable to protect herself.

Angela could not hear her phone ringing when she was rinsing the shampoo off; could not hear the phone ringing just after she had shut the front door to take the garbage down; could not hear the phone when she was asleep – drunk out of her mind.

The only calls Angela had received were from one increasingly snappy deputy editor. Each call had been increasingly curt. Angela's vague attempts at explaining that she had a stomach upset were not being swallowed. A doctor's certificate had been asked for.

Angela did not feel up to visiting her doctor. That man had never understood.

Pshemko was more interested by his reflection in the darkened glass of the mixing-room window than in what Max was doing beyond that glass. Pshemko had been shopping; he loved his new look. The black leather archer's glove by Vandervorst was a bit of fun, but *too much*? Pshemko wasn't sure. What was way over the top was the white sleeveless ruffle leather jacket by Warren Kade and the green leather Schönberger trousers.

'Rolling,' the sound technician said quietly, announcing the dull fact.

Max began to read from his spiral notebook.

'The only way to survive, however briefly, is by shutting oneself off *utterly* from every feeling, so that one becomes invulnerable, not like an armoured animal but like a stone. True or false?'

That was how he wanted the new album to begin. His voice would be treated: compressed, a little delay.

'Let's do that again,' he said.

The tape began to rewind. The technician nodded Max's way.

'Rolling.'

'The only way to survive, however briefly, is by shutting oneself off *utterly* from every feeling, so that one becomes . . .'

Pshemko had let them through, felt he had to. The atmosphere in the recording studio quickly changed. Max put down the notebook he had been reading from, pulled off the headphones he was wearing. The red light of the STOP button lit up in the control room as the tape stopped moving.

Here they are, Max sighed to himself internally, as expected.

His mother was in the middle of a Big Theatrical. She was standing, hands on hips, well into her What-did-I-do-to-deserve-this? mode as she stood snarling beside Max's father. First, they had cut their holiday short after reading press reports. Second, they had returned to a home which looked as if it had been burgled. Max's room – emptied of everything. Cash and a credit card missing, too.

Max kissed his mother, croaked a hi to his father. The man was taking in the sight of his son. That haircut, the white tracksuit he was wearing.

'Take your hands out of your pockets and don't stand there dreaming,' his father roared in a distinctly impatient voice.

Max felt both surprised and annoyed. He did what his father instructed – then thought about it.

'One, two, fuck you,' Max said with a Texas drawl. Time to take the piss out of his ol' dad. He felt it was justified.

'You have a lot of explaining to do, my boy.'

'That I have.'

Max's face was cherry red with what was not so much a blush as a volcanic eruption of embarrassment.

Pshemko came to stand almost between Max and his parents.

'Hey,' Max said to Pshemko, 'this ain't no boxing ring.'

He then moved towards his mother, pulled her towards him and hugged her tightly.

'I'm sorry,' he said, 'I've been so . . .'

The temp sitting at Angela's desk had deleted each of the messages from Max and Pshemko. No number, she thought, no call-back. She had enough to do.

Whoever had been there before her, some Max fan, was obviously a right weirdo. The drawers were crammed full of all kinds of shit, biscuits mainly.

The temp, who was way too good at the job to be leaving at the end of the week, had felt a little uncomfortable emptying all the former employee's bits and pieces into a box for collection.

No one said much about the woman she was replacing. Angela, that was her name. No one seemed to have a good thing to say about her. Everyone found her a bit sad. Seemed relieved that she had just . . . disappeared.

'It was like she went on holiday one day – and lost her return ticket,' the deputy editor remarked.

Gone a bit nutty, that was what everyone reckoned. Or gone freelance.

Angela tried hiding the cat medicine in the juice from a tin of salmon. No luck. So she wrapped the cat in a towel, to protect herself from any painful scratches, then knelt on the kitchen floor, placed one hand around the top of Minty's head and lifted until the cat opened its mouth. The liquid medicine was squirted in using the dropper. Angela only let go when she saw the cat swallow.

Job done, Angela left the cat there on the sofa – still wrapped in the towel.

A few seconds after Angela had locked herself in the bathroom, Minty was out of that kitty straitjacket and vomiting behind the sofa.

Angela felt guided, gently driven by voices. She was not alone. So many of the old selves were with her. Baby, Angel, Porky.

The tub was cool to cold. Not ideal, but easy to clean up afterwards.

The thick, hollow metal handle had popped out that blade so easily.

'Ready?' Angela asked the gleaming tip of the blade. 'I know *I* am.'

# 5

Angela wrote most of the letters sitting on the toilet, though some had been completed on the sofa, the last on the bench out by her old school playing fields.

Dear Max,

I have tried calling your cellphone number several times, but just keep getting your voicemail. It'd be nice to hear from you when you have a minute.

Angela

Dear Max,

Still haven't heard from you. Yeah, I've seen the papers, all the stuff on TV. You must be super busybusybusy right now what with all this media attention.

Call me when you have a minute.

Minty says Miaoooooow!

Angela

Dear Max,

You still haven't written or called.

I waited outside the studio for you. There was such a crowd, all those photographers! When you came out at around midnight (Friday, 17th) I shouted your name and waved as you got into some big, curvy, grey-green car, but you didn't see me. I felt like such a fool, such a fan – not a FRIEND – as you zoomed away.

I last wrote to you a week ago. It was registered but

obviously didn't make a very big impact on the right person. You probably didn't get it, after all – I'm probably just another one of the faceless beings who insist on writing stupid letters, making a lot of work for someone.

How much fan mail do you get? Too much, I expect.

Please call me. ASAP.

Angela

Dear Max,

I doubt this letter will get to you. It seems that I'm wasting my time. Your cellphone now seems to be OFF. This is confusing me a bit. You gave me your number, I called. Nothing. Lots of nothing. That's all for today.

How long can I keep this up? I really need to hear from you.

Angela

Dear Max,

What can I say? I find it really difficult writing to someone without getting anything back. I wonder if this letter is headed for the bin. All I seem to get from the fan club is merchandise updates.

Angela

Dear Max,

I can't say much right now – today was a bit too much for me.

I feel there's no point in anything. I just feel so empty and alone, like everything good has gone.

I just feel that there's no point.

4 Real 4 Ever.

Angela

Dear Max,
 Sorry about my last letter. I promise no more like that.
 Call me when you have a minute.
 Same number, same ol' place.
 Angela

Dear Max,
 You know where I am.
 This is my last letter to you until you make contact.
 I've had enough of this. Of everything.
 Today I stood at the top of the building where we spent our last evening together. I felt like jumping. Yeah, really. Then all this would be over.
 Angela

Things took a massive turn for the worse the day Angela logged on to Max's offical fan-club website. She had been totally taken aback on seeing that the latest pictures of Max were the photographs she had taken of him. Quicker than a click-hit fixer, Angela had taken in the vision of Max by the edge of the lake – covered in duckweed like some kind of Neolithic tribesman. Max, asleep on the beach – a fire smoking in the background. Max, high up on the edge of a building – the city behind him. Clouds. Sunset.

Along with the pictures came details of a forthcoming tour, planned for March of the following year.

Max will première his new album, *You Know Who You Are*, at a groundbreaking gig in Cuba on March 7th. Max will debut his fourth album at the 5,000-capacity Karl Marx Theatre in the island's capital, Havana.

Speaking exclusively to Oola Khan of the *Observer*, Max said,

'I'm rejuvenated in terms of songwriting and wanting to perform. The last year or so had left me feeling jaded with the whole process of releasing records and touring, that's why I needed to disappear for a while. I'm currently in the process of gathering a new team around me, I want things to be different.'

Angela felt like an outsider. Disposed of.

As she stood in her usual spot by the window, the look Angela wore on her face was both fixed and faded. Half smiling, half mourning. What she felt was bewilderment.

She stood there, doing nothing in slow motion, then yawned. Her breathing had formed a grey halo around her head. When she became aware of this she wrote her name backward through it, then erased it with the most tender part of her left wrist.

A light shower at eight improved air quality for a while, then a breeze started up. The sun was lazy behind layers of mist and gauzy cloud. The sky kept changing. It was soiled white, mainly.

Among red roofs, blue roofs, unlit neon and orange TV aerials, there were 750 variations of grey. The view Angela had was not old, but felt it. Most of what she saw had gone up over two previous generations. It didn't look so bad in sunshine or sunset, but in total cloud cover it was dreadful.

The smell of blackcurrant tea made only an hour ago was already fading, even with the windows firmly shut. She had been busy, hadn't stopped all day. A Things to Do list in the young woman's head still had many ticks to go.

Just about everything had gone. The furniture, the carpeting, all those books and CDs she had amassed over the years. She was amazed at what she had managed between the hours of two and seven that morning. Only the sofa remained. Angela felt that she owed that to little Minty.

As she drank a glass of tap water by the window, her eyes scanned the apartment building opposite. She knew each window so well. Some with curtains half-closed, some with blinds permanently drawn. Many with venetians turned to a precise angle.

Grey ferroconcrete.

One day the demolition men will go about their work with cranes, drills and hammers, pounding through the partitions of that block, smashing down exteriors, ripping out ironwork, reducing all to piles of raw materials to be sold for scrap, recycled or dumped. The bulldozers of the site-levellers will tidy away before men with brooms appear. Housewives will wipe their windowsills free of dust, then there'll be nothing left.

Daydreaming, Angela sat cross-legged where the kitchen table had once been, pinching her left nipple. Many was the time she had done that while watching a Max video. And more, much more. Now she was just fiddling with a part of herself unconsciously. Playing with a teat that would never feed.

Right then, what with everything so perfect and still, a point-blank bullet in her young head would have been lovely. But no kind person was there to pull the trigger. She would have to do everything herself. Every last, exhausting detail.

Pshemko was pissed off. Somehow he'd got a cigarette burn at the elbow of his new MA1 pilot's jacket. The butterscotch super-soft leather was tainted. He tried not to think about it as he watched from a comfortable purple velvet chair beside the mixing desk.

Max was laying down a guitar track. In the style of Jan Akkermann of the Dutch band Focus, he was producing a sound like a violin. He played a note while the volume on the guitar was off, then used the little finger of his right hand to turn on the volume again straight after playing. Swamped with reverb, the effect was eerie, something which pleased the electronic duo known as Röyksopp whom both Pshemko and Max felt would add something to the production. The arrangement, by Eriend Øye, was to feature a sample of wind from the top of Sandviksfjellet.

Max could hardly wait to play the new material to Angela. He had been planning for days to just turn up at her apartment, surprise her, but something had always cropped up. Always something.

Pshemko's right hand traced the line of each of the three pleats on the side of his trousers. Baggy was in. The recent Louis Vuitton collection had been one big orgasm for Pshemko – all those sexy black boys like himself, swamped in fabric. His fingers travelled up to the matching fabric belt. Shopping had long been his strategy to combat stress and, ultimately, attract cock.

The last few days had been tough on Pshemko, challenging. His team at the fan club were not coping. Ever since Max's disappearance it seemed that the floodgates had opened. Max's management had insisted that all names and addresses be computerised as they came in, and that merchandise information act as some form of response. It was a case of open the envelope, feed in the info, bin the letter, mail the brochures out, forget about it.

All kinds of presents were being delivered by one postal truck after another. There were the Max dolls that girl teens had sent in by the score, all of which went off to suitable charities. Word of someone having left a miaowing cat at reception towards the end of the day was a first. Word had spread quickly from reception to press office to Pshemko. Everyone thought it bizarre/hilarious, except the cat. The girl at reception had taken pity on the poor thing, deciding she would take it home with her. Give it some TLC. She liked cats. Had a similarly coloured variety herself: Tom.

Max had been told about the cat late in the night as he was about to start a rough mix on a new song entitled 'Hideaway'.

'What kind of cat?' he had asked, unnerved.

'It was *black*,' Pshemko said, savouring the mention of colour a while. 'Bag o' bones, by all accounts. No note or nuffin'.'

'Minty,' Max said under his breath in what was more the escape of a thought than an utterance. 'I need a cab,' he added loudly. 'Fast.'

He knew it was too late. *Knew*.

# 6

The night air was warm to cool. Perfect for walking.

Ahead, nothing. Just the glitter of the North Star.

No birds, Angela thought. No birds. The sky is swollen black.

A light rain started up, spattering sideways. Just enough to wet her, give her the feel of water.

Red tail-lights of cars heading out of the city blurred and linked together as if to form one long line of festive lights.

She sniffed. Tasted the saltiness of her tears. She was surprised to be crying. She thought she was all cried out. The closer to the bridge, she knew, the closer to the bottom of the bed of that river, the bottom of the sea. Wherever the tide would take her.

It had been a long walk. She was glad to arrive at last, coming to a halt in the middle of the bridge. She was aware that her brain had switched to autopilot, as if her fate had been added to that part of the cerebral hemisphere which handles the heart, lungs and coordination in tap dancing.

Under her ran water, miles of it. A whole world of water, polluted and fresh, stagnant and prehistoric. Ready. From her pocket came her keyring. No need for the keys, only that tiny penknife.

She dropped the keys, one by one.

She had considered writing a first and final suicide note. Didn't. Just couldn't be bothered. Couldn't see the point.

Her mouth had gone dry. She knew she would have to wait a while before she did what she had long considered: swallowing the penknife. Blade open, fully exposed.

Just for a moment she stopped breathing. No inhalation/ exhalation at all. Then a tremendous stillness filled her. She felt that she was invisible. Already gone.

The tip of the blade jabbed the back of her throat a little, then down it went.

Angela inhaled deeply.

She was surprised how quickly the thing had descended, how easily. For a moment she could feel the coolness of it in her stomach, then just a little warmth. She became aware that the back of her throat was bleeding. The taste was familiar. Soothing. Blood.

Floating in the insidious drag were blobs of toxic froth. The water did not smell rivery; there was a faint odour of mud, a faint chemical scent, something metallic. There was, too, an aroma of oil rubbed on a rifle – of an armoury. A heavy kind of oil, spreading rainbow-coloured smears over the surface. More than a smell, there was a stench of rust burned off by a blowtorch, the dark corners of a garage. And there, the hint of an igniter, gunsmoke. There, a puppy's wound, covered irritably by house flies. The odour of fallen leaves gone black. The sunny pop of a pistachio nut, and bones eroded to a browny white by rough waves of clear spring water some-where far off. The smell of all that and the dome of a great observatory after repairs and a black-and-white television thrown from a window for the low-budget filming of a pop video. The river. Below. Ready.

Currents whose motions were invisible to the eye drew occa-sional debris from the surface and, mysteriously, relinquished it again downriver into the central flow – back into the all-accepting sea, back into deep-water currents, cold-water layers.

The river did not look inviting, but it did promise to hold Angela to itself without judgment or question, letting her become a part of it. All she had to do was climb up to there, then there, then allow herself to fall fall fall.

You don't have to jump, just let go. That's all.
Just let go.

Pshemko drove like a maniac all the way. En route, Max told him why he had gone missing, what he had intended and how he had spent those days.

'Next left,' Max said, 'then all the way to the end.'

Pshemko skidded to a halt outside the shabby-looking apartment building.

'Wait here,' Max said, leaving the passenger door ajar.

'You sure you don't want me to come in with you?' Pshemko asked.

Max nodded back at him. He was certain. He had to do this alone.

Pshemko wasn't too impressed with the neighbourhood. He pulled the passenger door shut with a slam, then activated the internal locking device. Shoving both hands deep into the delicate pockets of his Maison Martin Margiela jacket was a comfort-searching action. Much to Pshemko's distress, he felt the thumbs of both hands force themselves through the delicate silk-feel polyester of the pocket linings. Left and right: simultaneously.

The spare set of keys to Angela's apartment had been with Max since the day he had left. His regret was that he had not *once* made the time to jump in a cab and go see her, not even for just an hour.

The keys were warm, worn smooth. Ready.

Max let himself in through the main door, then took the elevator.

'If that cat was Minty,' he said to himself as he rode up, alone, 'then fuck knows what Angela's gone an' done.'

When the doors of the elevator opened, Max felt that he was

walking on to a stage or film set, in a part for which he had been wrongly cast.

The corridor was too quiet. Too cool.

Max knocked three times. Nothing.

He stood for one long minute, looking at the lock into which the key he was now holding would soon turn.

His hands were shaking and his eyes felt peppery as he raised the key towards the lock.

The hinges let out a ghastly shriek that Max could not remember them having ever made before.

'Angela?'

Even with the lights off, he could see that the room was empty. Everything gone.

# DISCOGRAPHY

# DISCOGRAPHY

## The singles

Sweetly He Takes Us
b/w Road Into Fire

Up To The Edge
b/w Still And Moving Water

Come, Hear Us Rage
b/w In My Mind Always

The Devil's A Gentleman
b/w Rise And Walk (live)

Nothing is Sacred
b/w Desires Within Young Girls

Hidden Bruises
b/w Fragile Girl, Miserable Now (live)

Deep Love Scar
b/w Just Let Go

She's Suffering
b/w Brief, Flat, Final

Period
b/w Period (dub version)

## The albums

### TO BE PLAYED AT MAXIMUM VOLUME
A Mood For All Seasons / Isolation / Family Tree / True Teen / Scream Of A Mask / Sweetly He Takes Us / In Her Mouth / Fan-Tasy / Up To The Edge / Eyes Full Of Dreaming / Shriek And Faint / Road Into Fire / Angel

### THIS VERY MOMENT
This Very Moment / Edge Of The Screen / Great Day For A Breakdown / Broken Limbs / Nowhere Train / Rusty Nail / A Yard Of Skin / Deep Love Scar / The Devil's A Gentleman / Come, Hear Us Rage / Video Voodoo / Hidden Bruises / Accelerated Buddha

### TO THE MAX
Unhappy / Young, Pretty & Fucked / Simpler Than Life / I Want To . . . / NoNoNo / Brief Flat Final / Goodbye / Silence Broken Down / Inevitable Sunrise / She's Suffering / Tomorrow's Zero / Kiss Me Before I Die / Rain In The River / Time, Date / Period

# ACKNOWLEDGMENTS

Special thanks to the rock, pop and hip-hop stars, fans and fan clubs (official and unofficial) who helped provide source information for this novel in response to a number of editorial appeals in the music press and via fan club mailing lists, plus websites. Over the two years of research, it was the insightful observations and wonderful dreams of the majority, plus the maniacal fantasies of the minority, which fuelled much of this book.

The material was distilled from literally *thousands* of e-mails after a series of appeals appeared in *NME*; 250 hours of interviews, many of which were conducted in ticket queues; at concert venues, auctions of memorabilia, fan conventions and at signings; twelve hours of answerphone messages; over five hundred written accounts: replies to questionnaires, diaries and dream journals. Added to this, I was also allowed access to about three thousand letters written to many different celebrities by a number of official fan clubs which have requested not to be named.

Along the way there were innumerable brief encounters with rock and pop fans in the likes of Tokyo's Harajuku area, New York City's Astor Place, at events such as San Francisco's 'Out, Proud & Loud' youth convention and – in the UK – in places such as Manchester's Afleck's Palace and the Corn Exchange in Leeds. Not all of these individuals wanted to speak about the desires stirred by their 'idols' at first, and many more were reluctant to express the full extent of their feelings. Some were corresponded with and interviewed over a period of twelve months. In particular, I need to extend my gratitude to Andy, Helen A, Gracie Baby Nothing, Graham C, Mark C, Alexandra G, Vicki G, Cass K, Daniel L, Miss Lashes, Noriko N, Jasmin Q, Matthew S, Rachel S, Riot Starlet, Beth T, Kelly T, Howard W and Thomas W. All opened themselves so sincerely to this project, vividly showing some of the human reality behind the star-making industry. Also, many thanks to all those who communicated with me via www.1000deaths.com.

A number of books and periodicals have served as inspiration along the way, particularly *Starlust* (Comet/W.H. Allen & Co.) and *Fandemonium* (Omnibus Press) by Fred and Judy Vermorel; *Everything (A Book about Manic Street Preachers)* by Simon Price (Virgin); *The Manic Street Preachers – in Their Own Words* by M. Heatley (Omnibus); 'Adolescent Idolisation of Pop Singers: Causes, Expressions, Reliance' by Raviv et al. (*Journal of Youth and Adolescence*, 25, 5: 631–50); *From Blue to Black* by Joel Lane (Serpent's Tail); *The Adoring Audience: Fan Culture and Popular Media* by Lisa Lewis (Routledge); *A Bright Red Scream* by Marilee Strong (Virago); *The Language of Injury* by Gloria Babiker and Lois Arnold (The British Psychological Society); 'Treating Self-Mutilating Behaviour' (*Family Systems Medicine*, 6(1), 5–20); *Women and Self-Injury* by Lois Arnold (Bristol Crisis Service for Women); *Bodies under Siege* (Johns Hopkins University Press) and 'Repetitive Self-Mutilation' (*Psychiatric Annals*, 22(2), 60–3) by A.R. Favazza; 'Self-Mutilation and Eating Disorders' by A.R. Favazza, L. de Rosear and K. Conterio (*Suicide and Life-Threatening Behaviour*, 19(4), 352–61); *Patient or Pretender: Inside the Strange World of Factitious Disorder* by Feldman and Ford (Wiley); 'Self-Damaging and Addictive Behaviour in Bulimia Nervosa' by J.H. Lacey (*British Journal of Psychiatry*, 163, 190–4); 'The Impulsivist: A Multi-Impulsive Personality Disorder' by J.H. Lacey and C.D.H.

Evans (*British Journal of Addiction*, 81, 641–9); *Man against Himself* by K. Menninger (Harvest Books); *Multiple Selves, Multiple Voices* by P. Mollon (John Wiley & Sons): 'Adolescents' Use of Media for Self-Socialisation' by Jeffrey Arnett (*Journal of Youth and Adolescence*, 24, 5: 519–33); 'Psychological Determinants of Idolatry in Adolescence' by Sheung-Tak Cheng (*Journal of Youth and Adolescence*, 32, 127: 687–92); *Fashion as Communication* by M. Barnard (Routledge); *The Hunger Artists* by M. Ellman (Virago); *Fame – the Psychology of Stardom* (Vision); *Daydreaming and Fantasy* by J. Singer (Random House); and a collection of short stories entitled *Starf\*cker*, edited by Shar Rednour (Alyson Books). A weekly read of *NME* over the years has also been invaluable – from Julie Burchill in the days of punk to Sylvia Patterson's delving into the minds of musicians such as Radiohead's Thom Yorke. So, too, the writing of Sarah-Jane in *City Life*.

Certain pieces of music kept the mood simmering whilst I worked on this book, holed up in a nasty hotel in Malta's Bugibba. Useful pointers were provided by Robert Chevara, John Halliday, Julian Kalinowski, Dennis Nilsen and Warwick Thompson. I guess this list is the imaginary film soundtrack that has been playing in my head:

'The End Of The World' by **Laurie Anderson** (from *The Ugly One with Jewels*, Warner Bros.), and 'Big Science' (from *Big Science*, Warner Bros.); 'Twilight, Cripple and the Starfish', 'Atrocities' and 'River of Snow' by **Antony And The Johnsons** (from *Antony and The Johnsons*, World Serpent Distribution); 'It's My Life' and 'I'm Crying' by **The Animals** (from *Interesting Life*, A2 Records); 'You on My Mind in My Sleep' by **Richard Ashcroft** (from *Alone with Everybody*, Hut); 'Ghostchaser' by **Atari Teenage Riot** (from *60 Second Wipeout*, DHR); 'Theme from Midnight Cowboy' by **John Barry** (from *Best of John Barry*, Columbia); 'Help' by **The Beatles** (from *Help*, EMI); 'Nowhere Man' (from *Rubber Soul*,

EMI); *Casta Diva* by **Bellini**, (EMI); 'Ships in the Night' by **Be-Bop Deluxe** (from *Be-Bop Del Sunburst*, EMI); 'Fan Mail' by **Blondie** (from *Plastic Letters*, Chrysalis); 'Spaceball Ricochet' by **Marc Bolan** (from *The Slider*, EMI), 'Children of the Revolution' (from *Tanks*, EMI); Requiem – Kyrie by **Fernando Henrique Cardoso** (Gimmell); 'Starman' and 'Ziggy Stardust' by **David Bowie** (from *The Rise and Fall of Ziggy Stardust and The Spiders from Mars*, RCA) and 'Sense Of Doubt' (from the *Christiane F* movie, *Wir Kinder Vom Bahnhof Zoo*, RCA); Symphony No. 1 – second movement, *andante sostenuto* by **Johannes Brahms** (Deutsche Grammophon); Mass in E Minor – Benedictus by **Josef Anton Bruckner** (Harmonia Mundi); Missa 'Et ecce terrae motus' – Agnus Dei by **Antoine Brumel** (Sony Classical); Piano Concerto No. 1 – second movement. Romanze: Larghetto by **Frederic Chopin** (Sony Classical) and *Nocturne No. 18 in E major, Op. 62, No. 2* (Olympia); 'The Man Who Sold The World' by **Kurt Cobain** (from *Unplugged in New York*, MCA); 'Death Trip' and 'Sebastian' by **Cockney Rebel** (from *The Human Menagerie*, EMI) and 'Psychomodo' (from *Psychomodo*, EMI); 'The Partisan' by **Leonard Cohen** (from *Best of Leonard Cohen*, Columbia); 'Shiver' by **Coldplay** (from *Parachute*, EMI); 'Hard-on for Jesus' by **The Dandy Warhols** (from *The Dandy Warhols*, Capitol); Images I – Hommage à Rameau by **Claude Debussy** (Collins Classics); 'Personal Jesus' by **Depeche Mode** (from *Violator*, Mute) and 'I Want You Now' (from *Music for the Masses*); 'Black Eyed Dog' by **Nick Drake** (from *Way to Blue*, Island); *Cello Concerto* by **Elgar** (EMI); 'Stan' by **Eminem** (from *The Marshall Mathers LP*, Interscope Records); 'Spirits Drifting' by **Brian Eno** (from *Another Green World*, Virgin); 'Trouble in Mind' by Marianne Faithful (from *Trouble in Mind*, Island), 'As Tears Go By' by **Marianne Faithfull** (from *Strange Weather*, Island); 'The Day The Rain Came Down' and 'Sunlight Behind the Golden Glow' by **Felt** (from *Absolute Classic Master-*

*pieces*, Cherry Red Records); 'I Have The Touch' by **Peter Gabriel** (from *Plays Live*, Virgin); 'Runaway Horses' ('poetry written with a splash of blood') by **Philip Glass** (from *Mishima*, Nonsuch Digital) and Satyagraha – Act 3 Part 3 (Masterworks); Piano Concerto in A minor – second movement, Adagio by **Edvard Grieg** (CBS); Messiah – 'Comfort Ye' by **George Handel** (Hyperion); 'Those Crimson Tears' by **Ed Harcourt** (from *Here Be Monsters*, Heavenly); Ave, Generosa by **Abbess Hildegard van Bingen** (from *A Feather on the Breath of God*, Hyperion); 'Pretty On The Inside, *Mrs Jones*' by **Hole** (from *Pretty on the Inside*, City Slang), plus 'Beautiful Skin' (from *Celebrity Skin*, Geffen); 'Is This Really Going Down?' by **Hywyn** (Etcetera); 'Raw Power' and 'Your Pretty Face Is Going To Hell' by **Iggy and The Stooges** (from *Raw Power*, Columbia); 'Ain't No Sunshine' by **Michael Jackson** (from *Music and Me*, Tamia Motown); 'Isolation', 'Glass' and 'Means To An End' by **Joy Division** (from *Still*, Factory), 'Day Of The Lords' (from *Unknown Pleasures*, Factory) and 'Atmosphere' (from *Closer*, Factory); 'I Don't Know What I Can Save You From' by **Kings Of Convenience** (Source); 'Metropolis' and 'Neon Lights' by **Kraftwerk** (from *The Man Machine*); 'At The Edge Of The World', 'Give Me Time', 'Winter Academy', 'Blue It Is', 'Beyond The Sun' by **Billy MacKenzie** (from *Beyond the Sun*, Nude Records) **and** 'Baby' (from *Outernational*, Circa); 'Disposable Teens' and 'The Fight Song' by **Marilyn Manson** (from Hollywood – in the Shadow of the Valley of Death, Interscope) plus 'Dope Show' (from *Mechanical Animals*, Nothing Records); 'Die In The Summertime', 'Archives of Pain', '4st 7lb', 'This Is Yesterday' and 'She is Suffering' by **Manic Street Preachers** (from *The Holy Bible*, Sony Music); 'A Little Communication' by **McAlmont** (Hut); 'Dose Me Up' by **Tom McRae** (from *Tom McRae*, DB Records); String Symphony No. 8 – second movement, Adagio by **Felix Mendelssohn** (Kingdom); 'Casting No Shadow' and

'You See' by **Wim Mertens** (from *A Man, of No Fortune &
With a Name to Come,* Les Disques du Crepuscule), 'Circular
Breathing' and 'Multiple 12' (from *Vergessen,* Les Disques du
Crépuscule); 'Close Cover', 'Struggle for Pleasure' and 'Lir'
(from *Close Cover,* Windham Hill Records); 'The Fosse' (from
*Educes Me,* Factory); 'Exitium' (from Instrumental Songs –
Musique à une Voix, Lome Arme); 'Maximizing The Audi-
ence' (from *Maximizing the Audience,* from a play entitled
*The Power of Theatrical Madness* written by Jan Fabre, Les
Disques du Crépuscule); 'Wia' (from *Stratégie de la Rupture,*
Les Disques du Crépuscule); 'Lenige Spieren', 'Kruislings' and
'Song And Story' (from *Sources of Sleeplessness,* Les Disques
du Crépuscule); 'Part VII' (from *Vita Brevis,* Les Disques du
Crépuscule); 'Zo', 'Al', 'Et', 'Tot' (from *Alle Dinghe,* Les
Disques du Crépuscule); 'The Aural Trick' and 'Time Passing'
(from *The Belly of an Architect,* a Peter Greenaway film,
Factory); 'Von Ganz Unten', 'Gerausch', 'Weiter Und Weiter',
'Sich Polieren' (from *Der Heisse Brei,* Les Disques du Cré-
puscule); 'Often a Bird', 'Hors-Nature' (from *Best Of,* Les
Disques du Crépuscule), 'La Fin De La Visite', 'In 3 or 4 Days',
'Au Delà du Fleuve', 'Tout est Visible' and – so hauntingly –
the closing moments of 'Sidemen' (from *Integer Valor,* Les
Disques du Crepuscule); 'Angel, Angel, Down we Go To-
gether' by **Morrissey** (from *Viva Hate,* EMI Records); 'I Know
it's Over' (from *The Queen is Dead,* Rough Trade); 'Back to
the Old House' and 'Girl Afraid' (from *Hatful of Hollow,*
Rough Trade) and 'Well I Wonder' (*Meat Is Murder,* Rough
Trade); 'Janitor of Lunacy' and 'Le Petit Chevalier', by **Nico**
(from *Desert Shore,* Reprise); 'Queen Of The Night', 'The
Description of The Linen and 'The Garden Is Becoming a
Robe Room' by **Michael Nyman** (from *The Draughtsman's
Contract,* a Peter Greenaway film, Virgin); 'Song 1', 'Song 2'
(from *And Do They Do,* Ter Classics); 'Stroking', 'Gliding',
'Synchronising' (from *The Kiss and Other Movements,* Edi-

tions EG); The Humming Chorus from *Madama Butterfly* by
**Giacomo Puccini** (EMI); 'How to Disappear Completely' and
'Idioteque' by **Radiohead** (from *Kid A*, Parlophone) plus
'Packt Like Sardines in a Crushd Tin Box', 'I Might be Wrong'
and 'Knives Out' (from *Amnesiac*, Parlophone), plus 'The
Amazing Sounds of Orgy', Parlophone; Reciproco Amore –
'Lasciatemi Morire' by **Rascarini** (Deutsche Harmonia Mun-
di); 'Blood Flowers' by **Royal Trux** (from *Royal Trux*, Dom-
ino) and 'Up the Sleeve' (from *Cats and Dogs*, Domino); 'King
of Sorrow' by **Sade** (from *Sade Lovers Rock*, Sony); *Verklarte
Nacht* by **Arnold Schoenberg** (CBS); *Die Winterreise* – 'Gute
Nacht' by **Schubert** (EMI); Lieder, Op. 35 – 'Stille Tranen' by
Schumann (Teldec); String Quartet No. 8 by **Shostakovich**
(Barodin String Quartet, Virgin Classics); 'Pure' by **Siouxsie
and The Banshees** (from *The Scream*, Polydor), and 'Clock-
face' (from *Kaleidoscope*, Polydor); 'The Wisp' by **Simian**
(Source); 'Farewell Reel' by **Patti Smith** (from *Gone Again*,
Arista) and *Glitter in their Eyes'* from *Gung Ho*, Arista); *Le
Sacre du Printemps* by **Igor Stravinsky** (Brilliant Classics);
'Disappear' by **Sonic Youth** (from *Goo*, MCA); 'So Young',
'Sleeping Pills' by **Suede** (from *Suede*, Nude Records), plus
'Insatiable One' (Nude) and 'The Drowners' (Nude); 'Woman
In Chains' by **Tears for Fears** (from *The Seeds of Love*,
Mercury); Flute Fantasia No. 8 in E minor by **Georg Philipp
Telemann** (Denon); 'Nowhere Train', 'Uninvited Guest' and
'Persons Unknown' by **The Transmitters** (Ebony); 'The One
that Won The War', 'Curious' (Step-Forward); 'Every Day I
Die' by **Tubeway Army** (from *Tubeway Army*, Beggars Ban-
quet); 'Underdog (Save Me)' by **Turin Brakes** (from *The
Optimist LP*, Source); 'Stereo Porno' by **Vermorel** (Factory);
'Neon Wilderness', 'Sonnet', 'Catching The Butterfly' and
'Weeping Willows by **The Verve** (from *Urban Hymns*,
Hut); 'Evil Angel' by **Rufus Wainwright** (from *Poses*, Dream-
works); 'If You Go Away' by **Scott Walker** (from *Scott 3*,

Fontana); Moonlight Sonata by **Ludwig van Beethoven**, with Emil Gilels on piano (Deutsche Grammophon); Overture from *La Forza del Destino* by **Verdi** (Deutsche Grammophon); Prelude to *Tristan and Isolde* by **Wagner** (Deutsche Grammophon); 'Obsessed With You' by **X-Ray Spex** (from *Germ Free Adolescents*, Virgin).

I owe much to my guitar teacher, Norman Fisk.

A big shout out to Elaine Palmer at Pulp Books for permission to 'sample' and 'remix' certain sections from *Call Me, I Want to Fuck You* and *Mmm Yeah* (all first published by Pulp Books in the UK) for inclusion within *Rock 'n' Roll Suicide*.

Lastly, many thanks to North West Arts for a generous award which allowed me to research many aspects of this novel in Japan in the fall of 1999. So much of the mood within this book sprang from long hours in the consumer craziness of Shibuya, Shinjuku, the solitude of Yoyogi Park, Hiro-o's Arisugawakinen Park, plus Aoyama Cemetery.

Respect. Acknowledgement. Thanks.

P-P Hartnett
Colne, Lancashire, June 2002